PRAISE FOR SARIAH WILSON

The Friend Zone

"Wilson scores a touchdown with this engaging contemporary romance that delivers plenty of electric sexual chemistry and zingy banter while still being romantically sweet at its core."

—*Booklist*

"Snappy banter, palpable sexual tension, and a lively sense of fun combine with deeply felt emotional issues in a sweet, upbeat romance that will appeal to both the YA and new adult markets."

—*Library Journal*

The #Lovestruck Novels

"Wilson has mastered the art of creating a romance that manages to be both sexy and sweet, and her novel's skillfully drawn characters, deliciously snarky sense of humor, and vividly evoked music-business settings add up to a supremely satisfying love story that will be music to romance readers' ears."

—*Booklist* (starred review), *#Moonstruck*

"Making excellent use of sassy banter, hilarious texts, and a breezy style, Wilson's energetic story brims with sexual tension and takes readers on a musical road trip that will leave them smiling. Perfect as well for YA and new adult collections."

—*Library Journal*, *#Moonstruck*

The Seat Filler

The Seat Filler

a Novel

SARIAH WILSON

Published by Montlake, Seattle

www.apub.com

Amazon, the Amazon logo, and Montlake are trademarks of Amazon.com, Inc., or its affiliates.

ISBN-13: 9781542025713
ISBN-10: 1542025710

Cover design by Philip Pascuzzo

Printed in the United States of America

*For Adam Driver
and Arts in the Armed Forces*

CHAPTER ONE

"Juliet, I think we should go over the rules one more time," my best friend, Shelby, said to me while anxiously wringing her hands. I wanted to remind her that we were wearing gorgeous formal gowns and standing backstage in a massive theater filled with some of the most famous people in the world. This was the kind of moment we'd dreamed about having when she'd been sick. I wanted her to live in the moment with me.

But I knew why she couldn't, so instead I nodded. "Tell me again."

"When the cameras are on, make sure that you don't do anything that will draw attention to yourself, or else you'll get kicked out and then Allan's mom will hate me forever."

I reached over to squeeze her hand. Even while Shelby had been going through the worst parts of fighting leukemia, she was always so serene and calm. A year after she was officially declared to be in remission, she'd met Allan Standish, and they'd both fallen quickly and hard. I hadn't been the least bit surprised when he proposed to her two weeks ago, even though they'd only been dating for about three months.

Apparently Allan had an idiot for a mother (and I was supposed to call her by her actual name, Harmony, and not Satan's Evilest Minion like I wanted to) and she didn't like Shelby or the engagement. She had declared it was all happening "too fast."

She'd even gone so far as to offer Allan a vacation to Hawaii and a new sports car if he'd end things.

Which led to Shelby twisting herself into knots trying to impress Harmony. I truly did not get it. Allan told Shelby that his mom's opinion didn't matter, that he loved her and chose her no matter what his mom thought. Which made me like him and respect him even more, but Shelby apparently didn't believe him. She was determined to win Harmony over.

Harmony ran a company, SeatFiller Nation, which provided volunteers to dress up and attend the biggest Hollywood and music award shows to fill in empty seats. Producers didn't want any vacant chairs during a broadcast, because it would give the impression that their show was boring (it was) and that even the celebrities didn't care (they didn't). People in the audience would get up to go to the bathroom, hang out at the bar, accept and/or present awards. Allan had told us that sometimes nominees who hadn't won would leave after their category was announced (which was why they always saved the big awards until the end). But nobody wanted the people watching at home to see that the big stars had taken off, so they used seat fillers.

A couple of the volunteers and one of Harmony's staff members had canceled on her this morning, leaving Harmony in a (deserved) tizzy. She'd called on Allan to help her out. Shelby had overheard their conversation and had volunteered the two of us to fill in the remaining slots. Shelby had done it to be kind and to suck up; personally, I was impressed by the inherent brilliance of the offer, given that Harmony couldn't decline without coming across as, well, Satan's Evilest Minion. Or the pettiest one, at the very least.

I would have preferred to leave Allan's snobby mother high and dry, but Shelby was a much better person than me and didn't share my general disdain for People Like Harmony.

So she and I had run out and rented a couple of nondescript black gowns (another rule—we couldn't be too glitzy or sparkly, so as to not draw attention away from the celebrities). It was a great color on Shelby—her soft blonde hair, blue eyes, and bright-red lips looked perfect with her dress. I, on the other hand, felt a little like I was wearing a Morticia Addams costume as we waited backstage while Allan, working as a spotter, told the seat fillers where to go.

We'd been here since early in the morning, standing around in our gowns, waiting. The awards show had officially been going on for about an hour and a half, but since Shelby and I had the least experience, Allan was keeping us backstage. Which meant more waiting. I'd naively assumed being a seat filler meant more filling seats and less standing.

But Allan had said he needed us, so Shelby's way of preparing was to go over the strict rules that I'd already heard four times that day.

"Okay," Shelby said. "The next rule? Do not speak unless you're spoken to. You can't start a conversation with anyone, no matter who it is."

"Right! Otherwise it's off with our heads!" I paused before continuing. "But what if I'm a big fan and I'm compelled to share that with them?"

She did not look pleased with my joke. "Don't. You're only supposed to be seen and not heard."

I nodded back in what I hoped was a serious way.

"When you move down the row to get to your seat, be sure that you're facing the people sitting down."

I couldn't help myself, even though I knew better. "So, you're saying I shouldn't put my butt in Chris Evans's face when I scoot past him? That just seems like a missed opportunity."

Her death glare, one I had very rarely been the object of, was enough to make me knock it off and not ask her if I was allowed to make eye contact with anyone around me or if that had been forbidden, too. Seeing as how I was about to become the lowliest of peasants.

"And most important of all, the number one rule to rule all other rules: all seat fillers must be in a seat or backstage when the lights come on."

"Like the world's worst and stupidest game of musical chairs."

"I'm serious. If you're out there in the aisles or in front of the stage when they start broadcasting again, Harmony will murder all of us."

"I wonder who would play me in the Netflix documentary about it."

"Juliet!" Shelby protested. "Please!"

I took both of her hands in mine. It was just so ridiculous to me that Harmony didn't adore Shelby that I had to make fun of the entire situation. But it was past time to be serious to make my best friend feel better. "I promise I will behave and be a shining example to all seat fillers across this great land of ours. But I hope that you know that you do not have to kiss up to this crazy lady. You're marrying Allan, not Harmony."

She shrugged, and I saw the tears glistening in her eyes, which made me want to hunt Harmony down and punch her in her stupid face. "I want everyone to get along, and maybe if I can show her that I'm . . ."

When she trailed off, I filled in the blanks for her. "That you're what? Amazing? A survivor? One of the best people I know?"

"That maybe if she gets to know the real me, things will get better."

I felt like this was all a lost cause, but now was not the time to tell Shelby that. Her relentless optimism had gotten her through her cancer, and who was I to argue with success?

Shelby turned to look at one of the monitors, and my stomach grumbled. As if an answer to my hungry gut, a waiter walked by with a tray of tiny sandwiches. I reached for one as he got close, and he slowed down slightly to let me grab one.

But somebody slapped my hand as I got hold of the toothpick. I managed to hold on to my prize and glared at the woman staring at me.

If this was Allan's mother, very bad things were about to happen. Like, body bags might be necessary. Sensing this, the waiter fled.

"Are you new here? You must be, because anybody that's been to more than one of these events as a seat filler knows that the food is for the invited attendees only. Throw it away." She narrowed her eyes at me and got that judgy look some women had, as if they were assessing you based solely on your appearance and immediately dismissing you.

She took in my dark-brown hair and pale skin, and then her gaze lingered on the scars on the right side of my neck. Usually I wore my hair down, like a shield against this kind of attention, but Shelby had convinced me that my dress called for a good updo. That no one would pay any attention to or care about my scars, which had faded to a light silver color. And somehow I'd both believed her and convinced myself that they weren't that noticeable.

"Did you hear me? I said, throw it away!"

I hated that I let people make me feel self-conscious about the scars, and it made me angry. So after carefully removing the toothpick, I popped the food into my mouth, maintaining eye contact while I chewed. There were only two people in my life who got to tell me what to do, and she was neither one of them.

She made a sound of outrage when I ate my pilfered mini-sandwich (which was not all that great, but I was not about to let her know that) and stalked off to join another group of women, where she kept pointing at me and shaking her head.

I should have grabbed the entire tray. I was certainly hungry enough for it, and as an added bonus, it might have made Sandwich Monitor's head explode.

Harmony would have really been upset then.

Allan waved us over. He had light-brown hair and was as tall as I was, six feet. He had dark-brown eyes that were always smiling. I wondered for the millionth time if there had been an as-yet-undiscovered mix-up at the hospital, because I had no idea how he could be related to his mother. He had on a headset and was holding a clipboard. "Okay, Shelby? You're in row fifteen, seat J. You'll be climbing over some people. Don't run away with some movie star while you're out there."

"I'll try not to," she said with a giggle and kissed Allan quickly before going out to join the crowd.

"And Juliet?"

"Reporting for my first official assignment," I told him, saluting.

He smiled back. "You're going to be in row two, seat B. That's some prime seating, just so you know."

"Thanks!" I told him. I shot one final glance of annoyance at that know-it-all veteran seat filler before I headed into the auditorium. Glamorous and formal-clad people talked all around me; some were sitting, others standing. Lots of air kisses and handshakes as I made my way carefully through the crowd. I recognized a number of actors and actresses but remembered that I was not allowed to stop and gape at them with an open mouth.

Seats A and B in row two were both empty. I sat down in the B seat, wondering who had been sitting here before me. Shelby had mentioned that the award nominees and their dates sat on the ends of the first few rows. So probably somebody very famous.

There was a woman to my left who I almost bumped with my elbow as I removed my badge. The badge was attached to the front of my dress and said, "I'm temporarily filling this seat for camera purposes." I hadn't wanted to run afoul of another rule—I had to take the badge off so that it wouldn't be seen on camera. I put it in my small clutch, which also held my cell phone, my keys, and an emergency Snickers bar.

A Snickers bar I was seriously considering eating, given that I was still hungry and still annoyed.

Since I was tempted to observe everyone around me, I stuck to staring straight ahead. Like I was wearing blinders. I figured that was safest, considering that I was the kind of woman who lived for celebrity gossip. I had subscriptions to, like, three different tabloids. Fortunately Shelby shared my obsession, and we had spent many hours of her chemo poring over trashy magazines. I'd signed a very serious and very thick nondisclosure agreement for this event, and because I was already poor, I didn't need to make things worse by having Harmony sue me.

A man sat down next to me in seat A. I noticed that he was tall, as he was forced to turn his legs toward the aisle because he didn't quite fit. His hands were large and he was wearing an expensive watch that somehow seemed vaguely familiar.

"You're in the wrong seat." His voice was deep and, again, familiar. I was tempted to glance at him, but I fought off the urge. But that meant I wasn't sure whether he was talking to me or someone else. For all I knew, he might have been on his cell phone. I kept my eyes pointed toward the stage as the lights came back up and everyone hurried back to their own seats.

"The security is terrible at this venue," he mumbled as he shifted in his seat. "This should be one of the few places where I'm safe from stalkers."

Wait. Did he think I was stalking him? By sitting here and not interacting with him at all, carefully following Harmony's stupid rules?

Again, I was jumping to conclusions. He might have been talking to someone else. Maybe even himself. Out loud, where I could hear it.

They were presenting an award, but I couldn't hear what it was for, because the tall man in a black suit next to me was still muttering under his breath.

A winner was announced and a tiny actress I recognized from a TV show I used to watch went up to the stage to accept. The last thing I could remember reading about her was that she was bearding for a director in order to advance her career.

Huh. Looks like that worked out for her.

She started tearily thanking a long list of people for helping her win the award. That was some industrial-strength waterproof mascara she had on. I was kind of fascinated by how tears could stream down her face without marring any of her makeup. I would have looked like an oversize, drunk raccoon if it had been me up onstage.

"Are you seriously going to sit there and ignore me?" the man asked me.

"I'm trying real hard to," I finally responded, mostly because this actress was going on and on, despite the fact that they were playing music to get her offstage and she was in the midst of thanking every person she'd ever known, including her eighth-grade PE teacher, I kid you not. "So please be quiet."

"Did you . . ." His voice trailed off in disbelief. "I can't believe you just told me to be quiet. You stole my date's chair and I'm the one who should be quiet?"

I'd reached the end of my douchebag rope. The cameras were still pointed at the stage, where the hosts were now tugging on the actress's arm to get her to leave. I figured I could risk it. I turned to glare at him.

And my mouth dropped open.

It was him. The man who had played Felix Morrison.

And Malec Shadowfire.

He was the actor Noah Douglas, star of my favorite TV show growing up, and he had recently starred as the villain in a billion-dollar fantasy franchise about fairies. He was at this awards show for his most recent role as a young husband and father whose wife was dying of cancer in a film that aired exclusively on InstaFlicks. The movie was really good, but for the life of me I couldn't remember his character's name. Toby? Charlie? Phillip?

I was staring at him. In a very stalkery way, so maybe he'd had a point earlier. My heart was beating so fast I was afraid it might break free from all the veins and arteries that were (I think?) currently trying to tether it in place.

"You're . . . you're . . ." My mind had turned completely off. Of course, when I was twelve years old I had daydreamed more than once about what I would say to Noah Douglas when we met. Of how I'd win him over with my wit and natural charm.

That was not happening. I was floundering badly and couldn't even figure out a way to finish the sentence I'd started.

This was in large part because he was ridiculously, almost . . . animalistically attractive. He wasn't conventionally handsome; his nose was a little too big, his lips a tad too full. It shouldn't have worked, but for some reason on him his features came together in a way that made it hard to look away. He had dark-brown hair like mine, nearly black, and these intense, hooded light-brown eyes that made my stomach flip over and over.

What was I supposed to say to the man who had played Felix? And Malec? And that other guy whose name I still couldn't remember?

"Whatever you do," he said, his deep voice now so recognizable that I felt stupid for not having realized that it was him sooner, "do not call me Felix. Or Malec Shadowfire."

OMG, Noah Douglas was a freaking mind reader, too. This was bad. Very bad. I tried to banish every impure thought I was currently having about him.

Then, that flare of annoyance was back. Just because I was female and of a certain age, did that automatically mean I should recognize him? That I totally did was beside the point. He shouldn't have been egotistical enough to assume it. For all he knew, I could have been like . . . my mom. Who loved the theater and didn't watch television or movies because they were "less than." She wouldn't have known who Noah Douglas was.

So why was he so certain that I did?

"Why do you think I'd call you by those names?" I asked.

He gave me a look of weariness bordering on contempt. "Because that's what people always call me. But I do have an actual name. Use that."

That devilish little imp inside me—the one who was still mad at Harmony for stressing Shelby out and at that woman who'd tried to stop me from eating and then stared at my scars—broke free, triggered into a frenzy by Noah's very large ego.

And I told the biggest lie I'd ever told in my entire life.

"I'm sorry, I can't do that, because I don't even know who you are."

CHAPTER TWO

"What?" he asked, and again, he was totally entitled to the disbelief in his voice. He waited a beat before saying with a scowl, "In that case, I'm Noah Douglas. An actor who is nominated for one of these awards, which is why I'm here. How about you?"

I looked around for the cameras. The host had come back out, and they had segued into giving Ralph Ramsey a lifetime achievement award. His daughter—and Noah's recent costar—Lily Ramsey, was introducing her father. Both of those speeches were going to take a long time. I sighed. I was hoping that this segment would end quickly and I could make an exit and not have to sit here and keep lying to Noah Douglas.

"I'm a seat filler." I decided that was all the explanation he was entitled to.

"A seat filler? What kind of job pays you to fill seats?"

"I don't know, probably the same kind of job that pays you to pretend to be someone you're not." Like being an actor was so much better than being a seat filler. Pretentious, much? "Besides, it's not my job. I'm helping out my best friend's fiancé's mother. I'm volunteering. You should know what that is. Don't you celebrities love to volunteer?

Because you sure do get a lot of pictures taken while you do it." Not him, though. If he had a pet cause, I'd never heard of it.

I faced front again. My luck was only going to last for so long, and if I kept fighting with Noah freaking Douglas I was going to get kicked out and ruin Shelby's game plan to win over her future mother-in-law.

Drawing in a deep breath, I tried to calm my shaky nerves. They were alive, lit up with excitement from being this close to him. He was so . . . disconcerting. I wished, not for the first time, that my plan to steer clear of all men meant that I wouldn't feel any attraction to them. Especially not the kind I was feeling right now for this arrogant movie star sitting next to me. That would have been super helpful.

"What is your job, then?"

It took me a second to process this. Had he really just asked me what my job was? Why did he care? "A groomer."

"Of people?"

"What?" I asked, turning back toward him. *What the actual—* "No. Dogs. I'm a dog groomer. I have my own business. And what kind of weird world do you live in that you think I meant a people groomer?"

"I have a groomer. Annie. It's how this happens." He gestured to his face and hair. His dreamy hair that was in short, tousled waves pushed back from his face—it reminded me a little of a lion's mane. I had to curl my fingers inward to keep them from reaching out to touch it.

"That and good genes," I responded, shaking my head, trying not to get sucked in by his sexiness.

"I'll take that as a compliment."

"Up to you. I wouldn't."

A satisfied smirk settled on his lips. "Why wouldn't I? You essentially just said that I'm hot."

He so, so, so was. Blood rushed to my face, making my skin feel heated. "No. I said your genes were good. I could have been referencing your ability to fight off infection or your chances of not getting dementia when you're old. Anything past that is just your ego and you jumping to conclusions."

Noah still wore his smirk and he was just . . . staring at me. Like he was trying to memorize my facial features for the police report he probably planned on filing. I saw when his gaze slid down to the right side of my neck, and I swore to all that was holy if he asked me how I got my scars, no matter how much I loved Shelby, I was going to throat punch my favorite actor on live television.

But to his credit, he didn't say anything about it. The smirk turned into an actual smile, and it did funny things to the backs of my knees. I was glad I was already sitting down. He so rarely smiled at these kinds of events or on red carpets that it felt like I'd just been given the rarest of gifts. It lit up his whole face. And he had a completely adorable dimple in his right cheek.

Swoon.

"Are you negging me?" he asked, sounding almost delighted.

"What does that mean?"

"Some guys will make negative comments in an attempt to try and manipulate a woman in hopes she'll pay attention to them. It's called negging."

"Is that how you get women?" I asked.

"What? No!" His smile faded and he looked really insulted. Had that somehow been intentional on my part? Maybe I was subconsciously negging him and hadn't even realized it.

"Then how do you know about it?"

"I got this script where . . . never mind." He folded his arms across his very broad and appealing chest, and I forced myself to look away. His tone was dismissive, and I took it to mean that our bizarre interaction had come to an end.

Which I should have felt relieved about, but instead I found myself saying, "I bet women just fall at your feet, right?"

"That's usually how that happens, yes." He sounded sarcastic and I couldn't figure out his meaning. Was he just acknowledging the reality of his love life? Or was he indicating that I had no idea what I was talking about?

I didn't understand what he meant and it irritated me so much that I was back to being completely annoyed. Which made me remember how hungry I was. I couldn't recall any rules about not eating. Although maybe that fell into the don't-do-anything-embarrassing-on-camera category? Regardless, I was going to have some chocolate and calm myself down.

The zipper on my clutch was stuck. I tugged at it once, twice, three times. Nothing. I pushed at the fabric near the zipper, wondering if it was caught. Things were about to get really bad in this auditorium if I wasn't allowed to have something sweet to soothe my savage beast. Maybe I should use my teeth.

While I was thinking over the best way to get this thing open, Noah Douglas had reached over and taken the clutch out of my hands. He quickly and efficiently unzipped it and handed it back to me. I was so surprised by his actions that my fingers turned into Jell-O and my purse fell to the floor near my feet.

Of course.

I reached for it and heard him say, "Nice shoes, Cinderella."

I was wearing my pink Converse high tops. I loved these shoes; they were probably my favorite things in my entire wardrobe. They didn't really scream "Hollywood awards show," but I'd been told (rightfully so) that Shelby and I would be on our feet for most of the night and that nobody was going to see our shoes, so I'd dressed for comfort.

Straightening back up with my clutch, I said, "Like you have room to talk." I pointed down at his shiny black shoes. "What did you do, raid a funeral parlor?"

"I was told that these are worth several thousand dollars. I didn't get them off a mortician." That rare smile was back. As if I was amusing him. Which irritated me more.

"Huh. So in addition to being rude, you have bad taste and you're easily taken advantage of. Though on the plus side, when those legions of women fall at your feet, at least they'll be landing on some expensive shoes."

He made a sound that suspiciously resembled a laugh, but I was too angry to try to make sense of him. So instead I ripped open the wrapper to my candy bar and realized that at some point in the day it had gotten smushed. It was in bits and pieces.

Again, *of course.*

I carefully lifted up a chunk, trying to get the flaking-off chocolate to land in my clutch and not on me. The rental place would charge me extra if I brought this dress back with stains on it.

"Are you eating?" That indescribable tone was back in his voice, as if he was amused but hadn't experienced that kind of emotion recently so was rusty at expressing it.

"Yes. Did you want some?" I thought that was awfully big of me.

"No."

"Your loss." I got another bite of my squished and now slightly melting candy bar into my mouth. I blamed Noah Douglas for the melty part. Because him sitting there was having the same effect on my insides.

"Is that a Snickers bar? What if I had a peanut allergy?" he asked.

"Then you'd be dead and we'd both be happy?" Sucking in a deep breath, I turned to face him. "I'm so sorry. Stress and hunger are not my friends, and they make me into some kind of she-demon who says really inappropriate things. I didn't mean what I just said. That was awful. I don't want you to die. And if you do have a peanut allergy, I would . . . I don't know, stop eating and hold my breath. I'd call an ambulance and I'd try to find you an EpiPen. Do you have a peanut allergy?" My pulse was pounding. He was annoying, but I didn't want to actually hurt him. Or anyone else. I zipped my clutch back up.

His eyes twinkled at me. Like, literally sparkled with delight. "No."

15

Now I was mad that I'd apologized to him when he'd obviously said it just to make me freak out and be sad about the thought of him dying. Because I would be very sad. In part because then they couldn't film a much-needed sequel to Duel of the Fae where Aliana Morningsong goes to the Realm Beyond Realms to rescue Malec from death.

"You have chocolate on you. There."

Noah pointed toward my neck and reached forward with his massive hand, and I actually backed up as far as I could in my seat. "Dude, don't touch me."

He seemed surprised by my reaction and held both hands up, like I was mugging him. A cameraman noticed the movement and turned toward us.

"Put your hands down," I hissed as I ran my fingers along my collarbone, trying to figure out where the chocolate was. I found it, a pool of brown liquid. My skin was still flushed from interacting with Noah, and the chocolate had probably melted on contact. I didn't know if I'd actually cleaned it off or if I'd just made the mess worse.

"Are you always like this or is it just something I've brought out in you?"

I glared at him as my response. And even though I didn't want to, I asked, "Did I get it?"

He shrugged one shoulder. "More or less."

More or less? What? Was I covered in chocolate or not? A bolt of anger pierced my gut. I really was going to end up in jail tonight for having attacked a movie star.

Ralph Ramsey, who I had completely forgotten about, finished his speech, and everyone around us gave him a standing ovation, cheering and clapping. It took me a second to get myself together enough to rise up and do the same. And I noticed again how tall Noah was, how broad and masculine. He had to be six three, six four. I was the girl who joked about being five twelve, and he made me feel like I wasn't the tallest person in the room.

It was nice.

The lights went down, indicating a commercial break. Noah sat, and I realized my mistake. I should have squeezed past him immediately, because now I'd have to climb over him to get out. But was I supposed to leave? Shelby had told me to stay put until the original seat owner returned. And the original owner was Noah's date. Maybe she'd made a break for it after she found out what an egomaniac he was.

I sat down, ignoring him, still wiping at my skin and hoping I hadn't been on camera with melted chocolate all over my throat.

But it wasn't like before, when I'd just sat here minding my own business. Now I felt this weird, awkward energy between us. I'd read once that he had social anxiety and hated making small talk. Although what we'd just been doing wouldn't exactly qualify as small talk. More like "you suck" talk.

He cleared his throat. "So . . ." His voice trailed off, and I found that I was desperately curious to find out what he was about to say, but he got to his feet.

There was a gorgeous woman standing next to him. She had on one of those body-contouring dresses that had been made out of thin strips of white fabric. Almost like bandages. It showed off her perfect figure but also had me wondering if the national museum in Egypt knew she had escaped their exhibit.

I'd bet anything she didn't have an emergency Snickers bar in her clutch.

"Excuse me, but you are in my seat." She said the words through her clenched, perfect white teeth.

"I'm the seat filler. Just keeping it warm for you," I joked, but she glared at me. I stood up and was suddenly at a loss as to what to do. If Noah had moved over into the aisle, it would have been very easy for me to get out and head backstage.

But he stayed put, standing there.

Which meant that I would be forced to brush past him to escape, and honestly? I didn't think my shot nerves could take the sensation of full-frontal touching.

Then Barbie Mummy made the decision for me by coming into the row. I backed up as much as I could into the poor woman who had been seated on my other side, apologizing to her as I did so.

Noah's date took her seat, shooting me a look of triumph. I could go out the other way. But then I'd have to climb over, like, twenty people, and that did not sound appealing to me.

Time to swallow my pride and just get out of here. "Sorry," I said to his date, "I just need to . . ."

She didn't move her legs and in fact kept them close to the seat in front of her, as if daring me to hop over her. Did she think I wouldn't?

Not sure of how Shelby would want me to handle this, I just stood there awkwardly and weighed the pros and cons of going either direction. Whatever I was going to do, it needed to be soon. I was running out of time.

Noah had pulled out his cell phone and sat back down, which made the choice for me. Now that I didn't have to worry about being sandwiched between him and the seat in front of him, this would be the best way out.

I tried with his date again. "Excuse me. I just need to get past."

But she was also on her cell phone and ignored me. I tried nudging her legs, but she didn't budge.

Fine.

I hiked my dress up to my thighs and stepped over her legs, which apparently surprised her so much that her knees shot up into me, which made me lose my footing and fall headfirst against Noah's legs.

"Are you all right?" he asked as he reached out to help me.

"I'm fine," I said, brushing his hands away. I could feel dozens of eyes on us as I struggled to stand back up. He tried again to help me back up to my feet, and I resisted both him and the urge to kick his girlfriend in the ankle.

When I stood up, the only thing between me and the aisle was a still-seated Noah.

"Are you sure you're okay?" he asked with what sounded like real concern in his voice. He was such a good actor, putting on a show for everyone around us. Most likely for the benefit of his girlfriend.

"I told you, I'm fine."

I could see a smile hovering around the edges of his mouth. "Okay. Well, when you get backstage, remember the food goes in your mouth and not on your neck."

My hand flew up to my throat in surprise. Was the chocolate stain still there? "Listen up, you smug, arrogant, condescending pain in the—"

I was cut off by the lights coming back up, and a spike of adrenaline coursed through me.

They were back from the commercial break and I was stuck with no chair to sit in, and even if I climbed over Noah, there was no way to get backstage in time.

So I did the only thing I could think of.

I dropped to the floor at Noah Douglas's feet.

CHAPTER THREE

"What do you think you're doing?" his date asked before kicking me in the leg. She was not wearing sneakers, and it hurt.

"Ow!" I protested.

Noah put out his arm between the two of us. "Hey, Hannah. That's enough."

She let out a huff of indignation and then turned her body as far away from me as she possibly could, which was good, since it gave me some breathing room.

He leaned forward and asked, "So what is the plan here?"

"The number one rule is I either have to be in a seat or backstage when the lights come on, and obviously I can't do either one of those things right now. So I'm . . . here. Until the next commercial break."

"Which makes you . . . what? Schrödinger's seat filler?"

Okay, that made me smile. The man could be charming if he wanted to be. "You can't look at me or talk to me. Just pretend like I'm not here."

"Gladly," Hannah said, but it was like Noah hadn't even heard her. Or really even registered that they were, like, on a date, but I was the one he was talking to.

Why was that thought making my heart flutter?

Then he leaned forward and I wondered how I hadn't noticed before how good he smelled. Clean and crisp, with some kind of expensive, masculine, woodsy scent. "You know, when I said that thing about women falling at my feet, I didn't mean for it to be an invitation."

He said it so flirtatiously I couldn't even get mad. I just sat there on the floor, feeling extremely stupid. This was one of the most humiliating experiences of my entire life. Easily top five.

But not number one. Nothing could ever be more humiliating than number one.

And at some point a camera operator was going to realize that Noah was chatting with the floor and the jig would be up. "Look, I know I don't have the right to ask for any kind of favor, but I will get someone I love in trouble if you keep talking to me. You really do have to pretend like I'm not here."

He studied me for a moment, then gave me a little half smile. "Sure thing. But you owe me one."

What? I owed him one? What would that even entail? This night just kept getting more and more bizarre.

I heard one of the presenters say, "And the nominees are . . . ," and almost flew into a blind panic. What if it was Noah's category? And he won? Then there would be cameras everywhere and they would definitely catch me and Shelby would never speak to me again!

But it wasn't his category. I let out a sigh of relief.

This floor was gross. It felt sticky underneath me. I was definitely going to have to pay that stain-removal fee to the rental place, and there went my food budget for the next two weeks.

His date kept her distance from me, hostility radiating out of her every flawless pore, but it was almost like Noah had forgotten that both of us were there. Although he did keep accidentally bumping into me with his large feet and shooting me apologetic looks. Which surprised me, given that our conversation had begun with him accusing me of stalking him. And if anything was stalking behavior, I was pretty sure this was it.

Especially when I noticed he was wearing socks with pizza slices on them. That was unexpected, and I may or may not have accidentally brushed my fingers against them just to make sure they were real. He didn't seem to notice.

And despite telling myself not to stare, I kept sneaking glances at him. Even though he'd spent most of our brief time together being the worst, there was just something about him that made it so I had to keep looking. Like he was subliminally pulling me in and I was powerless to resist.

He seemed to always be in motion, crossing and uncrossing his legs, flexing and unflexing his huge hands, shifting from one side of his seat to the other. I wondered if he was bored. Or was just one of those people who had so much pent-up energy they hated sitting still.

Then he ran his fingers through his hair, and the gesture made my stomach quiver and my mouth go completely dry. I'd seen him do it a hundred times on-screen, but it landed completely differently in person.

To distract myself I tried listening to the speech of the winner, but it was almost like the entire world had faded away and Noah Douglas was the only real thing in it.

What was wrong with me?

Fortunately this winner was brief and to the point, and the lights went back down. Noah quickly got up and offered me his hand.

This time I took it, and it was like a thousand tiny atom bombs exploded across the surface of my skin. "Thanks," I said, and it shocked me how wobbly my voice sounded, how shallow my breathing had become. We stood there, our hands clasped, and something happened. Something I didn't recognize. And was most likely entirely one-sided.

I wondered if I should apologize for my earlier behavior or thank him for not making a scene and getting me in trouble or whether I should say goodbye or . . . I didn't know what to do, so I just let go and darted out into the aisle, wanting to put this entire evening behind me and hopefully leave with whatever dignity I still had left. I thought I felt his eyes watching me walk away, but I was too chicken to turn around and check.

In my haste to flee, I almost ran straight into the famous actress Dame Helena Lynch. "Oh, do slow down, dear!" she called out.

"I'm so sorry!" But there was no chance of that, even though now I'd nearly taken down a national treasure on the same night I bickered with Noah Douglas and then humiliated myself in front of him.

When I got backstage, my whole body sighed with relief. I was done. Safe. I bet if I asked Allan, he would pull some strings and keep me backstage. I could not go out into the audience again.

Although . . . what did I think was going to happen? What was I feeling so worried about? I'd told myself that it was my concern for Shelby, but nothing had happened. She was fine and I hadn't been caught breaking any of the rules. So why had my insides tangled themselves up in knots?

I grabbed one of the free water bottles and acknowledged that I was scared that Noah and I had just shared a moment. Of the romantic variety. Which was so dumb, because Noah was dating the Bride of the Mummy, and he would obviously never be interested in someone like me. I was the girl picked last for sports teams. The one who didn't get asked to the prom. I was always on the outside looking in. Not to mention that we'd just spent our entire evening being rude to each other. That wasn't exactly a recipe for romance.

Not that I'd go out with him, even if he asked. I didn't date.

I then reminded myself that he didn't know my name, so odds were I was getting worked up over absolutely nothing. Plus, I'd be so out of my depth that I would need scuba gear.

But what if . . . what if I could be with Noah Douglas, or someone like him, and not feel terrified the entire time? Wouldn't that be something?

I approached Allan. "Is it okay if I just hang out back here for a while? Can I be your last resort after you've put everyone else to work?"

He nodded, looking concerned. "Sure thing. You okay?"

"Yeah." I smiled, even though I felt like a fraud because I was still shaken up and was definitely not okay. My pulse had just finally returned to normal. "Everything's fine. My back just hurts a little." Along with my pride.

"I'll let you know if I need you. And if I didn't say it before, thanks for helping out tonight. You know how much it means to Shelby."

"I do." I wondered if he did. If he understood how truly awful his mother was. Because he'd grown up with her, and her craziness probably seemed normal to him, so he wouldn't be able to recognize how bad it was. But now was not the time to ask him about it.

It was time to hide myself in a corner and watch the rest of the event on the giant monitor hanging on the wall behind me. I found an abandoned folding chair and watched as a few more winners were given their little statues. My ears perked up when the host said it was time for the Best Actor award.

They announced all the nominees and cut to each one of them for a reaction shot. I caught my breath when they zoomed in on Noah, who looked a bit sheepish and was clapping for his fellow nominees.

The envelope was opened and . . . Noah didn't win. Chase Covington did instead. Noah leaned forward to slap him on the shoulder in congratulations while Chase kissed his very pretty wife seated next to him.

Why did I feel so disappointed? I was being so weird tonight.

I was getting hungry again when Allan stopped by to check on me. I assured him I was still fine, and he handed me a package of M&M's, which I took gratefully. "Shelby said I needed to keep you well fed."

"This is why you're my favorite out of all Shelby's fiancés."

That made him laugh, and he put a hand up to cover one of his ears, presumably to hear better. He pointed at his headphones, waved at me, and then went back over to the curtain as another commercial break started up.

The monitor showed the attendees chatting, and I couldn't help but search out where Noah had been sitting. He was still there, concentrating on his phone, not talking to the woman beside him. It gave me a tingling flush of pleasure that he wasn't interacting with his date.

I ate my bag of M&M's while the lights went back up and they announced that they were going to present the award for Best Dramatic Feature. I was interrupted from my visual stalking of Noah Douglas when Shelby joined us backstage. Allan said something that made her laugh, and she kissed him in return. While I was so, so happy for my best friend, I felt an all-too-familiar twinge of jealousy that I had no idea how to be like that with someone else.

And my worst fear was someone finding out the reason why.

It was better for me to put this whole night behind me and just move on like it never happened. Because, logically and realistically, nothing was going to happen.

In what reality would Noah Douglas be interested in someone like me?

They announced the winner, and it was the Peruvian film that had been getting all the buzz. I hadn't seen it. I preferred romantic comedies and fairy tales.

"How was your night?" Shelby asked when she reached me. She sat in another folding chair behind me, forcing me to turn around in order to see her. "I was seated next to George Wilcox. You know, the composer? He did all of the music for Duel of the Fae. He didn't win, though. I felt bad for him. But he was so nice to me. It was kind of surreal."

Ha. She had no idea how surreal I was about to make her night when I told her what I'd been up to. "Speaking of, you'll never guess who I was sitting with."

"Noah Douglas."

"What?" I asked with a laugh. "How could you possibly know that? Did you see me with him?"

Her eyes went wide and she repeated, "Noah Douglas."

"Yes, I know, we've established that I was sitting next to Noah Douglas. And I think I might have completely freaked him out. Like a sewer clown with a red balloon."

"No, um, Noah Douglas."

This time she pointed, and I turned to see what was going on. It took me a second to process that Noah Douglas was standing there, holding my clutch, which looked comically small in his hands.

The same clutch that I had completely forgotten on the floor in an effort to escape.

I stood up, stunned. My heart leaped into my throat, almost making it impossible for me to breathe. I wondered if my mouth was hanging open like Shelby's.

"Here. You left this." He held out my clutch to me, and I felt both totally weirded out and profoundly grateful. My phone was in there.

"Uh . . . thank you."

I took it back and just gaped at him, unsure of what to do next. Especially since the logical thing would be for him to turn around and leave. Why was he still here? Did . . . did he want to talk to me? Why? What was happening? This was like something out of a fanfic or a fantasy, and things like that did not happen to people like me.

"Hi!" Shelby stepped around me and held out her hand. "I'm Shelby Farmingham. Nice to meet you."

"Nice to meet you, too." He shook her hand, sounding oh so polite. "As you've already pointed out, I'm Noah Douglas."

That made Shelby laugh, and it was a laugh I'd never heard before. High-pitched and shrill. Like she felt just as hysterical and unnerved as I did.

"So . . . ," he said, once Shelby had calmed down, "I'm going to this after-party. I don't know how much fun it will be, but maybe—"

"Oh, good luck with that. Personally, I hate parties. They're not really my scene," I told him. I was much more of a crash-on-my-couch-and-eat-my-body-weight-in-chocolate kind of girl. And why was he bragging about going to a party? We already knew he was famous. He didn't need to remind us.

He raised his eyebrows. "Right. Okay." He paused, and I ignored Shelby, who was currently pressing down on my right foot and I didn't know why.

"Oh, that Juliet!" Shelby said, slapping me on the arm. Hard enough that I flinched. "She likes parties! Who doesn't like a party? She's the perfect girl to take to a party. You've obviously already met her, so you know that she's tall and gorgeous and fun and so, so sweet and kind." Was it my imagination or did mention of my sweetness and kindness make a smile ghost across his lips? "And she's an entrepreneur. She just started up her own mobile dog-grooming business."

"Yes, she might have mentioned that already," he said.

"Do you have a dog?" Shelby asked, her voice still too bright and perky. "Because you definitely want to hire Juliet. She will come to you and clean your pup. Anytime, day or night." She opened her purse. "Here's her card."

That made me blink rapidly. Why did she have my business cards in her purse? And why was she talking about me like I wasn't even in the room?

He studied it for a moment. "Thanks. I'll give you a call sometime, Juliet Nolan." He said my name like he was caressing it with his voice, and I almost passed out. "Have a good evening." He slid my card into his breast pocket, nodded his head, and then he was gone. Vanished as quickly as he'd appeared.

I would have wondered if I'd hallucinated the whole thing if not for Shelby jumping up and down and shrieking, "I can't believe we met Noah Douglas! What? How did that happen? Best day ever! And how deliciously awkward were the two of you? I loved it!"

"What was that?" I demanded.

Her jumping stopped. "What?"

"That . . . that word vomit just now? About me and my business?"

She tilted her chin defiantly. "I was helping you."

"I don't think so." That had been awful. If I hadn't scared him away before, well, Shelby had just made sure that I'd definitely never see him again. He probably thought we were psychos. "And why do you have my business card?"

"Duh, in case we need them. Which we obviously just did. Don't you have some of mine?"

"I don't even have mine in here."

Shelby took my clutch and put both my cards and some of her cards for her interior design business into it. "There. Now you do. Just in case one of the Hemsworths wants me to redo their bedroom."

"Do you think Harmony will get mad about you trying to drum up business?"

A look of dismay crumpled up Shelby's face. "Well, I do now!"

"No, don't get upset! I was kidding. I'm the only one who knows, and I promise I won't tell her. And you know Noah Douglas won't, so we're good."

"To be fair, the Noah thing was personal. It wasn't about business."

"What do you mean?"

"Uh, he's interested in you. He asked you out."

I could feel my eyebrows fly up my forehead. "What! He did not."

"Yes, he did. He was inviting you to that party, and you cut him off and then shot him down. After he was all gallant and returned your clutch to you. Which is something he absolutely did not have to do."

My heart started pounding fast. Was she right? I mentally reviewed what he'd said. He had never actually asked me to go. Shelby was reading into the situation. I couldn't let myself believe that she might be right. Time to put my defenses back up. It didn't matter how hot Noah Douglas was—nothing was happening and I wasn't going to buy into the fantasy. That was much more her thing than mine. I was the pragmatic realist here.

"People can be polite without ulterior motives. Plus, he was already on a date. With a very beautiful woman."

She waved her hand dismissively. "You know as well as I do half of the 'relationships' in this town are just showmances arranged by their respective PR teams. He doesn't seem like the kind of guy who would ask a girl out if he was on a date with another one."

"You don't know anything about him."

"Neither do you. Which is why you should get to know him when he calls you."

I wanted to roll my eyes. "He's not going to call me. That's just something you say when somebody forces you to take a business card."

"Noah Douglas is going to call you."

"No, he's not. Tonight did not go well."

"He is."

"He is *not* going to call me."

He totally called me.

CHAPTER FOUR

A week after the awards show, I was on my couch enjoying the second movie in the Duel of the Fae trilogy. Halfway through a box popped up on my screen.

ARE YOU STILL WATCHING?

"Yes, InstaFlicks, I'm still watching. I don't need your judgment on my movie consumption," I muttered. I clicked the "Yes" button. If they were going to question my life choices, they should create something that would appear in my fridge and ask, "Do you really want to eat that?" It would be much more helpful. Or remind me to take a shower.

My phone rang, and I picked it up to look at the screen. It said RESTRICTED. Before I started my business, I wouldn't have answered it, but now I couldn't afford to miss out on any potential clients.

The total upside was all the time I got to spend chatting with telemarketers about my insurance needs and potential credit card applications.

"Hello?" I asked, my mouth full of popcorn.

"Hi, is this Juliet?"

"Yep."

"This is Noah. Noah Douglas? We met the other night."

I sat straight up and shot all the popcorn out of my mouth, dropping the bowl to the floor. Then I fumbled with the remote, trying to hit the pause button. The last thing I needed was him hearing his own voice coming from my TV.

"Yes, hi. Noah. I remember. What can I do for you?" I cringed. I sounded so stupid.

"I know this is last-minute, but . . ." He trailed off, and my whole chest constricted. What if Shelby wasn't misguided by her pretty-girl vision filter and had called this correctly and he wanted to go out with me? "I find myself in need of some emergency dog-grooming services. Could you help me out?"

My shoulders caved in. Oh. "Emergency dog-grooming services? You know that's not really a thing, right?"

"In this case it is. My dog, Magnus, is obsessed with mud, and he managed to find some. Problem is that we have an interview and photo shoot we're doing together tomorrow, and we both need to look our best. Can you come over?"

It felt like a heavy weight was pressing down on my chest as my heart thumped loudly. This was a job, and someone like Noah Douglas was well connected in Los Angeles. This could lead to more clients and more money.

So why wasn't I saying yes?

As if he sensed my hesitation, he said, "I don't want to be that guy, but you do still owe me one, and I'm calling it in."

That was true. It didn't make that panicky feeling go away. "Okay. I'll do it. Where am I going?"

"I'm in the Hollywood Hills."

"Text me the address and hopefully I'll be there in about forty-five minutes." I shared an apartment with Shelby in Pasadena, and given that it was a Sunday evening, I didn't anticipate a ton of traffic.

"Sounds good. See you then."

He hung up, and I just stood there in my living room, phone in my hand, trying to process what had just happened. Why would he call me? There were a million other mobile dog groomers. This made no sense.

Shelby breezed into the apartment. She'd spent the day with Allan and was in a great mood. "Juliet! Guess what? Remember that first-year associate at Allan's office who was cheating on his pregnant wife with his secretary like a total cliché? Turns out the secretary is pregnant, too, and she showed up at his house and made a huge scene. His wife is divorcing his slimy butt." She had dropped her purse and keys on the kitchen counter but stopped when she saw my face. "What's up with you?"

"Um, Noah Douglas wants me to come over and wash his dog." I put my cell phone down on the coffee table and dropped the remote on the couch. My pulse was jackhammering all over the place, making my blood feel too thick for my veins. I had to suck in a couple of deep breaths.

"What?" she shrieked.

"Not one word," I said. I didn't want her trying to turn this into something it wasn't as I headed into my bedroom to get changed. I needed to calm down, not keep getting more amped up.

"That is not possible, because I have so many words!" she said as she followed me. "What are you going to wear?"

"Uh, my clothes?" What kind of question was that?

"You're not going to get dressed up?"

"To wash his dog? No." I went through a pile of clothing on my floor looking for a pair of jeans to throw on.

"I can't believe you're about to go over to Felix Morrison's house and that you're going to fall in love with him now. That man is so attractive. I'd let him Felix my Morrison any day of the week."

"You're engaged," I reminded her as I pulled one of my business's polo shirts out of my closet.

She sat down on the edge of my bed. "Obviously I'm speaking in a metaphorical sense, because I'm never going to date him. Mostly because I'm ridiculously in love with Allan, but also because he's so obviously interested in you."

"Asking me to clean his dog does not indicate interest," I said, tugging my shirt on over my head.

"Hard disagree." She paused. "If he asks you out, will you go?"

"No," I immediately responded as I opened my top dresser drawer to get a clean pair of socks.

"But *why* won't you date Noah Douglas?" She sounded like a little kid who'd just been told she couldn't have an ice-cream cone. "He seemed so nice."

"Your opinion is wrong. When I talked with him, he was infuriating, and I kind of wanted to stab him and I think God would have understood."

"Pretty sure you're not supposed to kill people. And you know that's an important one, because it made His top ten."

I sat down to put on my socks and shoes. "So did not gossiping, and yet . . ."

"And yet," she agreed.

"Look, I get it. I'm a woman. I have eyes and ovaries or whatever, and I can see how hot he is. But you are getting your hopes up a little high. Like, that castle in the clouds from 'Jack and the Beanstalk' high." I tightened my laces. "You know I'm on a man sabbatical."

"It's not a sabbatical when you've never dated. That's like saying you're taking a sabbatical when you've never actually had a job. It's not a sabbatical. You're just unemployed." She said this gently and I knew what she was hinting at, but she wasn't getting any answers from me about it.

"Why are you so interested in my love life?" I asked, getting to my feet and going into the bathroom to brush my hair and put it up in a ponytail.

She followed me there, too. "Somebody has to be!"

I went back to my old standby. "I'm focusing on building up my business right now. I don't want to worry about dating."

"No one wants you to worry. Dating is actually in the fun section of the program. I'm just saying that whatever happens tonight, maybe you should try pushing yourself out of your comfort zone."

"Which I don't want to do, because it's my favorite zone in the whole world. Much better than demilitarized or twilight. I prefer staying in it." I got my toothbrush, put some toothpaste on it, and quickly brushed my teeth.

"You know," she mused, "the one thing I regret is that we didn't get a picture with Noah. Because no one's going to believe that we met him."

"We know, and outside of us, who is going to care?" We had been best friends since our mothers met in a Mommy and Me playgroup, and whatever other friends we'd made over the years all fell by the wayside when Shelby got sick.

"That's true. Allan pretended like he was excited when I told him about it, but the only way he would actually care is if Noah got drafted by the 49ers."

I considered putting on makeup, but I knew what a mess I was about to make of myself, so there was no point. After a moment of internal wrestling, I reached for a pale-pink lip gloss and spread it across my mouth.

Her eyebrows lifted in excitement at my small effort, and she said, "You know I still plan on us having a double wedding, and I've got two years to make it happen."

This was something she'd decided when we were eleven, and she'd never gotten over it. "You saying something is a plan doesn't actually make it a plan. I love you, but I'm under no obligation to humor you."

"But I've had to let go of so many dreams," she said in a small voice, and it made me feel unbelievably guilty and sad for everything she'd been put through. I turned around to hug her.

"I know. And it's also okay to get some new dreams."

"But if I can't even get you interested in going out with a movie star, our double wedding is definitely never going to happen." She mumbled the words into my shoulder.

I stepped back and just shook my head. "Noah and I are going to have a strictly professional interaction. You know me—I don't like to mix business with disdain."

"You may feel certain things about Noah Douglas, but disdain is not one of them."

She hadn't been the one sitting next to him. She didn't know what she was talking about. "It doesn't matter. Don't you remember when that palm reader warned us about dating a guy with two first names?"

"That was my reading, not yours. You're free to date him."

"You know that's not going to happen. Tell me you know that I'm not actually going to date Noah Douglas."

"Probably not," she agreed. "But isn't it fun to daydream?"

Personally, I'd found daydreaming to be overrated and a waste of energy. Real life demanded too much of my focus. I had gone into the kitchen to search for my keys. I had a bad habit of dropping them places and forgetting where. "Have you seen my keys?"

"They're on the table. But before you go, take these." She handed me some business cards, both hers and mine. "Just in case."

It wasn't worth arguing about. "Thanks. I need to get on the road. Wish me luck!"

"I wish you kisses and a new boyfriend!" she said as I walked out our door.

Ha. Fat chance of either one of those things happening.

It took me a bit longer to get to Noah's house than I'd anticipated. He lived in a gated community, but the guard was expecting me and just waved me through. Then it was dark and the roads were winding and Google Maps was being strangely coy about where I should be going.

I eventually found it, and he had a long driveway with no lights. I turned on my brights and inched my way up the incline. I was surprised when I reached the top and found a tiny little bungalow that was well lit both inside and out. I'd expected a mansion, to be honest.

There was a strange lump in my throat as I turned off the van, climbed down from the driver's seat, and made my way to the front door. I heard a dog barking loudly as I stood on his porch, and for some reason that sound made me feel better. I rang the doorbell and braced myself for impact.

But to my surprise, it wasn't Noah who answered the door.

It was Lily Ramsey. His Duel of the Fae costar. She was holding a small white terrier that was yipping away with all his might, wriggling to get free of her arms.

"You must be Juliet!" she yelled over her dog. "Come in!"

While I adored her as Aliana Morningsong, she didn't have the same effect on me that Noah had. I was not bewildered and shocked like I'd been with him. I wondered what she was doing there and how she knew who I was, but my brain stayed fully engaged, and I was pretty sure I'd be able to have a conversation with her.

I followed her into the house and was even more surprised. This house was dark and small, with wood paneling and avocado-colored carpeting. I wasn't sure what he'd been going for, but the decor was log cabin meets 1970s shagadelic. The kind of place where after he'd been arrested for murder the neighbors would tell the media, "He was quiet and kept to himself."

Shelby would wail and gnash her teeth when I told her about this.

Lily led me into a living room that had a couch and nothing else in it. Not even any pictures. She sat down on one end of the sole piece of furniture, and I sat on the other.

"I'm going to let him go. He's harmless," she assured me in her lilting British accent. She and Noah had insane chemistry on-screen. Lots of online fans stanned them in real life and wanted them to be together, despite the fact that she was married. They would probably freak out if they knew they were friends who had playdates with their dogs.

I was a little in awe of how stunningly pretty she was, even without any makeup on and her long blonde hair up in a bun. Her features were delicate and her frame slight. She didn't seem so tiny on the big screen. She possessed one of those infectious smiles that made you smile in response, and I found myself feeling even more at ease.

I nodded, and she released him. He finally stopped barking and immediately ran over to me to sniff my hands. "And who is this adorable little fella?"

"This is Blueberry. I would scold him for the barking, but he's quite deaf. It was the reason I adopted him. I figured if anyone needed a home, it was him."

This made me like her even more. "That's really neat."

"He's been one of the best things that's ever happened to me. I adopted him right before the Fae trilogy started and would bring him to set with me, and he and Magnus became the best of friends. So whenever I'm in the same city as Noah, I tend to drop in unannounced so they can have a doggy playdate. And speaking of Noah, Magnus managed to get outside again and he's trying to coax him back in. He's quite the escape artist. Noah asked me to entertain you until he returns."

"Should we go help?" I asked.

"There's no one quite so capable as Noah. He'll wrangle him back in. He always does. It helps that the man is enormous and strong and could probably drag a polar bear inside if he had to. So how long have you known Noah?"

"We met last week. We only spoke for a few minutes."

Lily's eyes sparkled at me. "Really? How fun."

"What do you mean?"

"He's the kind of man who will exchange pleasantries with you and then two minutes later he'll ask about your relationship with your father. He loves to go deep and ferret out your emotional baggage and uncover your deepest secrets."

My heart lurched to one side. That wasn't good. I couldn't let that happen. I would remember that this was strictly business.

I was going to be strong when I saw him again. I wouldn't think of him as a gorgeous, delicious beast of a man. He was just a dog owner and he had hired me, nothing more. I would not melt like an icicle in the desert. I wouldn't.

Her phone buzzed, and she picked it up. If her smile was infectious before, it was downright dazzling now. "That's Todd, my husband. He's wondering if I've left already. I should get going. Will you be all right?"

She was just going to leave me here? "Of course."

"Great. I'm in and out of LA, and if you don't mind, I'd love to use your services in the future. I could always use a good dog groomer that I can rely on. And if Noah's letting you come to his home, well, it says a lot about your trustworthiness."

It did? "I'd love that."

"Brilliant."

It was then that I remembered the business cards Shelby had put in my back pocket. She was like some kind of seer. "I have a card, if you like."

"Oh no, it won't do you any good to give it to me, because I'll lose it. So I'll just get your number from Noah. Toodles!" She picked up Blueberry and made her way to the front door. I heard the door close and sat on the couch in silence. I was tempted to get up and explore but figured that would be rude and probably the worst way to start out our professional relationship.

I did look around, and from where I was sitting, I could see part of the kitchen with its orange cabinets and mustard-yellow appliances. It hurt my eyes to look at it.

I heard a sliding glass door opening and a dog barking and a man grunting. Something large hit a wall. It sounded like he needed help. I followed the noise and found them in a massive library that was filled with hundreds of books.

My breath caught when I saw him. Noah had on a black T-shirt and jeans and was covered in as much dirt as Magnus was, like they'd been wrestling around outside. He was every bit as overwhelming as the last time I'd seen him and somehow sexier as he held his very large and heavy dog in his strong arms with ease.

Every single bit of my resolve to be strong fled.

I was in trouble.

CHAPTER FIVE

"You made it!" he said, his deep voice tinged with exhaustion and amusement.

"I did. Hi. Um, Lily Ramsey let me in and we talked and she introduced me to Blueberry and then she explained about Magnus and then I heard you come in and it sounded like you needed some assistance, so I came in here . . ." I let my voice trail off. I sounded like I was having a stroke. "Is there anything I can do to help?"

"Yes. Can you shut the door and lock it?"

"Sure." I had to step around him and found myself struggling to breathe as I got close to him, feeling all of the warmth he was emanating. I cleared my throat and slid the door back into place, finding the lock in the handle and flipping it up. I backed up quickly. "There you go. All clear."

Noah's biceps flexed as he gently set his dog down, and Magnus came over to inspect me. I crouched down to his level and held out my hands for him. "You are one dirty boy," I told him.

"I am," Noah agreed as he brushed some soil off his pants.

My cheeks flushed and I said, "I was talking to your dog."

"I know." Then he winked at me and all the blood drained from my brain.

Magnus wagged his tail at me, bringing me back to reality, and I petted him. "He's beautiful. Is he part rottweiler?" He had the telltale black-and-tan color markings.

"He is. And part Newfoundland. And there's probably some other breeds mixed in. The adoption shelter wasn't sure."

The Newfie DNA explained why his fur was shaggy—he really was in need of a good brushing and bath. Which meant that Noah had been up front about why he'd called me and there was no ulterior motive, like Shelby had hoped for.

Why did that make me feel a little disappointed? This was so unlike me.

Noah crouched down next to me and Magnus went over to him, licking his face. I, surprisingly, found myself completely understanding the impulse. Noah told me, "I'm pretty sure he thinks he's part wolf and that's why he wants to escape into the wild. The problem is he's a good, sweet boy who doesn't have a mean bone in his body and thinks everybody is his friend. Which is why we don't want him to get into a fight with a pack of coyotes, do we, Magnus?"

He sounded like he was scolding him, but it was couched in so much gentleness and love that I was pretty sure Magnus had no idea he was being told to stop escaping.

I thought it was completely adorable how much Noah loved and worried about his dog. And a little ovary-melting, too.

Straightening up, I gestured around me. "This is quite a collection of books. I'm assuming you like to read."

"I do." He nodded and stood up, too. "When I got my medical discharge from the army, books are what helped me cope."

I knew that he'd joined the military when he was eighteen years old and had been discharged about three years later, after he was injured overseas. He didn't talk much in interviews about what had happened, but he'd often discussed his respect for the organization and for his buddies who had gone on to serve without him.

"What about you?" he asked. "Are you much of a reader?"

I picked up the book next to me, a collection of plays by Sophocles. I let out a little laugh. "Yes, but probably nothing you'd find interesting." For example, I adored the Duel of the Fae books that the movies were based on, and there was no way I could admit that to him.

Given that I'd told him I had no idea who he was.

"I doubt that," he said as he stood up and took a step closer to me. "You seem interesting to me."

My eyes widened, and I leaned against the bookshelf for support. What the holy frack did that mean?

So I decided to make a joke of it. "I'm not. I mean, while you're reading Sophocles, Proust, and Mamet, I'm usually rotting my brain watching television." I swallowed nervously, not liking the way he was looking at me. Or maybe the problem was that I liked it too much. "And you've definitely gone with some interesting decor choices here."

"I've been living in New York the last few years because I've liked the anonymity it affords me. But so much of my work is in Los Angeles that we moved here about six months ago. I wanted space for Magnus to run around in, so I planned on building a fence, but the homeowners' association is giving me grief. Anyway, this house used to be owned by a ninety-four-year-old woman. Her husband built it for her as a wedding present back in the 1950s. So I want to honor that history and restore it to its former glory, but I haven't found the right person to fix it up yet."

Maybe Shelby really was an all-seeing witch. "Actually, I happen to know the right person. It's my friend Shelby. Because if I tell her the way that this adorable bungalow is the victim of decorating abuse, I'm going to have to drive her to the hospital after she has a coronary. She takes her interior design very seriously."

I took out the small stack of cards she'd given me and sorted through them until I found one of hers. I handed it to him, being very careful to make sure that our fingers didn't accidentally brush, because I wasn't sure I'd be able to handle the sensation.

41

"Thanks for the recommendation." He slid the card into his own pocket.

That weird, awkward energy was back, and he was looking at me like . . . like he wanted to kiss me.

Panicky adrenaline flooded through me, and I cleared my throat loudly. "We should probably get started. Let me tell you a little about the services I provide."

I ran through what I'd do with Magnus, the brushing and bathing, the organic products I used that were environmentally friendly and didn't have any harsh chemicals, how I preferred towel drying and then stress-free toenail clipping. "I can also brush his teeth and clean out his ears, if you want."

"He probably needs the works. Let me get his leash in case he makes a dash for it once we go outside."

I nodded as he went into the kitchen. Talking about how I did my job had calmed me back down and made it so that I could appreciate Noah's broad shoulders as he went through the door. I thought again about how strong he was and how easily he'd hefted his dog. Magnus looked up at me expectantly, and I said, "You're the world's luckiest dog, did you know that?"

"Did you say something?" Noah asked when he reentered the library and attached the leash to Magnus's collar.

Other than a small part of me wishing I could switch places with Magnus? "No. I'm parked out front."

He led the way, which allowed me to walk behind him and enjoy the fact that his jeans were very well fitted and he filled them out nicely.

I tried not to sigh. I did not have nearly as much willpower as I thought I did. I was crumbling like a sandcastle at high tide.

To distract myself I asked, "So, you said they're doing a feature on you and Magnus?"

He glanced over his shoulder with a wry expression. "I know, it sounds pretentious. But yes."

It didn't sound the least bit pretentious to me. Because I was totally going to read that article and would probably even cut it out and put it in my old scrapbook. I'd started it back when he was starring on the teen show *Late for Class* as Felix Morrison. He played the mischievous ladies' man who was always getting in and out of schemes, to his principal's great frustration. The show was originally intended to be a showcase for the actress who played his homeroom teacher, but they quickly discovered that the teen girls were much more interested in Felix and he became the breakout star.

When I was younger, I used to clip magazine articles about Noah and the show, along with printing out stories and pictures of him from the internet, and put them all in my scrapbook. I wondered where it was. I hadn't seen that thing in years. My mom would probably know.

Noah opened the front door, and I made my way over to the van. He read the name on the side. "Waggin' Wheels. Clever."

"Thanks." I got out my keys to unlock the van.

He apparently had no concept of personal boundaries, as he stood close enough to me that if I moved even a fraction of an inch, my back would be pressed against his front. Flustered, I dropped my keys not once, but twice.

Shaking my head, I finally pushed the unlock and then the door open buttons to open the van. The lights popped on as I climbed in.

"Wow," he said. "This wasn't what I was expecting."

"It's nice, isn't it?" The inside was a pristine white with different stainless steel stations for each part of the grooming process, along with white overhead cabinets to hold all of my supplies. It almost looked like the inside of a spaceship. "Come in," I told him. "I call it my Hair Force One."

His expression didn't alter.

"Get it?" I said, just in case he didn't realize it was a joke.

"Oh, I got it. It just wasn't, you know, funny." I realized that he was teasing me in that sardonic tone of his, and it both annoyed and thrilled me.

Although the van had a high ceiling, Noah still had to duck when he got in and stand with his head slightly tilted. Magnus was sniffing everything in sight, and I shut the door behind us.

And realized just how tiny the space was with the three of us in it. I felt pressed to fill the silence with words. Any words. "Part of the benefit of using a mobile service like mine is that Magnus will have a chance to check this all out and get comfortable before we do anything. I'll also play with him for a little while and give him a belly rub and a treat, so that he's comfortable with me, too. There're no other dogs here, no scents or sounds that will stress him out. Hopefully it'll be an enjoyable experience for him."

He nodded and reached for one of the knobs on the cabinet closest to him. "Sounds good. Did you always want to be a dog groomer?"

"Like, since I was a little kid? No. My mom wanted me to be an accountant, and that's what I was studying in college, and then Shelby, the friend I mentioned earlier? You met her the other night. Her fiancé's mother is the one who ran the seat-filler thing for the awards show." I was veering into babbling territory and got myself back on track. "Anyway, a few years ago, Shelby got sick with acute lymphocytic leukemia, and it changed everything for me. One day I was looking at her lying in a hospital bed and it just hit me—what was I doing? I didn't want to be an accountant. Life was too short. I wanted to do something I loved."

"That makes sense," he said.

Magnus finished his exploration, and I sat down on the floor next to him and gave him a treat. I started scratching behind his ears, which he seemed to enjoy.

Noah was watching me, as if expecting me to go on, so I did. "Anyway, I tried a bunch of different things for a couple of years. And I realized that I didn't want to work in an office. I wanted to be my own boss, making my own schedule. My mom owns a housecleaning business and I was temporarily working for her, and she had this client who had bought this van for his third wife who wanted to start her own business, but it turned out she didn't like animals. And I'd always loved dogs. So I offered to buy the van and he sold it to me at a discounted rate. I pay him monthly installments."

"Was your mom disappointed?"

"She was furious," I said. "I think in part because she had given up on her dream to be an actress to take care of me and so she wanted me to have a sensible, reliable job, too. I think she finally realized that was more her issue, and she backed off." I let out a little laugh. "Wow. Sorry to drop my whole life story on you like that."

"No, I like it. I was the one who asked, remember?" I tried not to read too much into his words. I also tried to ignore how disconcerting it was to have him towering over me as I attempted to bond with Magnus. He asked, "Do you have a dog?"

I shook my head. "I don't. My mom was allergic and I currently don't because my landlord doesn't allow it. But someday I will. Someday I'm going to have my own ranch with a barn and tons of land so that I can bring in as many rescue animals as possible and take care of them. For now I get my daily fix from other people's pets. Don't I, Magnus?" I was scratching his belly, and his tongue lolled out of his mouth.

"I wasn't allowed to have any pets growing up, either, and now I wonder how anyone can be happy without a dog of their own. I had no idea how much you could love one until I got Magnus. I have a hard time imagining loving anyone more than I do him."

"I bet your girlfriend loves hearing that," I said.

"I'm not dating anyone."

But what about Barbie Mummy? I wanted to know, but decided it was none of my business. Maybe we had different definitions for the word *dating. Keeping it professional, remember?* I reminded myself. "I should probably get started."

"Yes," he said, handing me the leash. "I'm sure you have other things to do. I didn't mean to pull you away from any plans you might have had this evening. Is someone . . . expecting you?"

I led Magnus over to the table I used for brushing. He was a heavy beastie, easily 150 pounds, if not more. I did manage to get him up with the offer of another treat. "Expecting me? Other than Shelby? No."

"So . . . you're not seeing anyone? No boyfriend?"

"Uh, no," I said with a laugh that was tinged with a bit of frenzy. "No, definitely not." Never had, never would.

Wait. Why was he asking me that?

He immediately shot down any notion that he meant something more by it by adding, "Good. I felt bad about calling you over here last-minute, and I just wanted to make sure I wasn't infringing on your time. I'm going to grab a shower if you're okay here."

Maybe he'd felt obligated to ask me about my dating situation because I'd kind of asked him first. I went for some humor to relieve the tension I was feeling. "So what you're saying is that you're about to get groomed, too . . . Nope, I hear it out loud and I take it back. Too lame of a joke. I'll just see you in a little bit."

That hint of a smile was there, and I wondered what it would take to get that dimple of his to reappear. Not that I was going to try, but I did wonder.

He opened and then closed the van door, and I let out a sigh of relief. It was like my entire body tensed up around him, and I was glad to be able to calm down and focus on the job I'd come here to do. "We'll get you clean and shiny and soft, won't we, Magnus?"

Magnus barked in response, and I concentrated on making him beautiful. Muscle memory made it easy to go through the motions quickly. That Magnus was so cooperative helped, too. Which left me time to think. Like, would Noah come back out here to the van? Or would he expect me to come to the front door? It wasn't something

I'd ever considered before with other clients, but it suddenly seemed important.

Shelby sent me a text.

How are things going?

I took a picture of myself and Magnus's tail. Noah had always come across like a private person in his interviews, and I got the feeling he wouldn't want me to be taking pictures of his dog.

I'm washing a dog. So things are same old, same old.

I saw the three dots as she typed.

Has he asked you out yet?

No, and he won't.

He will.

I wasn't going to get into an argument with her over it, because the last time I did that, she had turned out to be right.

What if she's right this time, too? a little voice whispered. *Okay, universe,* I said. *If he likes me, he will come back to the van. If I have to go to him, he doesn't.*

It was childish, but now that I'd set up an imaginary test, we'd just see what happened next.

And I'll admit that now I was taking my time with Magnus, because a part of me was hoping Noah would come back to the van, but he didn't.

Giving in and acknowledging the sign the universe had just given me about Noah's lack of interest, I asked Magnus if he'd like a bow. I held up a blue one and he sniffed it, and so I took that as approval.

I tied it on him, and since he didn't rip it off immediately, I considered it a win. "Come on, boy, let's get you back inside before you mess up all my work." I attached the leash to his collar again and led him to the front door. I rang the doorbell, and even though I knew what was going to happen, even though I'd been expecting it, I still felt bowled over when Noah answered it.

Especially since his hair was wet and slicked back from his strong face. Although I'd always had definite opinions regarding what I preferred in men's haircuts (clean-cut), when it came to him, I didn't care what he did or didn't do. I was a fan of it all.

He'd changed into a different pair of jeans and a black hoodie. He smelled clean, like soap and shampoo, and I stopped myself from dragging in a deep breath.

"All done!" I said, too brightly.

"I can see that." His burning gaze floated down over my soaked clothing. Self-conscious, I pulled the wet cloth away from my body. "Do you need to come in and dry off?"

Heart pounding loudly in my chest, I said, "No, I'm good. It's all part of the job. Thanks." Not to mention that if he kept looking at me like that, my wet shirt was going to catch on fire.

And despite my saying it was fine, he stepped back to let me into the living room. My feet moved of their own volition so that it surprised me a little when he closed the door. Stupid, traitorous feet. I gave him the leash, which he undid.

Then he asked in a disbelieving tone, "Why is my dog wearing a bow?"

"Magnus likes it."

"He also likes to eat his own vomit, so he's not really my go-to guy when it comes to judgment."

"Well, I like it, too."

And despite his tone, he left the bow. It surprised me. Magnus yawned, apparently bored by us, and padded out of the room.

"How much do I owe you?" Noah asked.

"For a dog Magnus's size, I charge sixty dollars."

He pulled out a black leather wallet from his back pocket. "Sorry, I only have this. I spent the last month in Europe." He handed me a bill that looked like fake money. Like something from a board game. Was it real?

The only way I knew how to verify money was either by holding it up to the light or biting on it like they did with coins in old cartoons. Either way, I had no idea what I was looking for. "What is this?"

"Five hundred euros."

I didn't know what the current exchange rate was, but I figured that was much closer to five hundred dollars than fifty. "I don't have any change on me."

"Keep it. As a tip."

This was too much. "You can't tip me four hundred and forty dollars."

"They're not dollars. They're euros."

"You know what I mean," I said in frustration. "You can't tip me that much."

"Why not?" He seemed genuinely puzzled.

"It's extravagant and, I don't know, kind of . . . demeaning."

"Or it's incredibly generous." Now he was starting to sound annoyed.

I handed the bill back to him. "You can just Venmo me or something."

"I don't have any apps on my phone."

"You don't . . ." I was dumbfounded. "What do you have on it?"

"An actual phone. Email. Sometimes I text," he said defensively. "My fingers are big and those screens are small. It's annoying. Besides, I've never been much into social media."

That at least I understood. "Me neither."

"I know."

My lower jaw dropped slightly. "How do you know that?"

But he didn't answer. He went back into his wallet and pulled out a different bill. "The smallest denomination I have is a hundred euros."

"You say that like I'm being the unreasonable one. I'm not the one trying to pay for services rendered with Monopoly money." That got me a half smile, and my heart fluttered happily in response. Uh-oh. Time for me to go.

"Consider it hazard pay for coming over so late."

Nodding, I took the hundred euros, and even though it was definitely too much, I didn't want to prolong this whole encounter. "Okay, well, I should get going. Thanks for the opportunity. Magnus is a great dog. Enjoy your interview tomorrow."

"Wait." His hand was on my arm, and it was like being pumped full of thousands of volts of electricity all at once. "There's something I wanted to talk to you about."

CHAPTER SIX

"Oh?" My voice actually squeaked.

He took one step closer. "So, about the other night. When we met."

My brain rushed in to say something, to change the subject from wherever this was going. "Why did you call me to take care of Magnus? There are a thousand other mobile groomers in LA that you could have called."

He put his hands in his pockets and shrugged. "Most people in my life want something from me. Or they are blinded by my fame and treat me differently. You didn't. And I realized I could trust you."

"How?"

"When the story of us meeting didn't show up in a tabloid or on a website or splashed all over Twitter."

"Why would it?" Don't get me wrong, I loved gossip as much as the next girl, but what would that headline be? Seat Filler Bickers with and Puts Down Internationally Beloved Superstar? I didn't need that kind of backlash from the Noah Douglas Hive in my life, thanks.

"You'd be surprised."

Somehow he moved even closer, and my heart beat so fast in my chest that it hurt.

He added, "I was hoping that I could see you again. In a non–dog grooming capacity."

My breathing went shallow. Needing distance, I walked over to his front window and looked out at the incredible view—there were lights in the valley beneath us for what felt like miles. I found that I wanted to say yes. And that scared me more than anything else.

I didn't want to date anyone, and for reasons I couldn't say, Noah Douglas was the absolute last man on earth that I could ever date.

I turned to look at him. "Why?" I asked, having to know at least that. Why me? When he could, quite literally, have anyone? The most beautiful and talented women in the world probably routinely threw themselves at him. There was nothing special or important about me. I was just a regular person living a regular life.

"Why?" he repeated, sounding a little surprised. "Maybe I have a weakness for feisty spitfires who love dogs."

A large lump of regret formed in my throat. "Oh. Okay. Thank you. But that won't be possible." There was absolutely no way. It was such a no. A big no. The no-iest of nos. There was so much no here he would get to cruise through the no express lane.

Now he looked totally bewildered. He came over to the window to stand next to me, and my stomach fluttered at the way the moonlight lovingly bathed his profile. "Can I ask why not?"

"It's a long and really embarrassing story, and it's not one that I share with anyone."

"Not even your best friend?"

"Not even her." We stood in silence, and I felt compelled to keep explaining. "This really is a hundred percent me. There's something about me that makes it impossible for me to date."

I didn't want to sound overly dramatic, because when you got down to my reason why, it felt stupid: I couldn't kiss anyone. Whenever I tried, I had these full-on panic attacks. I was absolutely terrified by the idea of kissing, because the first time I'd ever tried it, it had gone unbelievably badly. In a truly humiliating way. No one had hurt me, but I'd so embarrassed myself that apparently I'd been unable to move past it. So relationships, and kissing, were completely off the table for me. The only way to avoid my freak-outs was to avoid being close to someone.

But right now, in this moment? Boy, did Noah Douglas make me want to say yes.

Only I couldn't. Even thinking about why I *had* to say no made me feel like I was at the beginning of an attack. My heart was thrashing around, and there was that nauseous feeling at the back of my throat. I had no intention of telling him the reason why I couldn't go out with him, but my body apparently thought I was going to and prepared to implode.

"Okay. Message received." He turned to look at me and that intensity was there, the one that would make me run across a bed of hot coals if that was what he asked me to do. But he broke it off, walking over to the front door. He pulled it open.

"Thanks again for coming over last-minute."

I hesitated. I was shocked to discover that I wanted to explain. But a rush of panic engulfed me and I knew there was no way.

The only thing left for me to do was to go home. I joined him at the door and said, "You're welcome. And thank you for the ridiculous tip."

That earned me a tiny smile.

"I'll share your business card with my friends, if that's okay."

Why did I like the idea of him telling other people about me? "That would be great."

I stepped outside, and I heard him say, "I'm glad I got to meet you, Juliet Nolan."

The door shut and that was that.

I crossed my arms, the January air suddenly feeling extremely cold against my still-wet shirt and jeans. I hurried into the van and turned the music on loudly so that I wouldn't think about what had just happened.

But it wasn't enough. I thought of all the men who had asked me on a date or suggested hanging out and how every time I had said no. I hadn't even been tempted to accept. The potential for humiliation had been too great.

This was the first time I regretted it.

And I had my regret to keep me company on the drive home, knowing my best friend would be waiting to hear every single detail.

Sure enough, she was sitting in the living room watching the second movie in the Duel of the Fae trilogy. She paused the movie when I came in and set my stuff down on the kitchen table. She announced, "It just can't be said enough how much better the second movie is than the third movie. Like, that director understood how to make Aliana a fully rounded heroine who is allowed to want a soul mate and a family in addition to beating up most of the bad guys. She doesn't have to be one or the other. And he also understands the female gaze when it comes to Malec. He lets us love him where the first director saw him as a two-dimensional bad guy. If you don't want us to love the villains and root for their redemption, then why do you give them soulful eyes, muscled chests, disheveled hair, and heartbreaking backstories? I'm just not that strong."

"You know I agree with you." We'd had this same sort of discussion many, many times. It frustrated both of us that the trilogy had ended up as a tragedy instead of a literal fairy tale because the director and writer of the third movie had done such a poor job.

"So that long-winded explanation of mine was just a setup so that I could say . . . speaking of Noah Douglas's soulful eyes and muscled chest, how did it go? I would very much like to have all the details, please and thank you."

"I need to get changed." Even though I'd had the whole ride home to sort through my feelings, my nerve endings still felt a little raw, and my stomach had that sunken feeling in it like I'd made a mistake. Much as I loved her, I worried that Shelby would make it worse.

"Are you trying to up my anticipation here? You don't have to. I'm already dying. Spill!" she said, following me into my room as I peeled off my wet clothes, threw them into my laundry basket, and changed into my pajamas.

"There's not really much to tell," I said carefully. I didn't lie to Shelby. Other than that one thing I never told anyone, she knew everything about me. "Oh! Except for Lily Ramsey was there. She let me in."

"What?" she shrieked. "I am so torn. I both adore the idea of them having a torrid affair in real life because I loved them together in the movie and am outraged that he would be cheating on you!"

I laughed and tugged up my pajama bottoms. "They're just friends. Their dogs like to play together, and she seems very happily married. Sorry to both burst your bubble and reassure you."

"Come into the kitchen," she told me. "I went out and got rocky road ice cream."

I knew it was a bribe to ensure I'd fess up, but when chocolate was involved, I did not care. "I'm right behind you."

"So . . . then what happened?" she asked, getting the ice cream out of the freezer. I grabbed bowls and spoons and met her at the table.

"Well, after Lily obviously became my new best friend, then I washed and brushed Magnus."

"And . . . where was Noah while this was going on?"

"He was taking a shower."

She grinned mischievously at me. "With you watching?"

"What?" I laughed, banning the images that conjured up out of my mind. "No! I'd prefer not to go to prison for being a Peeping Tom, thanks."

"I kind of think it would be worth it. He's in fantastic shape. There was this article in *American Weekly* that said he still works out like he did when he was in the military."

I'd seen him up close. I could believe it. "Sounds about right."

"He's so massive. It's like he's a reverse *Beauty and the Beast* character."

"What do you mean?" I asked after I'd taken a bite.

"You know how all the servants in that movie are people who were turned into objects? He's the opposite. Like a sexy refrigerator that was turned into a person."

That made both of us laugh.

"He's definitely not making a servant's salary," I said. "He tried to tip me over four hundred dollars and I had to talk him down to forty."

"You did that the wrong way. In business you're supposed to get as much money as possible. Plus, he's a celebrity, which you seem to have forgotten. If I'd been you, I probably would have swiped something from his living room as a memento."

"I think he would have noticed if I stuck his Golden Globe down my shirt." She had a point about the money thing. I recognized that it didn't make sense, but I hadn't wanted to take his money.

Maybe it was because part of me didn't want our relationship to be a purely professional one, no matter what I kept telling myself.

"I so needed this," Shelby said and took another big bite of her ice cream. After she swallowed she added, "Because I went down to check the mailbox while you were gone, and guess what I found?"

She reached toward the middle of the table and put a magazine in front of me called *California Architectural*.

"Oh no . . . is this what I think it is?" I noticed a Post-it tagged to one of the pages and flipped to it.

Sure enough, there was Millicent Nabors standing in her newly renovated condo. She was an actress from a show on the CW network and had met Shelby through Allan and hired her. Shelby had done a fantastic job, given these pictures, but at the last minute Millicent had fired her and reneged on her final payment by claiming that Shelby had violated one of the terms of their agreement (which she totally did not do), leaving Shelby in a financial lurch.

And now in the article, Millicent was claiming credit for the design, saying she'd always "had a natural instinct for it."

Allan had told us that, given their contract, there wasn't anything Shelby could do about it.

"I was counting on this," she said sadly. "I thought it was going to launch my career."

"I'm so sorry. You didn't need her and her tacky animal-print rugs. You're going to be a huge success." I sighed, not wanting to let her down but knowing that this information could bolster her spirits. "And something happened tonight that might make you feel better, although I don't want to get your hopes up, especially considering how badly this Millicent Nabors thing went."

"What?"

"Noah Douglas's house is a wreck, so I gave him your card and recommended you. His place is like if some supervillain from the 1970s was put into a cryogenic sleep and woke up today with the sole intent of decorating Noah's home badly with a seventies flair. I'm talking green shag carpeting and yellow appliances, my friend."

"Oh no. That's terrible." Her face crumpled slightly but then immediately brightened. "But yay that he might call me! I know it's a long shot, but hey, a long shot is sitting across from me right now."

I took a big bite of my ice cream. She wasn't wrong.

Shelby studied me and then announced, "I feel like there's something else you aren't telling me."

She knew me too well, and there was no way I'd be able to hide it from her. "There is." I set down my spoon, and she widened her eyes. That gesture meant I was serious and she'd immediately understood it. "He said that he would like to see me, in his words, in a 'non–dog grooming capacity.'"

"Like . . . a date? He wants to go out with you?" she squealed, bouncing up and down in her chair.

"Those were his exact words. Feel free to interpret them however you'd like."

"Oh, you don't want to say that." She had her hands clasped to her chest, and her eyes had a dreamy, faraway look. "Because he was very obviously saying he wants to spend the rest of his life with you and now our double wedding is going to be even more fabulous. Can you imagine the kind of celebrities we'll be able to invite?"

I shook my head, giggling at her silliness. This was why we were close. I brought her back down to earth when she went off on one of her flights of fancy, and she urged me to lift my head up and not get so bogged down by the daily grind of real life. She reminded me that it was important to dream and to fly.

"I don't want to be the one to burst your bubble here, but I told him I wasn't interested."

A look of pure horror crossed her face. "Why would you do that?"

"Because I'm not. I closed that door."

"Having worked with so many doors in my profession, I can tell you this—that's the thing about doors. Once you close them, they're designed to be opened again." When I didn't respond, she got up and rinsed out her bowl, immediately putting it into the dishwasher. I'd have to remember to do the same with my own bowl or else she'd get upset with me for letting it languish in the sink.

"Are you really not interested in him at all?" she asked, and I heard that tone in her voice again, the one that let me know she understood something more was going on with my love life but that she wouldn't press the issue. That she would wait until I was ready to tell her.

I didn't think I'd ever be ready.

"Noah is . . . different." It was the most truthful answer I could give her.

"Different how?"

I didn't have the words to explain, so I just said, "I don't know."

She closed the dishwasher door. "Is it because he played Felix and Malec? Like you're transferring your crush from them onto him?"

"No, it honestly has nothing to do with the characters he's played. It's him. He's just different, and this is the first time I . . ." I couldn't continue.

Thankfully she didn't press me further. Another thing I loved about her—she always understood when to push and when to back down. "Well, I don't think that's the last you've heard of him."

"How could it not be? I told him no thanks."

She shrugged. "I just don't think Noah Douglas is the kind of guy who gives up that easily."

Her phone rang, and she went into the living room to grab it. I could tell from the sappy look on her face that it was Allan. Again, I felt that pang of envy that I didn't have anyone in my life who made me feel the way Allan made Shelby feel.

Maybe you could.

It was dumb to think. Even dumber to hope for. I didn't know how to get over my terrified-of-kissing issue. If it was just mind over matter . . . but it wasn't. I wished it was, but I couldn't just force myself to be fine and not have a panic attack every time I got close to a man.

The problem was, as Shelby had so often bragged, she was usually right. And she'd been right about everything so far.

That was what had me concerned.

CHAPTER SEVEN

It turned out to be a lot of worry over nothing. I didn't hear from Noah again. My life continued on as it always had. I spent a lot of time going into different veterinarian's offices to leave a stack of business cards with them, hoping somebody would pick one up and call me. I also went out on the few appointments I had for the week and groomed some gorgeous pooches. I hung out with Shelby a lot more than normal because Allan was working on a case that was demanding a lot of overtime, and I chatted with my mom a couple of times about her upcoming play. Ran some errands, ate some chocolate, watched some TV. Normal.

There were no restricted incoming phone calls.

A week after I'd groomed Magnus, Shelby was hanging out with Allan, which meant that I had all the time in the world to watch Noah Douglas movies. It was strange watching them now, knowing that I'd had conversations with him and he wasn't just this actor performing on my screen, but a real, interesting, and all-too-attractive person.

I woke up and decided to have belgian chocolate ice cream for breakfast. Why not? Nobody cared when you had yogurt for breakfast, and it was basically the same thing. I was halfway through the first Duel of the Fae movie when my phone rang. I glanced at the screen. It was Shelby.

Before I could even say hi, she cut me off with, "Don't say no."

I paused the movie. I'd heard that tone in her voice before. She was about to beg me for a big favor, and she knew I wouldn't like it. "Why would I say no when you haven't even asked me yet?"

"Just promise you won't say no."

"Fine. I won't say no."

"Perfect. I need you to be a seat filler at the Academy Awards tonight."

"No," I responded. What if I did that and I ran into Noah? What if he thought I'd changed my mind? That I was sending him mixed signals? I mean, it would be a fair accusation, given that all I felt were extremely conflicting signals all the time where he was concerned, but I wanted to put that little footnote of my life down at the bottom of the page where it belonged and move on.

"But you were so good at it!" she protested.

"It's not really a skill."

She tried again. "You just promised you would!"

"I can't be held to any promise where you tricked me into agreeing first."

"Juliet, I need you."

I closed my eyes. She knew I couldn't resist when she said that. "But I have plans."

"Sitting on our couch eating ice cream is not a plan."

How did she know I was eating ice cream? "But I already threw away the lid. I feel committed to finishing."

I could almost hear her rolling her eyes over the phone. "Not an excuse."

"Okay. I don't have anything to wear." That ought to work.

"I rented your dress yesterday."

"What?" I stood up. "You knew this yesterday but you waited until right now to ask me?"

"Because I know you left things weird with Noah and I didn't want you to talk yourself out of it. Harmony called me yesterday and said she'd been so pleased with how well we did a couple of weeks ago that she wanted us to work as seat fillers again."

"As I've already mentioned, you do not have to do anything to try and please this unpleasable woman." Shelby's mother had died about a year before Shelby got cancer, and her dad had never been in the picture. Sometimes it felt like Shelby was hoping Harmony would become a replacement parent, and I wished she could see that it wouldn't happen.

Shelby sighed. "I get that, but I feel like she's making an effort in asking us to come back. If she's extending an olive branch, I have to take it. Please?"

It sounded less like an olive branch and more like a way to find a regular source of unpaid labor, but I wasn't going to rain on Shelby's parade like that. I put the ice cream in the freezer, although it was basically toast without a lid. It would get those gross ice crystals all over it. The things I did for my best friend. "Okay. Where's the dress?"

"Yay! It's in your closet. I put it in there last night while you were sleeping."

I went into my room and found the dress hanging there, just like she'd said. "You snuck this in here like some kind of awards season Santa?" I pulled it out, and it was another plain black formal gown in my size, and it was actually long enough. That was always pleasantly surprising whenever it happened. It was a simple one-arm dress that fell into a straight sheath. I wouldn't be able to climb over anybody's legs in this dress. I grabbed my Converse shoes. When it came to the rest of me, fortunately I had a best friend who loved dressing up, so I'd been taught how to manage hair and makeup well enough on my own.

"Yes, I'm your Academy Awards fairy godmother, and I'd do it again. Okay, I arranged for an Uber to come pick you up in half an hour and bring you here." She told me my name was on the list and then ran over how to get through the different levels of security. She reminded me to bring my driver's license.

"I'll see you soon," I told her. Then I spent the next half hour rushing around the apartment like a crazy woman, trying to get ready. I didn't let myself think about Noah.

Okay, that was a lie. I thought about him constantly. He was going to be there. He'd been nominated for Best Actor for *The Last Goodbye*. I thought he deserved to win, but Chase Covington had played an alcoholic drinking himself to death and for some reason professional people in Hollywood thought his performance was better and had been giving him all the awards. I didn't get it.

The car arrived and dropped me off at the first stage of security, where they went through my clutch. When they opened it, I realized that I'd forgotten to pack any snacks. This was very disheartening, since I knew I had hours and hours of waiting around in front of me.

I made it through the labyrinth of security guards and three other checkpoints before finally making my way into the Dolby Theatre. A guard directed me down a long hallway that he told me led backstage. There were even more guards standing along the wall who would stop me to verify that I was supposed to be there and kept pointing me down the same hallway.

The level of security was ridiculous—it was like a military operation. Like the president of the United States was going to appear.

Shelby was waiting for me backstage. She waved when she saw me, her whole face lighting up. She patted the empty folding chair next to her. Harmony had set up a quick meeting with her seat fillers to run over the rules for that evening. She passed around two clipboards together and told us there were two separate forms to sign. The first were the liability/publicity release forms that let them put us on camera. The second was a serious-looking nondisclosure agreement that said I wouldn't talk about being a seat filler at this particular show. Well, given that my mom would only be vaguely interested and my best friend was sitting beside me, I figured it was fine to sign, as I had no one else to tell. Especially since Allan signed his without hesitation. The meeting of hers dragged on for what felt like an eternity since so many people were actually reading the releases, so I ended up watching the monitors behind her instead.

They showed the red carpet, and I saw various entertainment reporters and television hosts arriving and joining their crews. Some of them seemed famous enough that they were taking pictures with the fans who were sitting in raised bleachers along the red carpet. The whole area buzzed with excitement and anticipation.

Then the celebrities started to arrive, and you could tell every time one of them got out of their SUV or limo, as a muffled roar went up from the fans. We could hear it all the way backstage.

Although I wouldn't have admitted it to anyone else, I was watching for Noah. Celebrities came in two by two, but no Noah. A jealous twinge went through me at the idea that he was going to bring a date. I wondered if it would be the same woman as last time. The one he claimed he wasn't dating.

As I pondered those possibilities, where time had been lagging, now it seemed to speed up. Allan went off to join his mother and go over seating charts, and I listened to the nominees and members of the Academy entering the theater and finding their seats.

At some point Allan called Shelby over and left me to Noah-watch alone. Most of the other men in his category had already arrived, and I told myself I was ridiculous for sitting here and doing this. Somebody started putting the folding chairs away, clearing a pathway. The sound level in the auditorium got louder and louder as more people arrived.

Was Noah waiting until the last minute to make some kind of grand entrance? That thought made me question why I felt so . . . I don't know, desperate to see him again. I was the one who'd said I wasn't interested. So why did I care? Wouldn't it be better for me to just spend the evening backstage and then go home to finish off my crystallized ice cream?

It was like I didn't even know myself anymore.

The orchestra was warming up when Allan found me. "I've got an assignment for you."

"Already?" Last time the first seat fillers hadn't been sent out until about twenty minutes into the ceremony, and only then to fill in the seats of the people who had won awards.

"My mom was told someone who was scheduled to come didn't make it, and to be honest, you'll probably have to sit in that seat the whole night." He took me by the elbow and walked me over to the curtain that separated us from everyone else.

"You're going to be orchestra center, in row A, seat nineteen. Got it?" he asked, and it was only then that I realized Allan looked awfully pleased with himself. It was a weird look on him. Usually he was either stressed about work or making googly eyes at Shelby.

Row A was the first row, right next to the stage. Wow. At least I wouldn't have to climb over anyone. I wondered if someone had been stuck in traffic. Why else would they be late to their front-row seats?

It wasn't just seat nineteen that needed to be filled. Seat twenty was empty, too. It reminded me so strongly of the last awards show and Noah that I had to take a deep breath. I wondered if Allan's little smirk had been because he was going to send Shelby to keep me company until the seats' owners arrived.

A very pregnant and very pretty blonde was seated in the chair to my right. She looked vaguely familiar, although I couldn't place her. She caught my eye as I walked to my maroon-covered seat and she said, "Hello."

"Hi." She was wearing what looked like a very expensive pair of silver-sequined high heels, and I wondered how she managed not to fall over, given how big her belly was. "I like your shoes."

"Oh, thank you. But look at yours! I love them."

I displayed my pink Converse proudly. "Thanks. So do I." I felt vindicated. Noah Douglas was full of crap.

"Much more practical than mine." She rested her hands on top of her stomach. "I feel like I'm pregnant every time I'm at one of these things."

"Congratulations. Do you know what you're having?"

She smiled at me. "A little girl. Just one this time, thankfully. Your name doesn't happen to start with an *O*, does it?"

That was kind of a weird question. "No. I'm Juliet."

She offered me her right hand, and I shook it. "I'm Zoe. Juliet? As in *Romeo and*?"

"Yep, Shakespeare."

"Huh. A Shakespeare name. That was something I hadn't considered but would make sense, given my husband's line of work."

I wanted to ask who her husband was, but it seemed nosy. "The only *O* Shakespeare name I can think of is Othello. And that doesn't seem like a good name for a little girl. Wait! What about Ophelia? She goes a tad crazy, but she does have a pretty name."

She let out a laugh. "I like it! You probably think I'm so strange. It's a family tradition to give our kids names starting with *O*."

Then Chase Covington walked over and kissed Zoe before taking the seat on her right side. "Chase, this is my new friend, Juliet. She suggested the name Ophelia. What do you think?"

"I like it better than Opal." He reached over to shake my hand, and I was nearly blinded by his megawatt smile. "Nice to meet you."

Wow, was he handsome. "Yeah. You too."

"And you're here with Douglas?" he asked. His tone sounded a little disapproving.

It took me a second to register what he was saying, and I turned to my left to see Noah sitting down in the chair next to me. "No. I'm just a seat filler."

"Are you sure about that?" Zoe asked me, and she sounded like she was about to break into laughter.

"Pretty sure," I told her, my voice suddenly sounding strange to my own ears.

"Hi," Noah said and asked, "is this seat taken?"

At first I could only look at him. He was in a black tux, and formal wear suited him very well. How did this make him even more attractive? He was so hot I was surprised that everything around him didn't spontaneously combust.

Once I shook off my feelings of overwhelming lust, I asked, "Are you serious?"

"What?" he asked.

"I'm sitting next to you?"

"And you think that's my fault?"

Somehow it was. I just hadn't worked it out yet. And if I was being honest with myself, I knew this was going to happen. Deep down, I'd known. And I'd wanted it. Even if I was protesting.

"You don't have a date?" I asked.

"She wasn't able to make it."

And there it was. Evidence of scheming. Because who would miss out on being Noah Douglas's date for the Oscars? "What happened? Did she have to go back to Egypt?"

He looked thoroughly confused. "You sound hungry. Here." Then he reached into his jacket and pulled out a Snickers bar, handing it to me. "I heard you got recruited last-minute, so I just figured . . ."

My heartbeat skittered all over the place. I took the candy bar carefully and just held it in my lap, staring at it. It was the most romantic thing anyone had ever done for me. To be fair, no one had ever done anything romantic for me, so it was a low bar, but still.

"Thank you." I felt like all the air had been knocked out of me, and it took me a second to add, "This was very thoughtful."

"You're easy to think of."

His words slammed into me, causing a whirlwind of sensations and feelings that overwhelmed me. I wanted him to know how much his gesture meant to me. "Did you want some?" I hoped he appreciated the magnitude of my offer. I didn't share candy with anyone.

"I'm good." He flashed the inside of his suit jacket to show me that he had two protein bars there. "Although I don't think we're going to be able to eat them here. The Academy doesn't allow it, and there's going to be cameras everywhere." Seated between Noah Douglas and Chase Covington? Yeah, cameras all over us was a pretty safe bet. He went on, "I know how important it is to you to follow the rules. Like how you have to stay in your seat until someone comes to take it."

It was then that I realized no one was coming to take my seat. This had Shelby's fingerprints all over it. "You guys lured me here under false pretenses."

"You weren't lured," he said. "Nobody set up a wooden box and a stick with a string on it."

"But there is a Snickers bar!"

"True. Only you didn't know about it until after you were already here, so not a lure."

"You did set me up, though," I protested.

"Which you'll either find charming or it's what you'll use as the basis for your restraining order," he said with a wink, and it sucked all of the fight out of me.

The orchestra started to play, and as the music swelled, the lights went up. The show was starting. I should have been upset. I should have texted Shelby right then and there to tell her what she had done was wrong on so many different levels.

But I didn't.

He'd brought me my favorite candy bar.

He wanted to spend one of the biggest nights of his life sitting next to me. How could I be mad about that?

Shelby was right. Noah Douglas didn't give up easily.

And I didn't know what to do next.

CHAPTER EIGHT

Because I was confused by the two competing desires inside me, one that wanted to run away screaming with my arms flailing and the other wanting to climb into his lap, I fell quiet. I watched the opening musical number and then the first two presenters walked out onstage, but I couldn't focus. Instead I was keenly aware of him.

As we all politely applauded, Noah leaned in next to me, that clean/expensive scent surrounding me. He whispered, his words hot and breathy against my ear, sending tingles to unmentionable places, "He's wearing a toupee."

The actor in question was in his sixties and known for his thick head of hair. "You're kidding."

"Nope. Saw it myself."

I couldn't wait to tell Shelby. "What about Melissa Wilton?" She was the copresenter.

"She is pregnant, but her husband is not the father."

I couldn't help myself. I gasped. "Who is?"

"The director of her latest miniseries. They're going to get married after she publicly announces her 'amicable' divorce."

There were a lot of things to like about Noah Douglas, but who knew that gossip would end up being one of them?

When they announced the winner, one of the most prestigious and beloved actors in Hollywood, now it was my turn to lean in and ask, "What about him?"

"He's dating his granddaughter's best friend."

"Ew, gross," I said.

He kept up a steady stream of commentary through each of the presenters and winners, delighting me in a way I didn't know was possible. I was having the best time as I found out who was having affairs (it was like ninety percent of them), the people battling addictions, the massive amount of plastic surgery for both men and women, and the ridiculous things they were willing to do for fame.

Like how the Best Supporting Actor winner pretended to have Lyme disease because he had a book coming out and knew he'd get a lot of publicity. Or how last year's Best Supporting Actress was in the habit of fostering dogs, getting a lot of press about it, and then having her assistant return them to shelters.

That one infuriated me. I was never going to watch a movie she starred in ever again.

"Are you having a good time?" Noah asked during a commercial break.

"Surprisingly enough, I am."

"Surprisingly? I feel personally attacked. I can be entertaining," he informed me.

"Duh, we're sitting here because of your ability to entertain."

Noah shook his head. "That's my ability to act, and to connect. Not entertain."

"They don't have to be mutually exclusive."

He smiled at me and I had to look away, lest I be totally overwhelmed by him. Someone came over to say hello to Chase Covington, and it reminded me that he was sitting so close to me and I inadvertently whispered Chase's full name under my breath when he stood up.

Of course, because this was my life, Noah heard me. "You had no idea who I was, but you've heard of Covington?"

I went absolutely still, my heart beating loudly but slowly. While I hadn't forgotten that I'd told Noah I didn't know who he was, it was something I'd shoved into the very back of my brain, never to be seen again. Like the old, broken Christmas decorations in my mom's hall closet.

I knew I should tell him. Confess that I could probably quote several of his movies verbatim. That I'd had a crush on him even before I knew what a crush was.

But something held me back. Maybe if he hadn't been so charming and fun tonight, I would have felt differently. I was having such a good time, and I knew that telling him the truth would ruin it.

Given that I wasn't going to see him again, as the Academy Awards was the last show in Hollywood's awards season, there was no point in destroying tonight. Maybe it was selfish, but I wanted this memory to be a shiny one.

"My best friend is a big fan of his and I've seen a couple of his movies. Plus, he's pretty famous."

A disgruntled look crossed Noah's features. "Yes, it's amazing how successful he's become with all of his obvious physical disadvantages."

I couldn't help myself; I laughed. "Yeah, okay, pot."

His eyebrows furrowed. "What did you call me?"

"I said you are the pot and Chase Covington would be the kettle in your he-got-ahead-because-of-his-good-looks claim."

"Come on," he said. "I know how I look."

"And how's that?" I asked, genuinely curious, given his self-deprecating tone.

"I've always been a little goofy-looking—"

"Goofy-looking?" I repeated, slamming my hand against the armrest between us. "What inbred, nearsighted, and totally-lacking-any-semblance-of-taste idiot told you that you were goofy-looking?"

Was this even possible? Did Noah Douglas really not know how deeply, primally attractive he was? I mean, when he was younger, he was definitely ganglier and had braces like the rest of us. He hadn't grown into himself yet. But now he had and it was some very excellent maturing that had taken place on his part.

Even if he had been a little goofy-looking once upon a time, I'd still idol worshipped him.

"That's good to know," he said.

"What is?" The fact that I thought he was hot? Wasn't that just, like, common knowledge?

But he changed the subject on me. "Chase Covington is just . . . a blonder, nicer version of me."

I heard the unspoken dig in his voice. "By nicer did you mean less talented?"

His eyes crinkled with a smile. "I would never say that."

"But you'd think it."

"Possibly."

Now it was my turn to smile. I'd never imagined Noah Douglas to be this relaxed, enjoying-himself kind of person. He seemed to be all intensity, all the time. Grumpy, even. "Now it's my turn to be surprised."

"By what?"

"You. I thought you were more . . . I don't know, one of those Method type of actors who takes himself way too seriously and thinks the world revolves around him. I wouldn't have ever guessed that you could be . . . chill. Or that you'd be into gossip."

"I am not into gossip."

Now I was confused. "Then why have we been doing that for the last half hour?"

Despite me calling him chill, the fiery intensity in his eyes was anything but. "Because you like it."

That made the air between us feel heavy and I meant to say something in response, but we were interrupted by a director that he'd worked with a couple of years ago who wanted to say hello. That continued happening for the rest of the evening—Noah would give me the 411 on everybody around us, and then there would be a steady stream of industry types who all wanted to chat with Noah and shake his hand.

Not that I could blame them.

When he stood up, I noticed his socks. They had pictures of his dog, Magnus, on them. Too cute.

During one of the breaks, I texted Shelby, because the only way he could have known about my love of all things gossip was from my best friend.

> What did you do?

> Me? I just helped things along. It seems like you're having a fun time.

I glanced up, wondering where she was. I was about to text that it was fine but hesitated because it was kind of a lie. Things were going much better than fine, but I didn't want to encourage her.

> Harmony invited Allan and me to a party at her place tonight. Will you be able to get yourself home okay?

> Yes, don't worry about me.

I was about to tell her to be herself and have fun, but she would have told me that she couldn't do both. She was going to spend her entire evening stressed out of her mind and trying to figure out new ways to gain Harmony's approval.

Then it was time to announce the winner in Noah's category, Best Actor. I tried my best to look neutral and lean out of the camera frame when they called his name, even though my heart was fluttering in anticipation for him. I was hopeful he'd win even though all those betting websites said that there was no way he would. I wanted to tell him good luck, but I was still a seat filler and probably shouldn't be caught on camera saying something like that. I wasn't Noah's date.

Even if it kind of felt like I was.

Sure enough, Chase Covington's name was called as the winner. He kissed Zoe, and she stood up and loudly cheered for him, ignoring the cameras that were capturing her every move.

When the applause died down and Chase began his acceptance speech, I said to Noah, "I'm sorry you didn't win."

Then I did something that shocked me. I rested my hand on top of his to comfort him. It was something I would have done for Shelby or my mom if they'd just lost a contest. It was just a natural reaction.

But then he put his other big, warm hand over mine, and it caused my stomach to hollow out and my galloping heartbeat to thump so hard in my throat it felt like it would strangle me. What was I doing? I counted out my breaths, inhaling one, two, three and then exhaling one, two, three before carefully extricating myself. I didn't jerk my hand away, which I thought was pretty impressive, given all the rampaging and conflicting feelings that were happening inside me.

Chase ended his speech and exited the stage as the music played, and the lights went down. Zoe jokingly told me to save her seat, as she was going to find a restroom.

"Tell Chase congratulations from me when you see him," Noah said, and she smiled and promised she would.

I thought that was very big of him. "I wouldn't have guessed that you're a good sport. I bet you're that guy that every time you have a game night you lose friends."

He blinked slowly, as if considering what I said. "In this situation it really is an honor just to be nominated."

"But you would have liked winning, right?"

"When you join the army, there is no such thing as losing or defeat. My company used to say we were only doing a tactical retreat. So yes, it sucks, and I would have much preferred winning." That sly smile of his played at the ends of his mouth.

"How competitive would you rate yourself? Like, on a scale of one to five?"

"To be fair, it would depend on what I'm doing and how much it mattered, but in general I'd say I'm maybe like a three." He paused. "Or a five-plus all the time."

I laughed at this, glad to know that Noah Douglas wasn't perfect and might actually have some flaws.

"Same," I told him. I'd always hated my sense of competitiveness, and it was a relief to find someone who operated on the same wavelength.

Somebody called his name, and Noah said hello to an older man. I briefly wondered what he did for a living—studio executive? Producer? Director? Screenwriter? As I ran through potential jobs for him, it occurred to me that there was only one more award to be given out, Best Picture, and then this night would be over.

I felt a twinge of sadness at the idea this whole thing was coming to a close. I pulled up the Uber app to see if I could schedule a ride when we finished here.

"That's not going to work."

The feeling of him so close to my neck did funny things to my gut, but I didn't even scold Noah for looking over my shoulder. "Why not?"

"The streets are all cordoned off for blocks. Only cars with permits are allowed in. And then once you get past all of the barriers, nothing will be available nearby. There's too many people affiliated with the show who don't have limos and will need rides."

He turned out to be right. Every ride I tried to schedule for my location canceled after I'd requested it.

"Great." I sighed. "I don't have a way of getting home."

"I could give you a lift. I just have to go to this one little thing first, if that's okay."

I should tell him no, thank you. I could figure this out on my own. I also felt bad about him going so out of his way to take me home. "I'm in Pasadena. It's not nearby."

"We're in LA. Thanks to traffic, nothing's nearby."

Wrestling with the decision, I blurted out, "That would be great. Thank you." And it actually was great. I didn't want tonight to come to an end just yet.

And even though I knew very little about men and their emotions, the look on his face made me think he was feeling the same way.

CHAPTER NINE

The Best Picture winner was announced, the final speech was made, and everyone started to leave.

"Stay close," Noah told me. For a second it seemed like he wanted to take my hand.

And for a second I almost let him.

But he put his hands in his pockets as I followed behind him. Thankfully he was tall and broad enough that it was easy to pick him out in the crowd. Everybody wanted to get his attention or touch him as he walked past. And these were his colleagues and employers. I could only imagine what it would be like if he were walking through a crowd of fans. They'd probably dismember him. By accident, but they'd all want a piece.

We went into a hallway, and he came to an abrupt stop. I nearly smacked into his back.

"And who is this?" the woman in front asked. She looked very confused. I saw her glance down at my sneakers, and I tried to hide them beneath the hem of my dress.

"This is Juliet. Juliet, this is Reina, my publicist; Morgan, her assistant; and Annie, my groomer." I figured it was a mark in his pro column that his whole team was made up entirely of women. Both Reina and

Morgan seemed on the shorter side, but that was probably only in comparison to Noah. Reina had beautiful, waist-length chestnut hair and Morgan sported a bright smile. Annie was taller, with a blonde pixie cut. All three women were dressed in black, just like me.

Reminding me that I was more like the help here and less like Noah's actual date.

"And where did you find Juliet?" Reina asked. It was a little disconcerting for her to be talking about me like I wasn't there. She was very nice about it, but still. He hadn't found me. I wasn't a lost wallet.

"Juliet and I are friends, and she's coming with me to the party."

That seemed to be good enough for everyone. Reina nodded and said she would take care of it. "The car is this way."

"Party?" I asked as we followed her. "I think I've mentioned it, but I hate parties."

"Yeah, me too," he agreed.

"Then why are we going to one?"

"It's for work. We'll stay for a little while, get some pictures and some food, and then I'll have Ray drive you home."

Ray? Was that his driver? And did that mean . . . he wasn't coming with me? He was going to put me in a car and that would be that?

When we stepped out of the theater, it was like a sound bomb had been set off. There was an explosion of noise as a throng of fans screamed for Noah, calling his name. The bright flashes from all the photos were blinding, and I had to look down at the ground to regain my bearings.

This was his life. It was incomprehensible.

The car ended up being a limousine. Not one of those big stretch ones, but it was bigger than a regular sedan with enough seating for all of us.

There was a flurry of movement off to the right, and I turned to see a woman ducking under the rope and in between two security guards who were just a second too slow in grabbing her. I wasn't sure what was happening and could only stand there and watch, my mouth hanging open. She pole-vaulted herself onto Noah, crying, screaming his name, telling him that she loved him as she clung to his back like a baby monkey. He tried disengaging her, but it was the four guards who ran over that successfully yanked her off, carrying her away.

It was terrifying.

Reina ushered everyone into the limo, including me. There was a second of stunned silence as we pulled away, and then there was a chorus of concern from everyone there, asking Noah if he was okay.

"I'm fine," he reassured us. To my shock, he did look totally calm. Annoyed, but he often looked annoyed.

"How are you not more shaken up?" I asked. My heart was still drumming a staccato beat in my chest, and the fight-or-flight adrenaline inside me had just started to dissipate.

He shrugged one shoulder. "That's not the first time that's happened to me."

"I think we should look into getting you a private security guard for these kinds of functions," Reina told him. At the look on his face, she said, "I know. I know how much you want to live a normal life, but I think we're getting to the point that things might need to change."

I totally agreed with her, but this wasn't a conversation that I needed to be a part of. So I sat quietly while Reina changed the subject and started prepping him for what would happen when we arrived and how he would need to pose for pictures despite not wanting to. Her return to normalcy was like a cue to the others—Morgan was scrolling on her phone, talking about the different outlets that wanted to speak to him at the party, while Annie ran product through his hair, making sure the waves set just so.

She had the best job.

He shot me a sheepish grin, as if to say he was sorry about all of this, and I shrugged. He didn't have anything to be sorry for. The crazy fan wasn't his fault. Then it occurred to me that he was talking about our present circumstances, where I sat quietly while everyone else talked to and with him. Admittedly, when we'd been sitting together in the theater, it felt as if we were almost like a regular couple. I don't know why I assumed it would continue to be just me and him. But now with three other people quite literally between us, he felt a world away.

Noah seemed so important. He had these people who were there just to take care of him and help him in his career. I sat in that car, feeling small and not liking it. Maybe when we got to this party, I'd see if I could find someone in the ride-share app to pick me up. Although I guessed we were heading into a situation similar to the one we'd just left and it might take some time.

The car slowed to a crawl, and I saw another wall of photographers, camera crews, and fans cheering and screaming. I hoped these guards would protect him better than the last.

"Morgan, would you mind getting out here and taking Juliet inside so that Noah can get his pictures?" Reina asked, and Morgan nodded.

"Juliet, is that okay?" Noah asked me, and I wondered whether he saw any discomfort on my face.

I smiled, because the idea of avoiding that red carpet actually sounded nice. "Yes. I'll just meet you inside."

"Can I get your number?" Morgan asked. "In case we get separated."

I told her my phone number and then she opened the car door. I went with her through a couple of security checkpoints, and it seemed as if none of the guards were too pleased about me being listed as Noah Douglas's guest. They hadn't been given a name, and they kept checking my driver's license. Which I didn't understand, because the word *guest* wasn't going to magically morph into my name if they looked at my ID often enough.

But we got inside and it was like a whole other glitzy, glamorous world. It was dark and it took my eyes a second to adjust. There was also music playing, and several people were on the dance floor already. Thankfully it wasn't too loud and allowed people to still have conversations. There were waiters wearing white tuxedo jackets circulating with champagne flutes, and a large bar to provide whatever other kinds of drinks people wanted. To one side there were dining tables set up with crisp linen cloths, and on the other there were soft-looking padded benches and sofas. It was all sleek and modern with different-colored lights flashing from the walls.

Everywhere I looked there was one famous person after another. It was like I'd walked into my favorite movie. Or all my favorite movies put together. Brad Pitt smiled at me as he walked by, and although he was old enough to be my dad, it did make me feel a little light-headed.

Morgan stuck to my side, asking if I wanted something to eat or drink.

But surprisingly enough, my almost constant dull roar of an appetite had gone totally silent. My stomach was still upset over what had happened to Noah with that fan. "No, I'm good. But thank you!" I wondered whether she was going to babysit me until Noah arrived. Which made me feel a little ridiculous, as she seemed to be about my age, if not younger.

"Okay, I'm going to grab some food. Do you want to wait here for me?" she asked.

I kept surveying the crowd and saw Zoe Covington. "I see someone I know. I'll be over there. Thanks!"

As I made my way over to Zoe, it suddenly struck me how presumptuous I was being. She might want to be alone with her husband or had other friends she wanted to chat with, and I was about to insert myself into their lives.

So I stopped, unsure of what to do, but Zoe saw me and waved me over.

When I got closer to her, I realized that her face looked pained. "Are you okay?" I asked.

"I'm just worn out. I know I've been sitting for the last few hours, but these shoes hurt more than I'd anticipated. I need to sit down and this is where Chase left me, so I'm afraid if I go somewhere else he'll never find me again, because I forgot my phone at home."

It might have sounded a tad melodramatic, but as busy and big as this party was, it was probably a valid concern.

"Let's get you off your feet, then!" There was a group of young women in a corner seat next to us. They were preening for their camera, making the same movements and faces over and over again, obviously filming it for an Instagram story or something similar.

"Excuse me!" I came close to them, and they all glared up at me when I spoke. "Would you guys mind scooting over? My friend is pregnant and needs to sit."

They looked me up and down and obviously found me lacking. Their ringleader said, "So? How is that our problem?"

These entitled little . . . Something inside me cracked with anger. "Listen, you look like you've never even sniffed a pizza, let alone eaten one, so I could probably snap you like twigs. But even worse, I will get my phone out and film you refusing to let Chase Covington's pregnant wife put her swollen ankles up. What will happen to your likes then?"

I'd only wanted them to move over, but at my threats they up and left, shooting me dirty looks. I did a "ta-da" gesture with my arms, and Zoe laughed as she sat down.

"I have to get your number. You are definitely someone I want to be friends with." She sighed with relief as she settled onto the seat.

This was a Cinderella fantasy. No way would she want to be my friend when I went back to my regular life. So I smiled at her. "Where's your husband?"

"I sent him off to get me food. They have In-N-Out at this thing, and I'm starving."

"Don't you have people for that?" I asked with a laugh.

"We do. But sometimes I make Chase be the people so his head doesn't get too big." There was a small table at kneecap level, and she put her feet up on it and sighed again. "I thought you said you were a seat filler. Who brought you to the party?"

"Well, Noah Douglas did. But not like on a date. He's just going to give me a ride home after he makes the rounds."

"Oh. Interesting. The *Vanity Fair* party is not really a place to bring a not-a-date. I mean, companies pay hundreds of thousands of dollars to be advertisers at this event just to score tickets to it."

Wow. I had not known that. "Honestly, we're not even really friends. I groomed his dog once."

Her eyebrows flew up, and I felt the need to explain. "That's not a euphemism. I have my own dog-grooming business and he has a dog."

"We just got a dog. His name is Nemo. If I had my phone, I'd show you a picture. He's a little cocker spaniel and the sweetest thing. My twins adore him, and he's so patient with them. We should probably have a groomer, too. Do you have a card?"

Shelby was going to punch me. "I don't have it with me. If you want to look me up online, my company name is Waggin' Wheels. Or I'm sure you can have your people call Noah's people and track me down."

"Sounds like a plan." She let out another big sigh.

While I knew about Chase, I realized I'd never read anything about his wife or kids. "Are you an actress, too?"

"Definitely not." Then we spent a long time chatting as she filled me in on how she ran an ocean conservation nonprofit with her husband and that they did their best to keep their family out of the spotlight. She said they'd met over Twitter, of all places, just before she graduated from college.

"Is it hard?" I asked. "Being married to a movie star?"

"It is. I wouldn't undo any of it because I adore him, but it is hard. Especially at first when you're not used to it. It felt like we came from two completely different worlds. There's fans and then there's groupies, which are at another level, and then you have stalkers. We've had to hire a lot of security. This isn't what I would have chosen for my life, but he's so good at what he does, I'd never want him to give it up."

"I know this is personal, and you don't have to answer," I said, "but do you worry about him cheating on you?"

"Never. I mean, when we started dating, yes, but that was because I was so insecure. And it's very common in Hollywood for that to happen. There are so many actors who cheat on their spouses while they're filming and think it's normal and then just go back to their regular lives. Chase doesn't do that because he knows I would murder him in his sleep. And I do trust him. There are trade-offs in any relationship, and this is what we have to deal with."

"What do we have to deal with?" Chase asked, handing his wife a cardboard box full of six cheeseburgers.

"People who think they're in love with you and all the other nonsense that comes with fame. But never mind that because I so love you right now. Thank you for all this protein," she responded, taking a burger out. "This is Juliet. From the ceremony?"

"Congratulations!" I told him.

He beamed at me. "Thank you!" He settled in beside her, and his demeanor changed. "Wait. Aren't you the one who is here with Douglas?"

"I'm not. Here with him. We're not dating."

Chase muttered "Noah Douglas" under his breath. I looked at Zoe questioningly.

She leaned in. "There's this guy I used to work with named Noah, and Chase never liked him, but I think this is more about the fact that Chase is jealous of your Noah's talent."

He wasn't my Noah, but I didn't correct her. "Why? Chase just won for Best Actor."

"Which he's obviously thrilled about. But he feels like this is more of a popularity / which studio paid the most money / which actor did the best press tour kind of award. Noah is the one winning all the film critics' awards at the festivals." She held the box of burgers toward me. "Would you like one?"

I'd been sitting here for a long time, which had allowed my appetite to return. I also didn't know how much longer I'd be waiting, so I thanked her and took one. It was a bit cold but still delicious. An entire multitude of people had apparently been waiting to talk to Chase, as they kept coming up to him and preventing him from eating. I felt bad for him, watching him smile and shake hands instead of getting to consume this deliciousness. I did note that Chase was holding Zoe's hand the entire time, which I thought was too sweet. Right when I finished my burger, I felt my phone buzzing. When I opened my clutch to check it, I spilled the contents all over the floor. Grumbling, I picked everything up and shoved it back in my purse except for my phone. I had a text from Morgan.

> Noah's on his way to you now.

Like some sort of spy operation. I texted back okay and put away my phone.

I wondered if we'd be leaving soon.

Zoe saw him before I did. She nudged me with her arm. "Your not-a-date is coming over."

Again, he was easy to spot, as he seemed to be a literal head and shoulders above everyone else around him. His gaze caught mine, and I swallowed hard at his expression.

"There's nothing going on between us." But whether that was for her benefit or mine, I wasn't sure. I felt like I'd said those words so often that they were starting to lose their meaning.

Or maybe it was that they weren't actually true.

Zoe gave me a knowing look and then patted me on my arm. "If anyone knows how you're feeling, it's me. Because I've been there, done that, and given the way he is staring at you right now, you are in very deep trouble."

CHAPTER TEN

Noah had nearly reached us when he was stopped by an older man who had his arm around a much younger, beautiful woman. At the man's request, Noah agreed to take a picture with the woman, who looked like she was in danger of spilling out of the top of her very tight, strapless, champagne-colored dress. And there was a lot that would have spilled out.

Now she was talking to Noah, and he had this weird smile pasted on his face and a pained look in his eyes. Like a hostage trying to communicate without his captors knowing.

I decided to be nice and rescue him.

"I won Miss Malibu last year," the abundantly bosom-blessed woman was telling Noah. "That's how I met Harold here. He was one of the judges. And, if you think about it, winning kind of makes me a queen. I've got the crown and everything."

Noah didn't seem to know what to say. "Oh. I hadn't heard that Malibu had incorporated as a monarchy."

That made me smile, but his words seemed to confuse both Miss Malibu and her sugar daddy.

"There you are!" I said. "Chase and Zoe are waiting to talk to you. If you'll excuse us?" I tugged at Noah's arm, and he quickly followed me.

"Thank you."

"You're welcome. But I hope you enjoy it. You only get one save per night, and you just used yours up. And what was that?"

"People just . . . tell me things. And try to impress me."

That seemed so strange. "Why?"

"I don't know."

I probably shouldn't fault them too much. At least they hadn't met him and immediately called his shoes ugly. "That's stupid," I concluded. "I would never do that."

"I know."

There was something behind his words, something I didn't want to examine, so I said, "Well, at least she was pretty."

"She wasn't really my type."

"Uh, she was gorgeous. Just like that girl Hannah was gorgeous. And you're trying to tell me you don't have a type that's physically perfect? Because yes, I'm sure you only date girls with personalities and brains that you can bounce a quarter off."

He laughed, and it was loud and joyful and glorious. I'd heard him laugh in movies and on TV dozens of times, but this was different. It was real, and I was the one who had caused it. It felt like something I should cross off a bucket list or something. *Made Noah Douglas laugh. Check!*

When his laughter faded, that electric we're-having-a-moment feeling returned, so I asked, "Don't you find it aggravating? When people try to impress you?"

He shrugged. "It annoys me, but it doesn't take much to annoy me."

"Same," I said and felt that click of connection again. I typically found myself generally annoyed with so many things. "Although I chose to be in a customer-based industry, which means I have to be nice. You are at a point where you could be a diva if you wanted to."

"I could, but it's a waste of everyone's time. Working on a set is a bit like being in the army—we're a team and we all have a job to do, and if one of us shows up late and throws tantrums, it ruins it for everyone. I don't ever intend to be the weak link. And I do have to be nice to people at events like this. Because you never know who might be in charge someday. Although I was tempted to blow off the documentary winners I met."

"You don't like documentaries?" I asked.

"They're just the news turned into kind of a movie."

Now it was my turn to laugh. "And here I was picturing you in a sweater-vest and fedora waxing on about the importance of documentaries to our cultural zeitgeist."

"I'm pretty sure I've never used the word *zeitgeist* in a sentence before."

We were both smiling when we joined Chase and Zoe. Noah greeted them both, congratulating Chase. The flashes from the photographers taking pictures of the two of them together seemed even brighter in this darkened room. Chase and Noah talked like the photographers weren't even there. Like they were members of some glamorous zoo who lived their lives and ignored the tourists.

They finished chatting, and Noah turned toward me like he was about to ask me a question, when a photographer interrupted him.

"Could I get a picture of you two?"

For a second I thought he meant Chase, but then I realized his question had been directed at me. "You don't want me in your picture. I'm just a seat—"

But Noah cut me off. "Of course."

We moved closer together. I rested my hand against his back, near his waist, and he wrapped his arm around my shoulders.

Without meaning to, I leaned into him so that our sides were pressed together.

I had the strangest feeling. Like this was where I belonged.

The photographer took several shots and then thanked us. He moved over to Chase and Zoe next, making the same request, but they stayed seated for their shots.

I stepped back, wanting to clear my head. Being that close to him made me forget myself.

Noah cleared his throat, looking a little uncomfortable, too. "So I've kissed all the right rings and taken all the pictures required of me and made all the studio executives' second wives happy. Would you like to, I don't know, meet some star? Dance?"

"Dance?" I repeated. "Oh, I don't dance. I don't like to inflict that on other people."

"What do you mean?"

"Don't get me wrong. I love music, but I lack that thing that makes your body move the way you want it to. One time at a dance in junior high, a chaperone literally pulled me off the dance floor because she thought I was having a seizure, so I don't do that in public anymore."

There was a devilish gleam in his eyes. "I was just being polite when I asked. I didn't really want to dance, but now you're making me want to."

I wrongly assumed he was commiserating with me. "You don't like dancing, either?"

"Oh no, I can dance. I had lessons as a kid and can definitely hold my own. But the picture you're painting, I can't lie—it has me intrigued. I feel like I need to witness it."

"Hard pass." There was no way. No matter how boyishly handsome he looked at the prospect.

"Is there anything else you'd like to do? Do you want to grab some food?"

I was about to say yes because I was already hungry again, and I was still in my mode of wanting this night to go on. To get to keep this shiny memory that I could tell my grandchildren about someday. If that photographer posted our picture online, I'd even have photographic evidence in case my grandchildren turned out to be little jerks who thought I was lying.

But it was then that I noticed his face had taken on a haggard look. As if tonight had been harder for him than he would probably admit.

I realized that I should put aside my desire to keep prolonging things and think about what would be better for him.

"I'm actually a little tired. Can we call it a night?"

There was definite relief in his eyes when he said, "Sure thing. Let's get you back home before you turn into a pumpkin." I couldn't figure out if it was a good or bad thing that Noah seemed to recognize the Cinderella-ness of my situation. Maybe he thought that tonight was our one shot at the ball, only I was telling him that I was ready to dash down the stairs and make a break for my carriage and leave my sole chance behind.

Because his assertion wasn't too far off. Every moment since I'd met him had taken on this sort of Cinderella filter that was coloring everything around me. Like I was in somebody else's Instagram story with mood lighting and hearts in my eyes. It wasn't me, and tomorrow my pink Converse shoes would turn back into . . . well, they would stay pink Converse shoes. But this whole Noah Douglas thing would be over, and my life would be back to normal.

But, as my mother would say, them's the breaks.

"Do you need to check in with anyone before we leave?" I asked, grabbing my clutch and making sure my phone was still inside.

"Reina and Morgan have other clients, and Annie's off the clock and enjoying herself on the dance floor, where no one thinks she's having a seizure. We're good."

I nudged him with my elbow as he enjoyed his own joke with a laugh. Then we said our goodbyes to Chase and Zoe, and she insisted on getting up to hug me. "I am going to look you up and I'll be calling you!" she said.

"Sounds good!" I responded. I hoped she would. I genuinely liked her.

Then she told Noah, "You've got a good one there."

He smiled, a real smile, and said, "I know."

I didn't bother protesting this time. Everybody seemed pretty set on their own interpretation of what was happening. Although my cheeks did flush slightly, and I hoped no one noticed.

"Let me just text Ray so he can meet us out front. Okay. Done. Shall we go?" he asked as he slid his phone into his pants pocket. Then he did the most adorable thing. He offered me his arm while his hands were still in his pockets. It was such an old-fashioned and sweet gesture it made my heart swoon. I wondered if he'd learned it when he did that remake of *Pride and Prejudice*. He'd been the absolute best Mr. Darcy.

I slid my arm through his, and as we walked out of the party, I was back to that upscale-zoo feeling. Flashes going off, people looking at us and whispering. "Everyone's staring at us," I told him.

"Are they?"

"Yes. And every last one of them is wondering if you lost a bet."

That got me a real, full-throated laugh again that still felt thrilling, and another part of my defenses melted.

"Not true. They're all wondering how I got so lucky."

I let out a grunt of disbelief. I had always been comfortable in my own skin and with my appearance. Sure, there were times I wished my thighs were a little smaller or my boobs a little bigger or that I could tan in the sun instead of frying like a lobster, but for the most part I was okay with me.

But I didn't have any delusions that I was on the same level with the typical women he dated, because I was not the double-D, fluorescent-white teeth, hair extensions, and fake eyelashes kind of girl. The kind that filled this room.

"More like they wondered how you got lucky when you had that Hannah person as your date."

"Hannah? That was a setup by my publicist."

I blinked in surprise. Shelby had called that one, too. "Do you do everything your publicist tells you to do?"

He took a moment, as if collecting his thoughts. "I started out my career on a kids' show. I played a character named Felix. A lot of actors never overcome that one role they are famous for. It becomes the only way the public can see them. I was in danger of that happening to me, but I have an amazing team who has guided me onto the path I wanted to be on. My agent, Sandy, and Reina are the best in the business. So when Reina said, 'Bring Hannah Fremont as your date,' I did."

"What about tonight?" I asked.

"They said I could make tonight about me."

The implication was there—that me being with him as his not-a-date was what he wanted. I couldn't deny what he seemed to be admitting without using the actual words.

When I didn't respond, he kept talking. "Sandy and Reina are the reason I'm where I am in my career."

He was really selling himself short, and it made me lay on the sarcasm nice and thick. "Yes, your talent has nothing to do with it, I suppose."

"Another backhanded compliment. You keep giving me those and I might get a big head."

"Might?" I teased. "I don't think you need any help there."

He laughed again, and the world around me became so dazzling and bright that it took me a second to come back down to earth. So it took me another second to realize that someone was calling his name from a distance. More than one person. But his long legs kept eating up the ground in front of us, and I was glad I could keep pace. "I think someone said your name."

"A lot of people say my name. I don't have to respond. I promised you a ride home, and right now that's what I'm going to do. My debt to this particular society has been paid in full for the night. I'm off the clock now."

His words made my toes tingle. Why did it make me feel brilliant and special that I was the only thing he was focusing on? That in this moment, keeping his word to me was more important than anything else?

The sea of photographers outside had pretty much cleared out, and there was only a handful of fans waiting near where the cars were picking up people leaving the party. We had to wait only about a minute, and Noah waved to the remaining fans who were calling to him.

I wondered if any of them were going to try to attach themselves to him like a baby sloth, but they were fairly outnumbered by the guards.

The car pulled up, and Noah opened the door for me. I got in, and he slid in next to me.

And closed the door. And the car left.

"Wait. Aren't we forgetting some people?"

"No."

"What about your merry band of work wives?"

A smile. "They can take care of their own travel. They can just call our car service. They'll be safe."

He had a car service? Couldn't he have just called that for me, too?

He wants to take you home. He still wants to spend time with you.

It seemed so dumb that I hadn't really figured that out before, that he wanted to be alone with me without his entourage around, but it was like it had just occurred to me and I didn't know what to think.

"Ray needs your address," Noah said. "Or if there's somewhere else you want to go, we can take you there instead."

Why was I getting the distinct impression that if I told him I was in the mood for Rio de Janeiro, we'd be heading for an airport? "Home is good."

I recited it to the driver, and Ray nodded. "We'll get you there quick as we can, but there's traffic."

It was LA. There was always traffic.

Then Ray pushed a button to raise the dividing barrier between the front and back of the car. The movement of that dark window sliding into place had this feeling of finality for me.

It made the space feel so small, and Noah was so big, sucking up all the room left in the back seat.

And I was back to being freaked out. Being at the party had felt less threatening. We'd been surrounded by people. Obviously he wasn't going to make a move with so many people watching everything he did. So my mind hadn't gone to the possibility that he might. The time we'd spent together had felt comfortable, and I'd allowed myself the luxury of not overreacting to every one of his movements and overthinking everything that was going on and just enjoying myself. Pretending to be normal, like every other woman out there.

That was all over now.

Because he might try to kiss me.

And then I would have a full-on panic attack.

CHAPTER ELEVEN

"Do you want something to drink?" Noah asked, leaning forward to open a compartment, from which he pulled out a bottle of champagne.

"No champagne for me," I said. "I'm such a lightweight." In my current living circumstances, I could afford neither alcohol nor the potential hangovers that might interfere with an early-morning appointment. "Plus, not being able to hold my liquor makes me very confessy."

And why had I felt the need to tack that on? I resisted covering my face with both of my hands as he put the bottle back.

"Do you want us to stop and grab something else? Water?" he offered.

I let out a sigh of relief. He wasn't going to home in on what I'd said. "No, I'm good. Thanks."

Then, of course, he made sure my relief was short-lived. "I take it that being confessy is a bad thing."

"It could be," I said honestly. At least one of my secrets was totally humiliating. The other would destroy this entire evening. I wasn't up for either experience.

"What is it that you don't want to confess to me? Do you have a deep, dark secret?"

"Doesn't everyone?" I was aiming for lighthearted, but I was afraid I'd missed the mark.

"Do you want to know mine?" he asked, and me being me, of course I desperately wanted to know it. I didn't know if that made me a hypocrite, keeping my secrets to myself while being way too enthusiastic about him spilling his.

"If you want to share it."

He looked at me thoughtfully before saying, "I haven't spoken to my parents in nine years."

As far as I could recall, he'd never mentioned his parents in any interview. Ever. "Really? Wow. Why?"

He settled back against the seat, unbuttoning his jacket to get more comfortable. "My parents were my managers. My mother was a child actor on a sitcom and never had a substantial role after that. My dad was a radio DJ. They met at some event, fell in love, and had kids."

Kids? My ears perked up. As far as I knew, Noah Douglas was an only child. He didn't have any siblings. Right?

Or maybe he did and he'd been protecting that fact all these years. He was so intensely private that it was shocking he was saying anything to me now. His interviews consisted of the same set of facts over and over again—he'd starred on *Late for Class*, had joined the army at eighteen, came home three years later, and did some small movies here and there until he broke out with the Duel of the Fae trilogy. Now every director in Hollywood wanted to work with him, and he was doing an excellent job of choosing roles that were getting him all kinds of critical accolades.

That was it. He'd never said anything about his family.

And knowing how private he was? Why was he telling me? I could totally betray him and tell this to, like, the ENZ website, and it would be everywhere.

Because he trusts you. Even though he shouldn't.

I was torn between guilt and selfishness. So I didn't choose. I stayed quiet and let him talk, let him make the decision.

"The one thing my parents wanted was for me to be a huge star. My dad quit his job, and they spent all their time managing me and my career. I paid the bills. Everything depended on me. There were no choices in my life, no normal childhood activities. I was either on set working or memorizing lines or with one of my instructors for acting, dancing, or singing. Nobody asked me if I was doing what I wanted. Or if I was happy. Nobody cared."

That made my heart break. I'd never imagined when I'd watched him as Felix that he'd been unhappy. "I'm so sorry."

He raised one hand, as if to wave off my sympathy. "It got worse when I was a teenager. I rebelled in the worst ways possible. I was a mess, totally acting out and partying all the time. The day I turned eighteen I got married, just to prove I was an adult."

Oh, I remembered. My fifteen-year-old heart had been entirely broken when he'd married one of his costars. A voodoo doll of his bride may or may not have been constructed.

"I just wanted to show them that they couldn't control me anymore. And they took my challenge seriously. They tried to get control back. They attempted to get a court to declare me incompetent and give them a conservatorship over me."

I gasped. I'd had no idea. "Who would do that?"

"My parents. They didn't want their cash cow to wander off into another field. It made me wake up and I realized I had to be out of their reach. I stopped partying, got my marriage annulled, and did what anyone in my position would do—I met with my local army recruiter and signed up."

I smiled slightly at his joke. "That couldn't have been easy."

"That's why I wanted it. I needed something hard, something authentic. I'd never lived in the real world with real problems, and I wanted it more than anything. To be my own man and be in a place where I'd be treated just like everyone else. My goal was to become an Army Ranger. If I was going to be in the military, I was going to be the best."

More than one director had talked about his incredible work ethic. I wondered if it was something his parents had instilled in him or if he'd found it in the military. "What happened? Why did you leave?"

"Because they made me," he said with a wry smile. "We were deployed to Afghanistan, and when we arrived, on our way to the base, we hit an IED. The blast pressure caused me to have a pneumothorax."

I was both horrified and enthralled. "What is that?"

"Basically it's when your lungs collapse. It was incredibly painful, and I couldn't breathe right. I thought I was having a heart attack and that I was going to die. Fortunately there was a medic in the jeep behind us, and he stabilized me. The explosion banged everyone up, but we all survived."

"Is that when you came home?"

He shook his head. "A little bit after that. They performed a thoracoscopy on me and let me heal up. Then they sent me home with a medical discharge. The doctors determined that I was at too much risk of a recurrence if I sustained another physical injury. It's why I can't do my own stunts in movies, either. Which is frustrating. Anyway, I was pissed off. I'd trained with my company for three years, and they were off to serve our mission while I was sitting in an apartment in Brooklyn with no idea what to do with my life."

"You didn't go right back to acting?"

"No. I considered becoming a police officer or a firefighter. Something where I could still serve and protect. But I went to this play, *A View from the Bridge*, and I was blown away. The way the lead actor played this character, how he channeled this rage and frustration into a work of art . . . I wanted that in my life again. I resisted at first, because I didn't want my parents to get credit for any of my success."

"Have they?" I had to admit it, I was dying to get my phone out of my purse and see if I could look his parents up. What kind of people would treat their son that way?

"I don't think so. Somebody on my team would tell me if they did."

"I'm sorry." It felt like such an inadequate thing to keep saying, but I was at a loss here. Things had worked out for him, but it couldn't have been fun to go through it.

"That's just how it was. Not everybody's parents are mentally healthy, and sometimes the best thing for you to do is move on with your own life. My army-appointed psychiatrist told me that and I agreed, and now here we are."

Now here we were. With him being nominated for the most prestigious acting award in the country. It was strange to think he'd almost walked away from all of it. "Do you regret your time in the army? Because your career might have been different if you'd stayed?"

"No. Joining the army was the best thing I could have done for myself. It taught me to work hard, gave me discipline and structure, and made me understand what was really important in life. It made me the person I am now, and I'm generally happy with who I am. Even if I can be a little impatient and annoyed with others."

My curiosity was eating away at me, and even though I shouldn't have asked the next question, I did. "Do you think your parents watched the show tonight?"

"I don't know. Maybe. I know they are still representing child actors and have opened their own acting school. For all I know they're putting my face on their promotional posters. But I can't spend all my time looking back and reliving the worst parts of my life."

I startled at that, my heart rate jumping. It was like he'd seen inside my head. Because all I did was look back and relive the most humiliating part of my life.

He put his arm across the seat behind me. "Do you ever find yourself doing that? Reliving hard times?"

"Recently? A whole lot."

"Is that what caused . . ." He trailed off, his hand hovering next to my neck, and I could feel the warmth from his skin, even though he didn't touch me. "And is this why you don't date?"

"My scars? No. I usually only feel a little self-conscious about them when somebody stares and makes comments. Usually I forget because it's just a part of me now and they're not that bad." It was one of the things I liked about Noah, that he didn't stare or say rude things.

"Can I ask what happened?"

"I was in an accident just after I graduated from high school. I got rear-ended by a drunk driver and glass from the windshield got embedded in my neck. The settlement from his insurance company paid for college, and I saved the rest. Which I'm using to live on now, because somehow I thought I'd start a business and people would just call me. I had no idea how hard it would be to get it off the ground."

"Sounds like you could have used a four-hundred-and-forty-euro tip."

"Ha-ha," I said, nudging him slightly with my hand.

Then he looked at me. The way that Malec had looked at Aliana after their first bout of hand-to-hand combat.

And I knew what that meant.

He wanted to kiss me.

Again I felt like I'd been lured. Only this time it was into a sense of complacency. Him sharing things, trusting me, telling me these stories about himself—it made me forget myself and my own fears. At his expression, they came rushing back.

As my heartbeat pounded out a panicky rhythm, I realized just how close we were on this seat. As if my body had been subtly making its way over toward him, like he was a giant magnet that I was helpless to resist.

So I started inching my way toward the door, wanting to put some space between us. Because he was too much and it felt a little like my throat was starting to close in on itself.

"Why are you afraid of me?" he asked.

I stopped moving. "I'm not."

"You are. I know I'm a big guy and sometimes that can come across as intimidating, but I'm harmless."

"No, you're not," I said with a laugh. I did not want to talk about this. I did not. I felt sweat break out on my hairline, and a wave of nausea made my stomach roil.

He looked really upset and pulled his arm off the seat, putting it back at his side.

I realized that I'd hurt him, and I hadn't meant to do that. "I'm not afraid of you in the way you're thinking. I don't think you're going to hurt me. That's not it."

He relaxed slightly while I wondered hysterically how much it would cost to steam clean the leather seat we were sitting on after I upchucked all over it.

While I concentrated on breathing in and out, he said, "You're so hard to read. Part of my job is figuring out what makes people tick. Why they do what they do and what they mean by it. And sometimes, sometimes I feel like you're attracted to me and you want me to touch you, and then other times you look at me like I'm a lion about to swallow you whole."

"If anyone is looking at anyone in a weird way, I'm not the only one at fault here." I felt tears at the edges of my eyes, which was so stupid. I was not going to cry about this. I wasn't. "It feels like you've spent a lot of time thinking about this."

"When I told you earlier that you were easy to think of, I was being serious. I find myself thinking about you a lot. Trying to puzzle you out."

What in the holy freak was I supposed to do with that?

He kept talking. "In the last couple of minutes, you've made enough space between us for a marching band to pass through."

That was true.

And I considered something I'd never considered before. Telling him. There was something inherently trustworthy and reliable about him. Like he was so strong that I could depend on him to help me carry my burdens. Maybe it was because he'd spent this car ride telling me all about himself, trusting me, that made me think that I could confess. I'd get through it, it would be embarrassing, but wouldn't it be a relief to have another person know?

I couldn't tell him every detail, but I could tell him most of them. And then he would understand. He was a logical person. He would see that we couldn't be together and nothing would ever happen and that while we'd had a nice time together, this was as far as things could ever go.

What would his reaction be? I wanted to imagine that he would be gentle and understanding. But what if he wasn't?

It was too scary, and I felt like I was going to pass out. I couldn't.

So I clung to what I was good at—putting off and discouraging men. "I can't explain it to you. I'm sorry. I can be friends and nothing more. That's all I have to offer you." And if he didn't want to be friends, well, I'd be okay with that. I was okay before we met, and my life would go on just fine without him in it.

Even if that thought did feel a little sad.

He stayed silent for a moment, considering. "Then I'll take whatever you have to give. I'd like to be your friend."

Relief coursed through me so powerfully that I felt a little dizzy. I sagged against the seat. "Good. So we're friends."

"Do friends hang out in a non–dog grooming capacity?" he asked.

I weakly smiled. "You did that tonight."

"Right. So I'll have to add in wanting to spend time with you in a non–seat filler capacity, too. Maybe this Friday?"

"I can't on Friday," I told him. "My mom is doing this one-woman show where she's giving birth to herself for one of her theater classes."

"That sounds like an oddly specific lie," he said.

"It's the truth. My mother's midlife crisis involves her going back to school to pursue that acting degree she's always wanted. You should totally stop by. Fun will be had by all."

The car came to a stop, and the engine turned off. I looked out the window and was surprised to see that we were in front of my apartment building. The night was officially over. And other than my one mini-freak-out, things had gone well and I'd enjoyed spending time with him. As friends did, right?

I put my hand on the door handle and was about to thank him when he said, "Wait. There's something else I need to tell you."

CHAPTER TWELVE

That worried, panicky feeling returned. Was he about to take it back? Say he didn't want to be friends?

"It's about Shelby," he said, and I immediately felt reassured.

"You mean how the two of you masterminded this evening? Don't worry, it doesn't take a genius to have figured that one out."

"No. I mean, yes, we may have schemed a little, but this is about something else." My mind went to a weird place. Like, if he told me right now that in the last week he and Shelby had fallen in love and were running away together, I was going to march straight into our apartment and set fire to all of her favorite lipsticks.

"What?"

"I've hired her to do renovations on my house."

"Oh." Yeah, that made much more sense. Shelby's makeup was safe. "Well, that was a good choice. She's excellent at what she does."

"I only did it because—" He stopped himself short, studying my face like he was hoping a clue would appear. "I guess that doesn't matter now. With us being friends and all."

The rest of that sentence felt vitally important, but I knew I didn't have any right to it. I was the one who'd said friends only.

"The important thing," he continued, "is that she agreed and we've already started. She's working on getting the permits."

I couldn't believe she hadn't said anything. She told me everything. Like, sometimes an uncomfortable amount of information. There was one time I couldn't look Allan in the face for a week because of her oversharing. How could Shelby keep this from me?

Because you've never kept anything from her? my guilty conscience asked me. I told it to shut up.

"That's good," I said. I knew how excited she must have been. And I'd bet she'd told Allan. While I understood that was how things were supposed to be, it felt a little like I was being replaced.

"Well," I said, realizing that I'd been sitting in his parked car for what was an unusual amount of time, and I could only imagine what poor Ray thought about what might be happening in his back seat, "I should go."

"Do you want me to walk with you?"

I most definitely did not. I needed to escape his appeal, not prolong it even further. "I'm good, but thanks."

I opened the car door and got out. I turned to shut it behind me, but he poked his face out of the opening. "Can I tell you something I've never told anyone else?"

"There's more?" I asked, again trying to be jokey and failing. I wasn't sure my nervous system could take it.

"I like you. Buddy."

His face was like an open book, and I could see what he meant without him speaking the words. Even with his qualifier, he wasn't saying he liked me as a friend.

"I bet you say that to all the seat fillers. Good night, pal." I smiled at him and then walked away, letting him close his own door. This was the problem with being friends with an actor who had hinted that he wanted something more. He had the ability to show every emotion he was feeling or to hide them all from me because it was his literal job. Which meant I could either be overwhelmed by what was on his face or left wondering what he was thinking.

Get out, get out now, that worried voice inside me whispered. *Stop this before it starts.*

I couldn't. There was this feeling of inevitability. Now that we had crossed paths—and had done so over and over again—it almost felt like I was destined to have him in my life in some way. I shook my head. So many women would have killed for this chance. And maybe I was being naive in thinking that I could dictate how this was going to go.

Because it felt a little like being on a runaway freight train heading toward the side of a mountain. I couldn't stop it or slow it down or jump off. I was on board for the full ride, wherever that was going to take me.

~

I woke up the next morning on the couch. My neck was stiff, and I groaned as I came to. I'd been waiting up for Shelby because we had so many Very Important Things to discuss. But I must have passed out, and instead of waking me up like I had wanted her to, she'd put a throw blanket over me and had gone to bed.

"Good morning!" She was in the kitchen turning on the coffee maker, way too cheery.

"How could you not tell me about the remodeling thing?"

She rushed over to the couch and sat next to me. "You have no idea how hard it was to not tell you. But isn't it the best news ever?"

I still couldn't believe that Shelby had sat on a secret that big. It was so unlike her. Not unlike me, but I wasn't the one being questioned here.

"The best," I echoed.

"This is going to be everything. His publicist put in a call to *California Architectural*, and they fell all over themselves to offer us the cover. The cover! I'm going to be launched into a different stratosphere."

"That is going to be so great," I said. I was happy for her, and it was selfish of me to be worried about how all this was going to affect me. Maybe it wouldn't affect my life at all. I'd already told the guy we could be friends. What that was going to look like I wasn't sure, but why would it be a bad thing if my best friend was fixing his atrocious house?

"And he is paying me so well. So. Well. He offered to double all of my fees and costs for doing rush work, and unlike you, I didn't talk him out of it because I've found that I like making money instead of throwing it away." She was teasing me, but it wasn't the same thing. Him paying her versus him paying me. Although if I'd been pressed about it, I couldn't have explained why.

I also hoped he'd pay her in actual dollars.

"And you know," she continued, "you're such an awesome person that he's basically hiring me based on the fact that I'm your friend. I mean, he went to my website and looked at my other projects, and I got a floor plan of his house from that friend of mine who works in the records office and I pitched him my ideas in that program I have that renders 3D schematics—"

"So, for more reasons than just being my friend," I interjected with a smile. "It's because you're talented and you're going to do an amazing job." But I didn't really want to talk about Noah Douglas. "How was your night?"

Shelby rolled her eyes and went into the kitchen. I followed her and sat on the barstool at our peninsula counter while she rummaged around for coffee mugs. "The less I say about that, the better."

"What do you mean?" I needed to go get changed. I had to return this dress, and it was feeling really uncomfortable. Formal wear was not meant to be slept in.

"Harmony pretty much ignored me for the entire evening. I was this close to getting up on her dining room table and doing my old tap-dance routine from junior high, just to force her to make eye contact with me. It's a good thing I love Allan," she said as she placed the mugs on the counter. "And I don't have to ask how your night was because . . . BAM!"

She reached for her laptop and flipped it up. "I wanted to slam it on the counter for the full effect but I don't want to break it and I need it for work, so . . ." She slid it across the counter toward me.

And there was a picture of me and Noah Douglas. He looked amazing, all self-assured and sexy with the barest hint of a smile. They'd published a picture of me gazing at him instead of at the camera, and it made me uncomfortable. Mostly because I resembled . . . the girl his mother had forced him to take out.

"We look like a set of Goth twins going to an emo prom," I told her.

"You're crazy," she assured me. "You look like a matched set with your dark hair and dark eyes. Like you were meant to be together."

I sighed. "You need to hurry up and get married so that you can get out of this isn't-love-so-wonderful phase."

The picture was listed with Noah's name on it. No mention of me. Which made sense. Then I scrolled down a little farther, and that's where the comments started.

Who is this fat ugly skank ho?

I would murder someone to stand next to him like that.

Ick. He could do so much better.

Call me instead, Noah Douglas.

I only ship Noah and Lily and I don't accept cheap substitutes.

I wish it was me!

And those were the comments that weren't riddled with spelling errors and grammatical mistakes, and I tried to ignore the ones with inventive swear words.

My stomach turned over, and I felt like I was going to vomit all over Shelby's laptop. Having gone through a bad round of bullying when I was fourteen, I'd pretty much steered clear of all social media since then, and this was reminding me why.

This was proof I'd made the right call last night when I'd told him I only wanted to be friends. I already knew what it was like to have to endure this type of venom on a daily basis. No way did I want to sign up for that mess again.

Gossip really hit differently when it was about you.

Shelby realized too late what I was doing. "Don't read the comments!" She shut her laptop screen and pulled it back. "It doesn't matter what a bunch of tweens and frustrated housewives think. It only matters what he thinks."

"To be fair, it doesn't really matter what Noah thinks, either. I told him I only wanted to be friends."

She stared at me, her mouth open. Then she reached for the most recent issue of *American Weekly*, rolled it up, and hit me on my arm with it like I was a bad dog.

"What? Why would you do that?" she demanded.

"Ow! Stop!" I grabbed the magazine from her and threw it onto the coffee table behind me. "I don't like him that way."

"You are my best friend and I love you, but that is quite possibly the stupidest thing you have ever said to me. You look at him like you've been starving for a month and he's a man-size vat of ice cream."

"Whatever" was my masterful reply. My phone buzzed, and I reached for my clutch. I had thrown it onto the counter last night when I got home. I emptied out the contents and noted that my phone was about to die. My heart had a moment of hope that maybe it was Noah. But . . . what if he'd seen the picture? That could be a bad thing.

It wasn't him. It was a text message from . . . my bank. Thrilling. I wondered what credit card I was currently eligible for or what their current low, low rate would be for refinancing my mortgage. The fact that I didn't have a mortgage never seemed to bother them.

"An uneaten Snickers bar?" Shelby asked. "Isn't that one of the signs of the apocalypse?"

I reached for the candy bar and put it back inside my purse. "Noah gave it to me." There's no way I could ever eat it. I would let it get moldy and stale, or whatever it was candy bars did when they went bad. (Having never let a candy bar go bad, I had no idea what happened to them.) I was going to put it in a box somewhere and pull it out to look at it when I wanted to reminisce.

Shelby's eyes danced. "So he gave you something and you're keeping it. For sentimental reasons. Nothing about that says, 'I want to be just friends.'"

"I keep stuff you've given me," I scoffed.

"Name one thing."

My mind went blank. I had nothing. "I'm not playing this game with you."

"Good plan. Because you'd lose." She poured coffee into one of the mugs before handing it to me. "You should have jumped all over that man. You're in the world's worst dry spell."

"It's only a dry spell if you're thirsty," I said, opting to drink without adding in massive amounts of sugar because I needed the caffeine kick. I grimaced after my first sip. I always forgot how much better coffee tasted after it had been sweetened.

She had both of her hands wrapped around her own mug. "How can you think you're not thirsty? You're like a dehydrated man who's been crawling through the Sahara on his hands and knees for two days with no help in sight."

"Why am I not a woman in this scenario?"

After she took a sip, she said, "Because only a man would do something stupid enough to get himself stranded in the Sahara." She set her mug on the counter. "You've got to give me something. Because I can tell that he likes you, whether or not you agree with me. There had to be a moment. I'm an old engaged woman. Tell me about the butterflies so that they may live on in my memory."

At that I laughed and said, "Fine. There was this moment last night where he looked at me like . . ."

"Like?" she prompted, urging me to go on.

"Like how Malec looked at Aliana after their first fight."

She reached across the countertop to grab my forearm while squealing in delight. "Are you kidding me? I would have *died* if he ever looked at me that way!"

"Hi, recently resurrected person here."

"Then what did you do?"

"I got out of the car."

"You didn't kiss him?" she asked in utter disbelief.

"We're just friends. I can't."

"You most certainly can! Often, and with a crap ton of passion."

I went to my old standby. "I'm not dating anyone. You know that. I'm focusing on my business. And kissing leads to dating."

"I really want to respect your choices and be supportive of you, but as your friend, please know that everything you're saying is still dumb. You should totally be making out with him."

When I just shook my head as my response, she came over to sit on the other barstool. "You know I only want the best for you, right?

Instead of drawing boundaries, I think you should go with the flow. See where the universe takes you."

"That's not really my thing. I'm more of a violently-struggle-against-the-flow type of person." Sometimes I did make things harder than they needed to be.

We sat in silence for a moment until she said, "So, just friends, huh? Does that mean you'd be good with him dating someone else?"

"Is he?" The words rushed out of my mouth without my approval. "I mean, if he is, that's fine. Good for him." My reaction was totally unwarranted considering he'd told me himself that he wasn't dating anyone. "As his friend, I would want him to be happy."

"I don't believe you," she said in a singsong voice.

Yeah, neither did I.

But even if I wanted to date him and wasn't desperately afraid of getting close to him, there still wouldn't be any way. I couldn't compete with the kind of women he could date. What did I have in common with the world's most beautiful actresses and models?

I mean other than the fact that we were all hungry all the time?

"Well, I have to get ready for *work*." She put an emphasis on the last word, clearly pleased to have a client again. She took her coffee mug to the sink. "Is there a message you want me to pass along to your newly acquired friend?"

"Nope, I'm good."

"Maybe I'll give him a good, rousing speech about how faint heart never won fair maiden," she mused, rinsing her cup out and putting it into the dishwasher.

"It won't do you any good. He accepted his defeat and retreated like a good soldier."

She seemed to consider this. "Or . . . he didn't retreat. Maybe he's biding his time and planning to attack from another position."

Shaking my head, I gathered up my stuff and then went into my bedroom, closing the door behind me. I dropped my purse on my bed and plugged the charger into my phone. I peeled off my dress. I needed a shower, but Shelby would need to use it first.

For her new job.

My phone buzzed again, and I let myself have that moment of hope again before checking. My bank again. They must really want me to go into debt. But this time I bothered to read the first line.

It said SECURITY ALERT.

I opened the message, and it said something about fraudulent activity and to call them as soon as possible to resolve it. My pulse began to beat frantically. I logged on to my banking app to see what was going on.

Zero.

My checking account had been cleared out.

CHAPTER THIRTEEN

I called the phone number in the text and pushed the numbers in the menu to report fraudulent activity. A woman named Karen answered and asked for my account number. I didn't know it off the top of my head, although I probably could have gotten it from my banking app.

She asked, "Do you have your debit card? You could read that number to me."

The last place I'd had my card was in my clutch. I dived for my purse, pulling out the candy bar, my driver's license, my lipstick, mints, and a thing of tissues.

No debit card.

"It's gone," I told her.

"Do you know when you lost it?"

"I had it yesterday." I specifically remembered putting it in my purse when I was getting ready for the Oscars, just in case I needed it for some reason. And now it was gone. I hadn't used it in days.

It was then that I remembered the party, how my purse had fallen on the ground when I was trying to read that text from Morgan. "I think I lost it last night at the *Vanity Fair* party."

There was a pause. "Did you say the *Vanity Fair* party? The one after the Academy Awards?"

"Yeah. I was there with Noah Douglas. It was kind of a date."

Another pause. "Like . . . in your dreams?"

"What? No. I was there." I realized too late how far-fetched and stupid it sounded, but it was the actual truth.

"Right. And Chase Covington and I were in his villa in Italy."

Were customer service reps supposed to be this snarky? "He was actually there at the party with his wife. I hung out with them."

She didn't respond.

I was completely aware of how crazy this all sounded. "I can send you proof. I have a picture of Noah and me together."

"Please hold." She was probably off to have a good laugh with her fellow customer service colleagues.

Dumb elevator music came on, and I wanted to raise my fists and shake them at the world. I'd spent a fantastic evening with one of the world's biggest movie stars at one of the biggest Hollywood parties, so of course the universe had to balance it back out by letting someone steal all my money.

I thought of the person who had taken my debit card at a party full of celebrities and wealthy people and how mad they must have been when they found out that there was so little in my account.

Shelby called out "Bye!" just before she slammed the front door shut, but I wasn't able to respond, as Karen came back on the line.

"Juliet?"

"Yes?"

She had me verify some of my personal information to locate my account. Once she had, she read off the suspicious charges to me. There were small purchases at two drugstores first, the criminal probably not realizing they'd spent a good percentage of my "fortune" on ChapStick and Slim Jims. Their next stop was at a gas station and a liquor store, where they'd bought enough alcohol to make an entire frat house black-out drunk. Then once they saw that there was no alert on the card, that

I hadn't reported it as stolen, they went online to a jewelry store website and tried to purchase a six-thousand-dollar pair of earrings.

Which my bank's algorithms noticed, because I was so broke that they probably would have sent me an alert if I'd ever tried to buy two-ply toilet paper.

When I denied all the charges, Karen told me she had canceled my debit card and would mail me a new one. She then told me that the bank had up to ten days to investigate the fraudulent charges and that once they'd determined they were in fact fraudulent, they had another business day to replace the missing funds.

"But my rent is due in four days," I told her. I didn't have however many days they were going to take to give me back my money.

"It could be worse," she told me sympathetically. "You reported it within two business days, which means your liability is limited to fifty dollars. If you'd waited more than sixty days, your liability could have been up to five hundred dollars."

"Wait, what? Someone stole from me and I'm liable for fifty bucks?" I know it didn't sound like much, but it was a lot of money to someone like me.

"Because they used your debit card and it was processed as a debit instead of a credit transaction, it's not under the same sort of protection, and you do have liability."

My mom had told me once to always use my bank card as a credit card, and now I was finally understanding why. "But isn't that why the cards have those chips in them? To force them to input my PIN?"

"Not every vendor has an updated card reader, and there are places that will take a swipe instead."

I put my head in my free hand. What was I going to do? I felt totally defeated. "Okay. I guess it is what it is." It didn't sound like there was a whole lot I could do. I assumed Karen was only doing what she was supposed to do. "Thanks."

"Sure thing, Juliet. Is there anything else I can help you with?"

"No." There wasn't anything else she could do to help with the rest of the mess that had become my life.

"You have a good day, and thank you for doing business with Regional Advantage Bank." Pause. "And say hi to Noah Douglas for me the next time you see him."

She hung up, having shot that last barb at me with a slightly sarcastic tone. Someone nicer probably would have assumed she was being polite, but I knew my own kind and how we threw shade at others.

I needed money. Like, now. Not fifteen days from now. And business days were stupid. Our world was international and open 24-7. There should just be days, and weekends should count when someone took all your money.

A cold chill enveloped me, and I shuddered a little. I was just now understanding what had actually happened—and there was a sense of violation that some unnamed person had stolen from me. Taken everything I'd worked so hard for and blown it all in just over twelve hours. It seemed so unreal that I'd been robbed. My normally dim outlook on humanity had grown even bleaker.

I glanced at my phone. I needed to take that shower and get ready. I had an appointment in a couple of hours. I relied on muscle memory to carry me through the motions as I considered my options.

There was always my mom, but she had a major hang-up about me not repeating her mistakes. She didn't want me to marry someone older than me who had a reputation as a player like my dad apparently had (I found that hard to believe) and who would walk away when things got too hard. She'd always counseled me to be sensible and get a steady, well-paying job. She had not been pleased when I'd graduated with an accounting degree but no plans of becoming an accountant. That I would figure out what I wanted my job to be.

When I told her about my plan to buy the van and start Waggin' Wheels, she reminded me that I wasn't prepared and didn't know how hard it was to start your own business (which she had done, so she knew better than I did). I kept insisting that I could do it and she didn't have to take care of me. There was no way I was going to run to her now and admit that she'd been right about everything and I needed financial help.

Especially since she was being so careful with her own expenses because she was pursuing her degree full-time. I knew her concern came from a place of love and that she would help if I asked, but it was important to me to be independent.

I could ask Shelby, given that Noah was paying her *so well* and all, but I wondered if that would be akin to him giving me money, and I definitely did not want that.

It was something I kept running over in my mind. Part of me hoped that the bank would do their investigation quickly and that I didn't need to worry about bringing in some extra money, but I knew I couldn't depend on it.

I spent the day helping out at an adoption fair for a local animal shelter. Volunteering always put me in a good mood. While there I also handed out fliers offering one free grooming session to anyone who adopted a dog. There was nothing better to me than knowing animals were going to a good home, and I could definitely use the karma points. The hours flew by and thankfully distracted me from my current circumstances.

After the fair ended and we'd packed everything up, my problems came rushing back. What was I going to do? What could I do?

I could sell my plasma. I could try to get some gig job like delivering food or doing people's grocery shopping. The problem was that I didn't have a car, just my van. And by the time I added in the gas costs, I probably wouldn't be making any money. I could try to borrow Shelby's car, but now that she had a full-time job again, I knew she'd be driving all over the place to meet with her contractor and look for samples to show Noah and pick up band saws and jackhammers or whatever she did with her day, and her car would not be available.

When I got into the van, my phone rang. It was Shelby.

I answered and said, "This is a coincidence. I was just thinking about you."

"Juliet, I need your help."

I put on my seat belt and said, "I swear, if you're calling me because you're claiming that Noah is in desperate need of mouth-to-mouth resuscitation . . ." I mean, I would probably be too freaked out to do it, but if it meant keeping him alive, I could probably take one for the team.

Maybe.

"No, it's nothing like that." It was then that I noticed the frantic edge in her voice, making me feel like a jerk for teasing her. "I'm at Noah's place with the movers and there was someone here watching his dog because I told him we'd be in and out all day and that guy just took off and I remembered that you mentioned that the dog tries to get out and run off and everybody's asking me what to do but I'm so distracted and I cannot start this job by losing Noah Douglas's dog."

Honestly, she was extremely lucky that Magnus hadn't run away already. "Okay, there's a leash hanging up in the kitchen. Put it on his collar and hold on to him until I get there. Things are going to be fine. I'm on my way. I'll take care of him."

Traffic was terrible and I could hear my phone buzzing, presumably with texts from Shelby asking if I was almost there yet. Shelby had never really liked animals, and I could only imagine that this was freaking her out. Magnus was a sweet boy, but he was a big dog and might not be all that easy for her to manage.

When I arrived, Shelby was waiting out front with tears streaming down her face. "I'm so glad that you're here!"

I hugged her briefly and moved to take the leash. "Are you okay?"

She nodded and gulped. "This has to go well. It just does. I cannot blow this again. This is my last chance."

"I've got this," I told her. And I meant it. I was going to do whatever I had to do to make sure that this was a success. Shelby was my framily (my friend who was also my family), and I had her back. "Go and do whatever you need to do. I'll take him for a walk." Magnus wagged his tail at me, apparently pleased to see a slightly familiar face. Or maybe he understood the word *walk*.

"Thank you," she said. "I owe you one."

A mover stepped out of the front door. "Are we taking the mattress or leaving it here?"

"Leaving it here. I'll be inside in a second to tell you what else goes and what stays," she said. Then she whispered to me, "Can you believe Noah Douglas has a mattress on the floor? Like he's still in college? I can't wait to buy him an actual bed."

I didn't want to think about Noah in any bed. "Sounds fun. Anyway, we're off."

She waved happily to me, her good spirits restored now that I was in charge of Magnus.

"Come on, boy."

We'd only been walking for a couple of minutes when I noticed a dog sitting across the road from us, watching. He looked like a black poodle mix. He had on a collar, but I didn't see any people with him. The road had a sharp bend here, and I was afraid he might run out into the street at the wrong moment and get hit.

I tugged Magnus to come with me, and I crossed the road. The dog growled slightly, as if warning us not to come too close, but there wasn't any real conviction behind it. In fact, he looked like he was trembling a little. I put the loop of the leash handle around my wrist to free up my hands. I told Magnus to sit and he did as I asked. I crouched down and pulled out one of the treats I still had in my pocket and offered it to the dog. He waited a few moments, sniffing the air between us. In the end his hunger won out, and he came over to scarf down the treat.

"Good boy," I said, and then I reached out carefully and picked him up. He was light and easy to carry in one arm. I took a look at his tag. His name was Sunshine, and I put his address into my maps app. When I asked it to give me directions, it told me to walk about a minute south to get to his house. I had to turn my phone around to determine that south meant left.

"Let's get you home," I told him. "I bet somebody is missing you."

Sunshine's house was a bungalow that reminded me of Noah's place, and I knocked on the door. An older woman with long white hair answered the door. "What?"

Did she not see that I was holding her dog? "I found Sunshine here on the side of the road."

She shaded her eyes and stepped forward. "I didn't realize that he'd gotten out. How were you able to carry him? Sunshine doesn't like strangers."

"He seems to like me." I was good with difficult dogs. We had an understanding. The understanding was that I would ply them with treats if they made a minimal effort to do what I wanted. It had worked out well for me so far.

"I suppose you better come inside," she said with a grimace, and I followed her in. A real curmudgeon, as my mom would say. "I'm Gladys Kravitch."

"Juliet Nolan," I responded.

"You out wandering the neighborhood looking for lost dogs?" She closed the front door once I'd stepped inside.

"I was just up the road at Noah Douglas's house, helping out with Magnus." I lifted his leash, in case she hadn't noticed him, either.

She fixed her annoyed gaze on the dog, and Magnus hid behind my legs. "Bah. The movie star." She said the words with disgust, the same way I'd say *the spinach and kale salad*.

"This way." Magnus followed us as she led me down a narrow hallway into her living room, and it struck me how sparse it was. My own grandmother had died years ago, but I remembered her house being full of tchotchkes and knickknacks. While there was definitely a grandma vibe to the decor, with heavy burgundy drapes, a lace doily on the coffee table, and older oak furniture, there were no mementos out. No collectibles or walls full of pictures. There was, in fact, only one picture.

"Is this you and your husband?" I asked.

"Yes." She paused. "Was. Was my husband."

"I'm so sorry. When did he pass?"

"Last year." I heard the way her voice caught. "My Bruce and I were married for forty-seven years." She sat down on the couch and pointed to a stuffed, quilted armchair and said, "Sit. There." Like I was one of the dogs.

I just did what she told me. It was easier. I usually dealt well with prickly people, because I realized that everyone had more stuff going on in their lives than they usually cared to admit, so it was easy to ignore the small, offensive things. I put Sunshine down, but he immediately turned around and tried to get back up in my lap, so I let him.

"You expecting a reward?"

"No! I just wanted to bring Sunshine home."

She pointed to the writing on my polo shirt. "Waggin' Wheels?"

"It's my company," I told her proudly. "A mobile dog-grooming service."

"Do you ever do dog sitting?"

Huh. I'd never considered that. Maybe it would be a good idea for me to include more services beyond grooming. It could mean more clients. "I haven't, but I guess I could. Why?"

She pointed toward the hallway, and it was then that I noticed a large suitcase. "My fool sister broke both her legs when she was taking down her Christmas lights. I'm her only living relative, and I have to fly out to Montana to look after her. Her condo complex doesn't allow any pets, so I need someone to take care of Sunshine. He already seems to like you."

"I'd love to, but I can't take him home with me. My apartment doesn't allow dogs, either."

"Stay here. I have a guest room."

"Here?" I asked, surprised by how sudden this all felt. "But you don't even know me."

"I was going to call a service and have them send a stranger over that I'd make the same offer to. How is this any different? At least this way I already know that Sunshine won't bite you, which gives you a leg up over anyone else. I'd need you to be here for two weeks. I can pay you fifteen hundred dollars. Half now, half when I get back."

I didn't even know what to charge her, or if that was fair or maybe even too much. I didn't want to take advantage of her. "If you're on a limited income, you don't have to—"

She cut me off. "I can take care of myself just fine. My Bruce made sure of that."

I felt like I was going to insult her if I refused or offered to do it for less, so I said, "I'd love to." This was definitely going to solve my money problems, and it presented me with a way to diversify my business for the future.

"Good." She nodded. "I tend to trust my gut, and it's saying you're the right person for the job. Can you start tomorrow?"

"Yes." That would give me a chance to go home and pack a bag.

"Come on. I'll give you the tour."

As I stood up and looked out of her window, I caught a glimpse of Noah's house.

And it was only then that I realized I was about to become his closest neighbor for the next two weeks.

CHAPTER FOURTEEN

Gladys's house had three bedrooms and two bathrooms. She showed me the guest room and where she kept the spare linens and towels. In the hallway there was a picture of Gladys and Bruce on their wedding day. She was wearing a long, flowy yellow dress and had a wreath of flowers in her hair.

"You look so beautiful in this photo," I told her.

"My Bruce convinced me to elope. I wore my prom dress. He always did have fool ideas about things."

In the family room, she showed me the TV and the various necessary remotes. I was instructed not to mess with the DVR recordings of her "stories."

"My Bruce was always messing with the timers," she said. I could hear the ache in her voice every time she mentioned her husband. She probably just thought they had been average people in a regular relationship, not knowing how many people probably looked at them and hoped they would find what she'd already had.

I know I did, even if it was impossible for me to have that in my own life.

We went into her kitchen, and she pointed out several places where the wood floors were buckling. "We had some water damage a few years ago. My Bruce always intended to replace them but he never had the time, and then he got sick . . ." She trailed off and shook her head. "Just keep an eye out when you're in here."

She showed me where she kept Sunshine's food. She had already written out her daily routine with her dog, and it boiled down to feeding him at specific times in the morning and evening and taking him for two daily walks. Easy.

Sunshine also had an orange teddy bear that he adored but was often misplacing. She told me to keep an eye on it. I told her I would.

"Any questions?" Gladys asked.

"Not that I can think of."

I put my phone number into her cell phone and then called it so that we'd have each other's numbers. She told me she would Venmo me the seven hundred and fifty dollars, and I tried not to look surprised that she knew how to do that. She then went to a drawer to give me a copy of her front door key. "I'll be leaving for my flight at six in the morning tomorrow. You should come over sometime after that."

"I will," I said as I tucked the key into my front pocket. "Thanks for the opportunity. I will take really good care of Sunshine."

She walked me to the front door, and when Magnus and I stepped out onto the porch, she said, "You feel like an answer to a prayer, although I haven't spoken to God since my Bruce died."

"You're kind of an answer to a prayer for me, too."

But apparently that was too much emotion for her, as she just muttered, "Bah," and shut the door in my face.

I grinned. I liked Gladys.

I walked back up the road toward Noah's house while Magnus tried to sniff every rock and twig we passed. The moving crew's van was gone, but Shelby's car was still out front. I let myself inside the house, calling her name.

She came out of the kitchen. "Hey! You were gone awhile."

"Yeah, I just got a job with Noah's neighbor. She's going to pay me to dog sit, so I'll be there for a couple of weeks." Then I told her about how my morning had gone and my checking account situation and that the down payment Gladys had given me would tide me over until the bank put my money back.

"That's a relief," she said. "And yay for you for expanding your business. Speaking of business, have I mentioned that this is my dream job?"

"Maybe once or twice," I teased.

"Noah said not to go too crazy but that I had no budget. He would trust me."

Wow. That was a mistake of epic proportions. "Does he know how you are?"

"I won't go nuts."

"Ha. Famous last words. Maybe you should give him solid-gold countertops."

"Don't be ridiculous." I expected her to tell me it would be too tacky, but instead she said, "The weight of them would crush the cabinets underneath." She grabbed her sketchbook and put her laptop into her purse. "I need to get home and start ordering some stuff. The permits should come through by this Friday, and then we can start construction first thing next Monday."

"Okay," I said. "See you at home."

She hesitated. "Aren't you leaving, too?"

I gestured toward Magnus. "I feel like I should keep an eye on him and explain the situation. When did Noah say he would be back?"

"Six." She took her keys out but had that knowing look I hated. "And you're, what, going to wait for Noah to come home? Because you miss him and want to see him again?"

My stomach flipped over lightly that she could read me so easily. "It's not like that."

"Oh, I think it is."

"You're entitled to your delusions," I told her.

"You say delusion, I say complete and total fact."

"See you at home," I repeated so she would take the hint.

"Or not," she responded, waggling her eyebrows at me. "Dealer's choice."

"Just go," I said with a laugh.

She waved and gave Magnus a wide berth as she headed for the door. I heard it close and then realized I was hungry. Noah was supposed to be home in an hour. I could probably wait until then. I considered going into his kitchen but decided that was rude and possibly invasive, although technically I was doing him a favor, and feeding me was, like, the least he could do.

I messed around on my phone for a while but it started getting low on battery, so I put it away. Magnus came in carrying his food bowl in his mouth.

"Are you hungry, boy?" I asked, taking it from him. "Me too. But let's get you taken care of first. Where's your food?" I followed him to a skinny pantry and found a massive bag of kibble. I filled up his bowl and put it down for him. "Here you go."

And that was the most exciting thing that happened to me for the next few hours as five turned to six and then seven and eight and finally, a bit after nine o'clock, I heard the keys in the front door. Magnus ran to greet Noah, barking loudly.

No part of me was excited that he was home. I was sitting at the kitchen table, drumming my fingers, and I was so thoroughly annoyed with him. Plus, I was now starving. Why did he say he'd be back by six when he wasn't? Maybe six meant something different where he was from. But we'd both been born in Southern California, so that couldn't be it, either. Maybe it was because he never went to a real school and was just really bad at counting.

I heard him telling Magnus hello and I couldn't resist calling out, "About time!"

"Juliet? You sound pleasant." There was muffled movement, like he was taking a jacket off and hanging it up in a closet.

"Yeah. Because there's this movie star I know who hired a flaky dog babysitter who then said he'd be home by six and it's now nine, so I've been stuck waiting here for him."

He was talking to Magnus, and then he called back, "You didn't have to wait. Magnus would have been fine on his own for a little while."

Nope. There was no way I was letting this go south for Shelby. She was going to do what she did best and would be a huge success and every movie star in Hollywood was going to put her on speed dial to decorate their houses. I was about to explain to him how responsible she'd been in calling me so that Magnus didn't escape again when he walked into the kitchen and . . . and . . . and . . .

. . . and . . .

He was dressed as Malec Shadowfire. He had on the wig with the long black hair and his trademark suit of black leather armor. I even saw folded wings.

OMG, I was going to die. I was going to shatter into a million pieces and nobody would ever be able to put me back together again.

Noah walked over to the fridge, took out a half gallon of milk, and drank it straight from the container. It was such an incongruous sight—Malec drinking a modern thing of milk—that my brain couldn't process what was happening.

Maybe that was because I couldn't get enough oxygen to it. How had he sucked all the air out of the room just by being dressed that way?

"Could . . . could you go . . . and . . . could you go change? I can't . . ." *control my involuntary hormonal reactions to you.* "I can't take you seriously when you're dressed like Malec" was what I settled on.

It was amazing I was able to form words at all. I felt like I was having a series of mini-strokes.

"You know who Malec is? Did you finally watch the trilogy?" he asked, not moving to go change like I'd very nicely asked him to. I had asked him, hadn't I? I couldn't remember.

And had I finally watched the movies? I owned them all in three different formats. I'd come this close to ordering a life-size cutout of him as Malec. Had I watched the movies?

"Yeah. Yes. Shelby and I binged them after the first time you and I met." That was technically true, although probably not in the sense of what he would consider the full truth.

And there was no way I was telling him the whole truth now—that I'd lied to him the first night we met about not knowing who he was. Because Shelby had her dream job and it was going to make her career take off, and I would do anything to help ensure that happened.

If any part of her belief was true—that he'd hired her solely because she was my friend—well, what happened if he and I stopped being friends because I'd lied to him? He would fire Shelby.

Which would be all my fault, so the best way to prevent that from happening was to say nothing to him. It might have been a big deal if we were in a relationship, but we weren't. Friends could have secrets from each other. And it wasn't something that could hurt our very platonic friendship, so I was okay.

I could not make direct eye contact with him. It was like staring into the sun.

"Let me pay you for watching him," he said, and I saw him reaching for his wallet.

"Put your euros away," I told him. "I don't want your fake money." Our relationship was already weird enough, and I was not going to have him paying me on top of everything else. "But I won't object to being fed."

"Yep. You definitely sound like you need to get some food in you." He went to one of his cabinets and pulled out a box of chocolate puff cereal. He walked over and put it down on the table in front of me. "Do you want some milk, too?"

"The same milk you just drank straight from the container? No thanks, Captain Hygiene." I tore open the plastic and took out a handful of cereal and shoved it into my mouth. My shoulders slumped inward with relief. "I don't know what I'd do without chocolate."

"My guess is twenty-five to life."

I smiled and shook my head at his remark and kept feeding my complaining stomach.

"If you're okay here, I'm going to take a shower."

"I'm okay." I drew in a shaky breath. I was going to tell him that I didn't really want him to leave and take off his Malec outfit, but I recognized that it was probably for the best since I was feeling so weak-willed anyway. Him leaving the room and not being in that really, um, hot costume would let me calm my nerves. I could fill up on cereal so that I would feel like myself again. Everything would be fine.

Just so long as I didn't imagine him in the shower.

Oh crap! I was making it worse.

He left the room, whistling to himself, and I realized that I probably should have left. He was home and there was no reason for me to be hanging around. But I hadn't offered to go and he hadn't asked me to leave. Friends could hang out together, right?

Plus, I was really hungry.

Magnus was sitting near my feet, giving me pathetic looks.

"Sorry, you can't have chocolate," I told him. "Even the processed kind."

He hopped up when Noah walked back in the room wearing a dark-gray T-shirt, black sweats, and a pair of socks that had pineapples on them. His hair was wet, and I almost fell out of my chair.

This was not any better.

"I'm going to make some wild rice–crusted halibut," he said. "I was up for a role as a chef a few years ago and had zero kitchen skills, so I hired a professional to teach me. I didn't get the role, but I did learn my way around a kitchen. Do you want some?"

Wild rice–crusted halibut? Professional chef? Classes? Was he serious with this? "Sure."

For a second I thought he might confess to joking around, but he got out a skillet and started gathering up ingredients.

Gah, now he was going to cook, too? I wasn't going to survive the night.

I was the one who said *just friends*. That was definitely how it needed to be. Why was this so hard? Why was he so hot? It wasn't fair.

I needed to talk. Something to distract me from this visual. "So where have you been?"

"The children's hospital. I went to visit them as Malec."

I blinked slowly in surprise. I'd never once heard of him doing something like that. "Do you do it a lot?"

"Every chance I get. What, you think it's normal for me to run around in my Malec costume?"

"I don't know your life," I said, eating some more cereal and trying to ignore the way my heart was softening at the idea of him dressing up to entertain sick kids. Serious swoonage. That giddy feeling was being balanced out by the guilt I was feeling about being angry with him for not being home on time when he was busy lifting children's spirits. I was the worst.

He started cooking dry rice on the stove. "The kids love it, and normally it's a fun time for everyone."

"You don't sound like you had fun."

"One of the kids, Joey, he's always the most excited to see me. But the doctors told me the next time I come, he won't be there. I asked if it was a matter of money, because I'd take care of it, and they said it wasn't. There's nothing anyone can do. Cancer pisses me off."

"I'm sorry. That's awful."

"Thanks. So I was already in a bad mood when I left the hospital, and on the way out one of the board members chased me down and offered me ten thousand dollars for my charity if I'd take a picture with his wife in my costume. I said no."

I spilled a couple of chocolate cereal balls on the table and grabbed them before Magnus could go after them. "You have a charity?"

"I started it when I got back from Afghanistan. A buddy of mine was medically discharged at the same time as me and he had a hard time finding a job and taking care of his wife and new baby. I forced him to take money from me to help him out, but I thought there should be something to help veterans start over that didn't have a ton of red tape and oversight. So I have this nonprofit, and it provides career training and scholarships and has an emergency component for veterans and their families who need money and food to tide them over temporarily."

My mouth dropped. How did I not know any of this? "And somebody would have given you money for that and all you had to do was take a picture?" Was I missing something?

Now he was using a spatula to transfer the rice to some paper towels. "That's not the point. I want people to donate because they want to help veterans. Not because of Duel of the Fae. It makes me uncomfortable, and it feels like they're missing the entire point."

"No offense, but that's kind of stupid. There are so many great charities out there and good causes to support. Probably nine times out of ten if someone supports yours, it will be because you're the head of it. I can't really see where that's a bad thing. And if you're uncomfortable, well, maybe find a way to get comfortable with it. Are you in a position to be turning money away because it's not coming in the way you want it to?"

He seemed to consider this. "I guess not. Maybe you're right."

"I typically am."

"You're going to ruin your appetite," he said, watching me eat more cereal.

"Not likely," I responded. "By the way, Karen from Regional Advantage Bank says hi."

He was pouring the cooked rice into an expensive-looking blender. "Who?"

"She works in customer service. I talked to her today because I lost my debit card at the after-party and I told her I was there with you, which she totally did not believe. And as a parting shot she said to tell you hi. Like I'd made up the whole thing."

"Wait." He stopped what he was doing. "You lost your debit card?"

"And somebody used it and cleaned out my checking account."

"Everything?"

I formed my fingers into a circle. "Zero balance. And don't go for your wallet again."

"But you have money in your savings account, right?"

"No, Mr. Movie Star. I don't have investment or retirement accounts, either. It's all gone."

A look of guilt crossed his features, as if that was exactly what he'd been thinking. "I'm sorry. I feel responsible."

"You're not responsible for the actions of a criminal."

He put the lid on the blender and then looked at me for, like, a really long time. It was starting to make me uncomfortable. "People just usually depend on me for this kind of stuff."

"I'm not in the market for a sugar daddy," I said teasingly, and that put a smile on his face.

"I've given you money before," he reminded me.

"You overpaid me for a service I performed for you, and that was before we were friends. It would be weird now."

"I don't think so."

"It's not your decision to make," I told him.

"Okay. But know that it's here if you need it."

He turned the blender on high, and his offer touched me in a way I wouldn't have imagined possible. Not to mention how it sent little shivers of happiness rushing through me.

We were getting into dangerous territory. He had taken out pieces of fish and was dunking them in different bowls that had flour, eggs, and the rice mixture, and he told me about his day. About the little girl who said she wanted to be Aliana when she grew up so that she could marry him (a sentiment I understood all too well) and the little boy recovering from cancer who said he'd grow his hair out as long as Malec's when it came back in.

The fish smelled delicious and took less time to cook than I would have imagined. He brought a serving over to the table for me, along with a fork. Then he sat down across from me and told me to dig in.

I took a bite. It was incredible. Light, flaky. "Why are you good at everything? This is amazing."

He grinned. "Thanks. I probably should have made a salad or something, but it was a long day, and I'm tired."

I was going to tease him that tired people didn't usually make wild rice–crusted halibut for dinner but decided to be nice.

We ate in silence. It was just too good to let sit and get cold. When we finished, I offered to clear our plates, but he wouldn't let me. "You're my guest."

"Thank you for that dinner. And for cleaning up. You know, I could get used to this," I told him as he walked over to the sink to rinse off the plates before he put them into the dishwasher. "You waiting on me."

He smiled and said, "I live to serve."

I smiled back and . . . I realized I didn't have a reason to stay. I'd returned Magnus to him safely and he'd fed me both cereal and halibut, and now it was probably time for me to head home.

"It's getting late," I told him.

"You're right." He came back to the table but didn't sit down. I took that as my cue to go and stood up.

"Or . . ." He let his words trail off.

"Or?" I repeated, far too hopeful.

"You could stay for a drink. I think we both deserve one after the days we've had. What do you say?"

The right, clearheaded choice was obvious. Go home. Pack my bag and get ready to start my new job in the morning.

Walk away from Noah Douglas and all his dangerous sexiness.

Problem was, I didn't want to.

CHAPTER FIFTEEN

"Just one drink," I said.

"Do you have a preference?" he asked. "Beer? Wine?"

I grimaced. "Not wine. We no longer speak after this wicked one-night stand we had years ago."

That made him laugh as he headed for a bar cart in the corner. "Do you want me to make you my supposedly favorite drink?"

"Sure. What's your supposedly favorite drink?"

"Whiskey sour."

"I've never had it." Which meant I didn't know how much alcohol was in it. "Are you trying to get me drunk?"

Noah had pulled out a bunch of different bottles and a metal shaker. "If I was trying to get you drunk, I would have grabbed the vodka."

"Should I be worried about how fast you said that?"

"No. I was in the military. I know the best way to get drunk fast." He was pouring syrups and liquids into the shaker.

"Were you a bartender in a movie, too?"

"There was an offer, but the deal didn't come together. I did my research, just in case."

He poured the drinks into glass tumblers and handed me one. "Do you want to go sit in the library?"

Again, that felt a little dangerous. But I said, "Yes."

I followed behind him, remembering the room from before. I planned on sitting in one of the armchairs, but when we got there the only piece of furniture left was a couch. A very small, two-seater one.

"Shelby's really cleaning you out, isn't she?" I asked when I sat. He sat down close, facing me, and I had to refrain from scooting away. But whether that was to prove something to him or something to me, I wasn't sure.

He took a sip of his drink. "I'm planning on staying here during the renovation, so she's leaving me what she thinks I need and we'll just move everything around as they work on different rooms. I couldn't go to a hotel. I hate hotels."

"That must be fun for someone who travels as much as you do."

He raised an eyebrow in agreement, taking another drink.

I decided to take a drink, too. I grimaced after my first taste.

"What do you think?" he asked.

"I think this tastes like lemonade's hardened older brother who has a full tattoo arm sleeve and a criminal record."

He laughed, but I did take another drink. It tasted better now. Maybe his laughter had done that.

Or it was the alcohol.

Probably the alcohol, which was warming my insides and making me feel very relaxed. It really had been a long time since I could afford such quality liquor. "So if this is supposedly your favorite, what is your actual favorite?"

He leaned forward, a gleam in his eyes. "If I tell you, you can't tell anyone. It would ruin my street cred."

"I'm pretty sure you don't have any street cred, but I promise not to tell." With my free hand, I made an X across my chest. "Cross my heart."

"So I went to Hawaii, trying to vacation."

"Trying to vacation?" I couldn't help but interrupt. "How does that work?"

"My agent wanted me to relax, but it didn't work so well for me. I'm one of those people who needs to be doing something, working, or else I get in my own head, and that's not good. Anyway, I went down to the hotel bar the first night, and the bartender recognized me and gave me their house special. It was a piña colada."

I gasped with joy. "Please tell me you drank it out of an actual pineapple and that a tiny pink umbrella was involved."

He held up one hand, as if telling me to slow down. "No, it was in a regular glass. I didn't want it, but I tried it just to be polite. But it was literally the best drink I've ever had. I kept ordering them and then had to be helped back to my room."

That made me laugh, and some detached part of my brain wondered if it was a little too loud.

"Whenever I've ordered them anyplace else, they're never as good. And if anybody saw me drinking it . . . my reputation would be shot. Our captain once said that real men drink whiskey sours, so . . ."

"So that's what you drink in public?"

He shrugged one shoulder. "I don't really drink in public because of that whole thing with my parents. The last thing I would need is to be out of control where somebody could take a picture of me. But it's what I drink when I hang out with my army buddies."

I took another drink. It really was improving with familiarity. "Do you see them very often? The guys from your unit?"

"My company, not my unit. I'm one of the few bachelors in the group. So they're busy. I'm busy. Our lives are pretty radically different, but we do try to keep in touch via email and text. It helps with the guilt."

"The guilt?" I questioned. "Why would you feel guilty?"

"From leaving them early. I really struggled with it in the beginning, and it still flares up from time to time. That I was pretending to be a warrior in movies while they were actually fighting. Logically, I understand that it wasn't my fault and things just happen, but that doesn't stop you from feeling what you feel."

If anyone knew that you couldn't stop feeling what you feel, it was me. And this was actually a really good drink. Why had I thought it tasted bad before? "You did what you were supposed to do."

"I know that, but it's like getting cast in a part, going to all the rehearsals and all the fittings, and working with your director and castmates. Then it's opening night and it's time for you to go onstage, but you're the only one who isn't allowed. You've put in all this time and effort, but you don't get to see any fruits from your labors."

"You sound like you miss it."

"I miss a lot of things about it. The structure, the discipline, how everything had meaning and purpose. I miss my buddies the most."

"That makes sense," I said. "And back to your guilt thing, you didn't ask to get blown up and sent home. And I hope those friends tell you that."

"They're some of the best men I've ever met, and yes, they've done their best to help mitigate my guilt. They've been some of my biggest cheerleaders and encouraged me to keep making movies and helping veterans out. But if I'm being honest, I'm the one who envies them. They've shown me what I'm missing out on."

"The white picket fences and family?"

"Yes." He took a long drink this time, nearly finishing it off. "Speaking of family, you should tell me about your parents."

"That was a very smooth transition," I assured him. "Not at all awkward."

"Thank you."

"Why do you want to know about them?"

"Finding out about someone's parents makes you understand them better. What makes them tick."

I had another quick drink. "And you like understanding people better?"

"It's kind of my job. Plus, I want to get to know you better, chum. Also, I told you all about my dysfunctional parents."

That was true, and it seemed only fair that I do the same. "Well, Dr. Freud, my story is fairly boring. I'm close with my mom, who was pretty much a single parent my entire life. She and my dad got divorced when I was two years old." My glass was nearly empty, which seemed very sad to me.

"Why did they split up?"

"Mostly because my father was a player who wasn't ready to settle down and then cheated on her. I also think it had something to do with my older sister dying as a baby. From SIDS," I added before he asked how. The few people I'd ever told about my sister always asked how it happened. "I think I was supposed to replace her and it didn't really work that way. Sometimes when I was younger, I used to blame myself for not being enough. Not filling her shoes so that he would want to stay with us. But he slept around and that, understandably, ended things."

"I'm sorry. I had an older brother who died."

Before I could stop myself, I totally overreacted. My eyes flew open wide, and my mouth hung down slightly. "You did? I didn't know you had a brother."

"How would you?"

Right. I wasn't supposed to have any knowledge about him or his family. I tried to compose myself, because I was not behaving normally. I might have been a bit buzzed. "What happened?"

"He had cerebral palsy. He died from pneumonia when I was four. I only have these vague memories of him. And sometimes I wonder if they're actual memories or just photos I've seen that I've transformed into memories. I sometimes think that's why my parents were so focused on me, because they'd spent so much of their time caring for him and they just transferred all of that to me."

"I'm sorry, too. I'm glad you have some memories of him." Now I understood why it was important for him to visit sick kids in private.

"Yeah." He shook his head, as if to clear it. "But we were talking about you, not me. Are you close to your dad?"

"Not really. He moved to Arizona and got remarried and has a new family, new kids. I just wasn't ever very important to him. I mean, sometimes he emails or texts. When he remembers he sends me birthday and Christmas cards. I have half siblings I've never met. His wife is super into social media and I've found it's painful to see pictures of their happy family, so I stay away from it. But that's not the only reason I stay away from it."

Wow. Had I really just said that last part out loud? I hadn't meant to. Or maybe I'd just imagined it. It was currently hard to be sure.

I was guessing it had been completely internal when he took the tumbler from my hand and put both of our glasses on the floor. "I'd offer to get you another one, but you might have to drive home later."

Wait. Had he said "might"? Or did I imagine that, too? I was a tiny bit tipsy, and in the past I had misinterpreted things people had said when I was drunk. Like the time a woman in college said to me, "I like your shirt," and what I'd heard was, "You should come over here and pour your beer on me and scream in my face because you think I insulted your clothing."

So, I could have misheard him.

"Are you going to ask your parents to help you out financially?" he asked.

"Nope, it's fine. I got a job today. I'm going to dog sit Mrs. Kravitch's dog for the next two weeks. You and I are going to be neighbors! Do you know Gladys?"

A look of disgust curled the edges of his mouth. "I know Mrs. Kravitch. Rhymes with—"

"Hey," I cut him off. "Be nice. I like cantankerous old ladies." I planned on being one someday.

"She's the lone holdout on the HOA board and is the one keeping me from getting my fence for Magnus."

Oh. I hadn't known that. "Maybe I can talk to her when she gets back."

"I already tried laying on the charm. It didn't work." I had a hard time picturing that such a thing could be true. I mean, I was only barely resisting it, and he wasn't even really trying with me. I tried to picture what it would be like if he focused his full-blown charm on me, and I imagined it would probably be a little like walking out onto a darkened stage and having a bright spotlight beamed right into your eyes.

Gladys was a stronger woman than I'd given her credit for.

He rested his arm across the back of the couch, and it reminded me of us being in the car together last night. But this time, instead of feeling afraid that he was going to make a move, I found it oddly appealing. And wondered what he would do if I laid my head against his forearm.

He had really nice biceps. Did he know that? He must, since he obviously worked out to have them.

"Thank you," he said with a grin.

Oh crap, that part had definitely been out loud. It seemed that my inhibitions had been lowered without me realizing it. "You know you have good genes. I already told you that."

"You did," he said with a smile. "So, is your father the reason you don't date?"

He was a little like a dog with a bone, wasn't he? But I found myself only slightly annoyed. "No. You're not going to give that up, are you?"

"It just doesn't seem fair to deprive the men of this great city the opportunity to date you." He thought he was so adorable, didn't he?

To be fair, he was.

That feeling I had last night was back. That Noah Douglas was trustworthy. Considering all he'd told me about his life and his family, it was clear that he kept his own secrets locked up tighter than Fort Knox . . . Wouldn't he do the same for me? And maybe if I said the words out loud, to somebody else, it wouldn't feel like this ridiculous, terrible secret. I might find relief saying it.

I mean, it was so dumb. What I'd been carrying around was stupid. And the accompanying panic attacks were even dumber. He was going to think I was ridiculous. How could he not when I already did?

I knew it was supposed to be a bad idea to tell him, but I couldn't think of a single reason why. He was my friend. My good friend. And very, very, very trustworthy.

"I am trustworthy," he agreed.

Okay, I was definitely tipsy, and all the things I thought were just inside my head I was apparently saying out loud. Maybe that was a sign that I was meant to say them. Meant to tell him. My mom was a big believer in signs, and I'd always dismissed them. Maybe I shouldn't have.

And he was just my friend. That was the boundary we had agreed on. So there wouldn't be any temptation to make it more, right?

"Do you have secrets?" I asked.

"That's the thing that's hard about my life—when someone's interviewing you and you've developed this rapport, there's this constant struggle between opening up and giving everything away but wanting to keep something for myself. I live in this twilight kind of world where my ability to do my job relies on my ability to be human and live a regular life, but I can't do that. I'm always straining for normalcy and settling on what I can get. It's one of the reasons I read. I get to experience so many different parts of humanity through stories and plays that I wouldn't get to otherwise."

"That's a long-winded way of not answering my question."

He laughed and said, "There are parts of my life I keep private from the press and the public, but they're not secrets. I think a real secret, something I had to guard from everyone in my life, would be too hard for me to keep. It would weigh me down."

That's how I felt. Weighed down. And I didn't want to keep feeling that way. Did that mean I was going to confess? My mind was a little muddled, but this seemed like the right move. I needed a moment to decide without him possibly overhearing my brain talking to itself. "I'm thirsty. Could I have some water?"

"Yeah, absolutely. I'll be right back."

I'd never even come close to telling anyone else. I thought about things he'd said to me, how he'd joined the military to have a life that was more authentic, more real. Was I guilty of not being my truest self because I kept something like this a secret? Normally it didn't consume a lot of my mental or emotional energy because I stayed away from attractive men and just lived my life.

Until I didn't.

Until I ended up on the couch of a movie star that I was desperately attracted to, and maybe the best way to make sure that I didn't have a full-blown meltdown in front of him was to tell him the truth so that he'd see why we had to stay just friends.

Although, to be fair to Noah, he was so . . . compassionate. Empathetic. He'd been nothing but respectful toward me. And I didn't think he'd make fun of me. Because he was a mature adult who had really lived and had his current life together. He wasn't a frat boy or a high school football jock. Perhaps someone who had devoted his career to understanding the human condition would be understanding toward me.

Maybe it would be cathartic. Liberating.

He came back in the room and handed me a water bottle. He'd poured himself a bowl of cereal.

Cold fingers of fear wrapped themselves around my spine, and I tried to temporarily distract myself. I was going to do it, but I was afraid, and my body was trying to buy some time to convince my mind it should choose differently. "You're eating again?"

"It happens all the time. I eat a ton of cereal. I don't really ever feel full."

If I had been looking for a sign, there it was. That connection of "we're the same" sparked again. He would get me. He already did.

My heart pounded so loud in my ears that I felt light-headed. I breathed in deeply and realized that my limbs were shaking. I wanted to stop feeling this way. So I was going to tell him and get it all out.

"I want to tell you why I don't date."

CHAPTER SIXTEEN

"Okay." He kept eating, which surprised me. It felt like such a monumental occasion that it deserved him putting down his food and giving
me his full attention. Or maybe this was better. He wasn't staring at me,
which would have made this worse.

"You can't laugh," I told him. "If you laugh, I am walking out your
front door and I'm never coming back. I'm serious."

He swallowed his mouthful. "I won't laugh."

"Promise me."

Now he was the one making an X over his heart. "I promise."

This was it. I was going to do it.

Swallowing back that nauseated feeling that was growing in my gut,
I said, "I don't date because . . . I'm terrified of kissing anyone. Like,
just the idea of doing it makes me freak out. The times I've come close
have caused full-on panic attacks."

There. I'd done it. I'd said it out loud, and despite my body telling
me otherwise, the world hadn't ended. I let out a shaky sigh of relief as
the adrenaline started to fade away.

And in the same moment, Noah coughed and sprayed milk out of
his nose.

"Are you okay?" I asked.

"Yeah. Sorry. That just went in the wrong way."

"More like it came out the wrong way," I said, trying to lighten things up. Because other than hosing down his couch with two percent, he hadn't responded, and his reaction seemed desperately important. But instead of letting him speak, I had to keep going, nervously. "I had that happen with a Twix bar once. That tasty cookie layer really hurts when it's coming out of your nose. Then I smelled chocolate for, like, three days. Which wasn't necessarily a bad thing."

He hadn't laughed. He might have turned into a milk sprinkler, but he hadn't laughed. I at least had that.

"Does that mean you've never kissed anyone?" he finally asked.

"Not technically, no. Is that so hard to believe?"

I could seriously almost hear the record-scratch sound as we descended into awkward silence.

"It's unusual. Which is why you heard disbelief in my voice. But that doesn't mean it's, like, a bad thing you should be ashamed of," he said, putting his bowl down on the floor. "Does that mean you're a virgin?"

Heat rushed to my cheeks, bringing out my inner snark. "Of course not, because in between all the being terrified of kissing I was hooking up constantly."

"No, right. That makes sense. Sorry. I just need a second to wrap my head around this."

Now I was annoyed. "People can be virgins."

He held up both of his hands for a second, like he was trying to ward off my anger. "I know! That's not what I . . . Sorry, I'd never considered that this might be your deep, dark secret. Being scared of kissing. And what do you mean, you've never technically kissed someone?"

Might as well give him the full story. I took one of his throw pillows and put it in front of me, like a shield. "When I was fourteen, I was the only one out of our friend group who hadn't been kissed, and it was really embarrassing. Everybody except Shelby used to tease me.

So at Anna-Marie's birthday party, they all decided that it was time for me to get kissed. And they announced that we were going to play Seven Minutes in Heaven."

His eyebrows furrowed.

"Haven't you heard of that game?" I asked.

"I didn't have a normal childhood, remember? I'm assuming it's a kissing game."

"It is."

"Why is it seven minutes? That seems like an arbitrary amount of time."

What did that matter? "Because it rhymes with heaven? I don't know. That's not really important."

"Right," he agreed. "I'm just trying to make sure I'm understanding everything."

"In that case you should know that it's basically a couple being put into a closet or a room, and they're supposed to kiss for seven minutes. The people outside keep track of the time and then they throw the door open when it's over. They had me go in Anna-Marie's bedroom."

I closed my eyes for a moment, trying to strengthen myself. This was the worst part. And it was the part I could not give him every detail of. "So I was waiting for Chris Quintana. He was the cutest boy in school—everyone had a crush on him."

Noah's eyes narrowed. "I already don't like him."

"It gets worse. So I'm in there waiting, feeling completely anxious and nervous because this was going to be my first-ever kiss, and Anna-Marie had this pillow. And the pillow had a picture of my celebrity crush on it."

That celebrity had been Noah as Felix Morrison. Which I was never, ever going to tell him.

It was also part of the reason why I could never kiss him. I was worried it might be like reliving that moment again.

"And since I'd never been kissed, I thought I'd practice." My whole face felt like it was on fire.

"And this Chris kid caught you?"

"Well, yes, but there was a problem. The face was like one of those puffy decal types and . . . my braces got caught on it. I was stuck. So he found me, my face pressed against a pillow, and he had to help me get free."

"I mean, that's embarrassing, but was that enough to put you off kissing forever?"

"That's not all of it. Don't get me wrong—that in and of itself was completely humiliating. I begged him not to tell anyone, and he was actually a pretty decent guy. He said he wouldn't. And then . . ."

"And then?"

"Then he suggested that I should try kissing an actual boy, because it was a lot better. And I don't know if it was just a mixture of embarrassment and adrenaline or what happened, as my brain wasn't actually functioning in that moment, but I pretty much leaped on him with my teeth bared and smashed our faces together while attempting to 'kiss' him. I knocked him over and landed right on his face."

His eyes widened in horror.

"I completely cut his mouth up. There was blood everywhere. He ran out of the room. As far as I know, he didn't tell anyone the details, but it was pretty obvious what I had done. Everybody called me BB, for Bloody Braces, the rest of high school. The online bullying was relentless. Which meant that I wasn't going to date any guy I knew, because everybody teased me constantly."

"Understandable." He paused. "To be honest, I thought you were going to tell me that someone hurt you. And that was why you steered clear of men."

"No. Nobody hurt me. I was the one committing face felonies with my teeth blades."

He smiled slightly at that, and it emboldened me to go on. "Then I went to college. And it was really awkward to be so far behind everyone else. I'd hated that feeling in high school, like there was this race everybody else was running, but I was still stuck at the starting line wondering when it was going to be my turn. Everybody else was having sex, and I'd never even kissed someone. So freshman year I decided to find a guy to make out with. I was friends with this girl from one of my math classes, and she said her boyfriend's best friend was into noncommittal make outs and hooked up with different girls constantly. And I wasn't going to sleep with him, but I thought kissing someone who knew what he was doing would be a good option."

"I'm guessing it didn't go well?"

I hugged the pillow tighter. "This friend brought along her boyfriend and the four of us were hanging out and watching a movie, and then she came up with an excuse to leave. So here I was, alone with this guy in his living room, not knowing what to do and feeling fully freaked out. Waiting for him to make a move."

"And what happened when he did?"

"He didn't. The guy who was known on campus for cycling through every available woman wasn't interested in me. Which was this total blow to my self-esteem and put me off the idea of dating for a long time. And then when I tried to get back into dating again, there was this boy in my statistics class who seemed decent and interested in me, and we went to a movie and ice cream and I was like, *This is it. I'm going to kiss this guy.* I thought I was too old to keep waiting." I stopped for a second, worried that if I brought it up again, I'd be back in that moment, feeling the way I felt. I took in a deep breath and let it out slowly and then kept going.

"So we were at my front door, saying good night. And he was moving in, getting closer and closer to me, and then it was like I'd been hit by a truck. I seriously thought I was having a heart attack because my heart was beating so hard. I was shaking, I couldn't catch my breath, my chest hurt, I wanted to vomit. I couldn't feel my hands or my feet. I thought I was going crazy. Somehow I said good night and went inside and I was about to call an ambulance, but after a couple of minutes on the floor, I was able to calm down."

"That sounds awful."

"It wasn't fun. And I didn't know where it had come from or why it had happened. And I couldn't face that dude again. So I tried going out with someone else. And it happened again. Every time I got close to somebody, where it was possible they would kiss me, I was so terrified that I thought I would die."

"Is that . . . is that how you feel when you're with me?"

"I haven't gone that far, because we haven't come close to kissing. Obviously you're super attractive and confident and charming and I respond to that, but all of that scares me to death at the same time. That's why I said we have to be just friends. I can't be more than friends, and this is why."

"Do you have attacks at other times?" he asked.

"Nope, never. I thought maybe I had an anxiety disorder or something, but it seems to be centralized just around the kissing thing."

"Have you ever seen a professional about it?"

I let out a laugh. "Before tonight, I couldn't imagine even telling someone else, let alone a therapist. I don't know why I'm telling you." I paused. "That's not true. It's probably a little bit the alcohol, but I just . . . I know I can trust you."

He smiled. "I'm glad you feel that way."

He pursed his lips together, seeming to be mulling something over. Then his eyes lit up. "Wait. Hang on. This would be a really weird coincidence." He walked over to his bookcase, where there was a large stack of bundled papers. He dug through them until he found one and pulled it out. He flipped through a few pages. "Believe it or not, I've actually heard of this before. You might have philemaphobia. A fear of kissing. My agent wants me to do a romantic comedy, and she sent me this script that's about what you're describing."

He handed it to me. It was titled *The Worst First Kiss*. I could almost hear my mom's voice saying, "There's no such thing as coincidences." I'd never subscribed to that particular theory of hers, but I was much closer to believing it now. Jeez, if I was looking for a sign, you couldn't ask for a bigger one than that.

As I glanced at a couple of the pages, not sure what I was looking for, he said, "In this script the heroine has that phobia, but it's about germs. Is that a problem for you?"

"No. I don't think about germs. I mean, more than one dog has licked my face, and I didn't freak out about germs or anything. I'm not grossed out by kissing. It's the act itself that is paralyzing for me." I hesitated to ask my next question, but curiosity took over. "How does the heroine deal with it? Does she get over it?"

"She does. She learns to ground herself to deal with the attacks."

"What does that mean?"

"Basically that instead of avoiding the feelings associated with the panic attacks, you let yourself feel them but stay in control by grounding yourself. Hold on, let me look it up real fast." He turned pages until he found what he was looking for. "You're supposed to think of five things you can see, four things you can feel, three things you can hear, two things you can smell, one thing you can taste. When your mind is racing, going through those steps is supposed to bring you back to the present so you can focus on what's happening to you physically instead of being caught up in your brain. And deep breathing is supposed to help, too."

"Really?" I was skeptical.

"In the script it works, and she also practices kissing with the hero, who is also her best friend, and she overcomes her phobia. There was a note that the scriptwriter overcame this thing in real life. I'm not an expert or anything, but it seems to me that it's kind of similar to being afraid to fly or being terrified of tarantulas. You get over your fear by repeatedly exposing yourself to the thing you're afraid of and working through your reaction."

Logically it made sense. It also made me feel better that somebody else had been through the same thing as me, even if hers had happened for different reasons.

It was also the first time in a long time that I'd felt hope over my situation—what if I could overcome this? What if I could be in a normal relationship and actually be able to kiss someone without feeling like I was going to die?

That would be amazing.

As if he could read my mind, Noah asked, "Is that something that interests you? Trying to work through it? Or are you happy with the way things are?"

"I've never been happy that I'm like this—I just resigned myself to it. It's been this shameful, dark, scary thing that I've been carrying around for a long time. And overreacting the way that I have, it's made me avoid romance and men altogether. I would like things to be different." I didn't want to be alone for the rest of my life.

Noah nodded, his expression serious. I liked how calmly he seemed to be taking this in, how matter-of-factly he was processing it and looking for a solution. Which I supposed was a very male thing to do, but I appreciated the approach.

"Then I think I could help you."

"And how are you going to do that?" I asked. Run me through meditation exercises? Find me the world's leading expert on . . . whatever the name was for my kissing phobia that I couldn't remember? Knowing the kind of guy he was, he'd probably insist on paying for my sessions and I'd have to tell him no and then we'd argue and—

He interrupted my train of thought and said, "Let me help you get over your fear. You could kiss me."

CHAPTER SEVENTEEN

I don't know why that was the last thing I expected him to say, given how our conversation had been going, but it was. A bolt of fear spiked inside me. "Oh." I was going to ask him if he was serious, but I could see from his face that he was.

He said, "We're friends, and I want to help you. Not to mention that I'm probably the best guy you could pick for a project like this. I have kissed a lot—and I mean a lot—of women. Both personally and professionally."

"Maybe you shouldn't sound quite so proud of that," I said.

"I'm just giving you my CV so that you understand why I'm the best candidate for this job. I'm perfect for it—I can be whoever you want me to be. I could even go put the Malec costume back on."

"Oh. No. Don't do that." It would be too weird. Right? But maybe it would work? Could I picture myself kissing Malec?

Little bit, yes. I could.

But I couldn't ask him to do that. Or maybe I could. Or it would be a step too far. Maybe it would stress me out even worse, because I would know he wasn't actually Malec, so it would be weird if he was pretending like he was.

On the other hand, I had really, really liked him in that costume.

"Have you worked it out in your head yet?" he asked in a teasing tone, and I immediately flushed in response.

"No. I wouldn't want you to do that. If I said yes, I would want it to be just you." Because Noah was the one I knew and trusted.

He was the one that would take care of me and wouldn't let anything bad happen.

"Good." He made it sound like that had been the right answer. "And in a way, you'd be doing me a favor, too. If I took this part, it would help me to have actual, personal knowledge about the material. Because so far my experience has been the opposite."

"Can't keep the women off you, huh?" I'd bet he'd never met another woman who didn't want to kiss him.

"Occupational hazard," he told me. He didn't sound like he was complaining.

"I don't know," I told him. I was so worried it wasn't going to work out, and then on top of everything else, I also would have wrecked my friendship with Noah, and I would probably get Shelby fired, too.

"I can't believe I'm trying to convince you to kiss me," he said.

"It does seem a little far-fetched," I agreed.

"What are you worried about?"

Why did it feel like he could read my mind? There were so many things I was worried about. How badly this could all go. What his reaction would be when I inevitably freaked out. How if we started kissing, then it was entirely possible we might develop feelings for each other.

And I didn't want that right now. "If I said yes to doing this, there would have to be some boundaries. Because the truth is, I don't want the pressure of romantic feelings or emotions being in the way. It would be hard enough trying to fix my dysfunction without also worrying about relationship issues and problems on top of it. I think it would be too much."

He looked confused. "You're not interested in dating me? Why?"

I remembered my conversation with Zoe Covington. How hard things could be, how much they struggled to keep their personal lives private. The fans who didn't understand the difference between reality and fantasy. "Even if I didn't have this phobia, I don't think you're the kind of guy I could see myself with. Look at your life. I'm obviously a private person. I don't share myself with many people, and some parts of your life have to be on display for the entire world. You're hot and talented and women all over the world are dying to be with you. I think I'd always be worried that you couldn't be faithful to me. And what if some crazy stalker attacked me for being your girlfriend? It would be a lot."

I was trying to convince both of us, latching on to every negative thing in his life to make sure that we wouldn't date. Because I couldn't deal with it. Noah Douglas was not the kind of man you dated. There was no way he'd ever stick around, and I knew I'd never be able to deal with him walking away from me if I kissed him and fell in love with him.

Which probably had something to do with my father leaving me, but I wasn't really up for examining my daddy issues.

"I disagree with just about everything you said, but I would respect your boundaries." He sounded a little wounded, and I immediately felt bad. "So we don't date. But if we are able to help you overcome your phobia, you will want to date somebody eventually, right? In that case, think of me as your seat filler until that guy shows up."

"That doesn't seem right," I said. "I wouldn't want to use you." I worried that maybe I was being a little presumptuous. He might not want to date someone regular like me, either, who wouldn't understand his lifestyle and wouldn't be able to easily navigate the Hollywood landscape. Only unlike me, he was way too polite and respectful to list all the reasons why I wasn't good enough to be his girlfriend.

Because you know, deep down, that you would never be enough for him. You don't measure up, a voice inside me said, making me sad.

But he made things better by sporting a wicked smile that I felt deep in my gut. "I don't object to being used in whatever way you'd like. But I'm aware of the situation and the parameters, and since I'm an adult, I can make my own decisions. I'm still in."

He was giving me everything I could have asked for. Before I could talk myself out of accepting, I said, "Me too."

His eyebrows lifted, like this wasn't the answer he'd been expecting. "Okay. Do you want to start now?"

The panic returned, making my chest feel like it was on fire. "No, no, I do not. I need to, I don't know, get mentally prepared for it. Like, I need some time to realize that this is going to happen. With you." Because that was a lot. "I should probably head home. I'll just find a ride."

I got out my phone. It felt like we'd been chatting for a long time, but it hadn't been long enough that it was safe for me to drive.

"Put your phone away. It will be expensive to take an Uber. I'll text someone from my car service."

Now that I'd decided something so utterly earthshaking and life changing, I wanted to flee to deal with my conflicting emotions. It was a testament to how confused I felt that I didn't argue with him about financing my way home. In that moment I didn't care. All I cared about was that I couldn't wait around and I needed space to work through this. "Isn't that going to take forever?"

"Nope." He typed something on his phone and then said, "They have a car that's about ten minutes out."

Then he looked at me expectantly, and it made me think that he wanted us to sit here and continue this conversation, which I was not up for. I needed to retreat, so I stood up. "I have to go lock my van up, and I'll just wait for the driver out there."

I saw his confusion. "You can wait here."

"No, I don't think I can. Is that okay?"

"Whatever you need. Let me walk you out." And he didn't seem disappointed, which was a relief for me. It made me feel less pressured.

He opened the door, and I stepped outside. "So, um, sorry about all the baggage I dumped on you tonight."

Noah leaned against the door frame, and as my pulse beat hard, I wondered why that motion made him desperately more attractive. "You may not know this about me, but I'm very strong and can handle it. I have to special order supersize weights just so they'll be enough of a challenge."

Him teasing me made me feel better, made the pressure subside just a little bit. "That's good, because I'm pretty sure my baggage is over the weight limit."

He smiled, and I felt that moment of connection again, even though we were standing six feet apart.

Then he cleared his throat and said, "I should be home at about eight o'clock tomorrow night, if you want to come by."

That made my heart squeeze painfully. The idea that we were making plans to meet up and kiss. "I can do that. And by eight o'clock do you mean eight o'clock, or do you mean, like, two in the morning?"

"Ha-ha. If something comes up, I'll text you."

"Okay." At that point I should have said goodbye and walked away and hidden from him in my van. But I just stood there, like I wanted something else to happen.

Like there was something I still wanted to tell him. "I hope you know . . . what I told you? I've never told anyone else, ever."

"I know. And it's not an honor I take lightly."

That connection returned, only this time it was urging me to walk back over to him, tell him I'd changed my mind and that we should immediately go inside and start practicing kissing right now.

"So . . . ," he said, and I realized that I'd been standing there for an uncomfortable amount of time wrestling with myself. "Good luck with the new job tomorrow. I can't imagine any job working for Mrs. Kravitch is going to be a fun one."

"It won't be the worst one I've had. I've done some truly terrible things for money."

"Like?"

"Like get up at seven in the morning," I said. He broke into his infectious laughter and, figuring I couldn't ask for a better exit than that, I headed off toward my van. To distract myself, I ran through a mental list of what I still needed to do.

When I got home I had to pack a bag, avoid Shelby for the rest of the evening—because if she pushed me at all about what had happened tonight, I feared I might break and tell her everything—make arrangements to get a ride back up here tomorrow, where I would take care of Sunshine and two of my other clients, and then . . .

Then I was going to come over to Noah Douglas's house and I was going to kiss him. A shudder of dread and excitement passed through me.

Everything would be just fine. Probably.

~

When I got home, it all proceeded according to plan. Shelby was out with Allan, so I was able to pack up in peace. By the time I got up the next morning, she was already gone for the day, so I left her a note reminding her about my new gig and to call me if she needed anything. This also allowed me far too much time to think about what was going to happen with Noah later.

I took an Uber up to Gladys's house, and as Noah had predicted, it was ridiculously expensive. I was glad I had some extra money to help cover the expense.

Sunshine was excited to see me, and I wondered for a minute if Noah was up at his house or if he'd already left for the day. I got

Sunshine fed and watered and took him out for a walk to retrieve my van. I decided to take him with me for the two grooming appointments I had scheduled for the day. I texted Gladys to ask if she was okay with me bringing him along, and she texted back a single word.

> Fine.

And that was it. So I was taking it as a yes.

After my first session, I stopped to grab something to eat and ended up sharing half of my hamburger with a very sad-eyed and beggy Sunshine. While I was considering running back inside to order a second one, my phone buzzed.

If it was Gladys telling me she'd meant, "Fine, keep my dog at home, I don't want him driving around with you," she was out of luck. And I was going to have to lie.

But it was a text from Noah. From his actual phone number and not a restricted one.

> What do friends, who might occasionally kiss, text one another?

I smiled.

> Hi usually works.

> Hi.

> How are you is also good.

How are you?

Eating lunch, so I'm happy.

So...anything interesting happen to you lately?

I got to hang out at the Academy Awards.

With anyone amazing and dashing and completely kiss-worthy?

Just this actor.

Yeah? How are things going with him?

Confusing. Complicated. But good.

> **Sounds like you should see him again.**

Why did that make my heart flutter?

> **I will. But we're just friends.**

> **Yep, you should definitely hang out with him again. He sounds awesome.**

I sent him a smiling emoji and then added him to my contacts. That little interaction made my soul lift and feel like nothing bad could happen to me. My next dog was a Great Dane, and I didn't even care about all the splashing that soaked my entire outfit and the floor. It was fine. I felt happy and hopeful for the first time in a long time, and I was going to get to see Noah again.

Although I wondered how I could both wish for and dread something at the same time.

Sunshine and I went out for dinner, and as the hours passed, that mixture of anticipation and fear became a potent cocktail that almost made me cancel no less than half a dozen times.

But every time I got my phone out, I couldn't bring myself to do it. Even if I told myself I didn't want to see him again, I did.

I made some brownies, thinking that it would be a nice gesture to bring them over, since he'd fed me last night. But then they smelled so good, and while I knew chocolate was not going to mitigate what was about to happen, I figured it would put me in a better headspace to emotionally deal with everything.

And then I accidentally ate seven pieces.

So when seven thirty rolled around, I felt a little sick to my stomach, which I attributed to gorging myself on brownies. But I went into the guest bedroom and got dressed. I threw my hair up into a ponytail and put on jeans and a T-shirt. Dressing up for it felt like it would make it too much of a big deal. I was just going over to my new friend's house to hang out.

And possibly smooch him.

I brushed and flossed my teeth really well. Really, really well. Like, I almost made my gums bleed. I also put some mints in my pocket, just in case.

I tried to psych myself up and hang on to that sliver of hope that this was going to work. I would conquer my fear of kissing and, as a side bonus, have a fantastic story to tell at parties someday. Even though no one was going to believe me.

I said goodbye to Sunshine and walked the short distance up to Noah's house. When I got to his door, before I could even knock or ring the doorbell, Magnus was barking. I heard Noah call out, "Come in!"

Although it felt a little awkward to just walk into his house, I did it anyway, petting Magnus and saying hello to him. Once he'd been properly greeted, he trotted off.

It concerned me a bit that Noah didn't keep his doors locked. Although maybe he'd specifically left it open just for me.

"Hello?" I called out. For one second I was worried that Noah was in his bedroom and expected me to join him, and I nearly bolted back out the door.

"I'm in the kitchen!" His mouth sounded muffled, like he was eating.

Sure enough, he had another bowl of cereal that he was eating over the sink. He'd apparently just gotten out of the shower again, his hair hanging down in wet strands. I was struck with a desire to push it off his face, but he beat me to it. I sighed. I loved when he did that.

"You just missed me clearing out my fridge. I saw on the news that romaine lettuce was recalled."

I liked how he seemed calm and mellow. Like this huge thing wasn't about to happen and we were just hanging out together. "Do you know what doesn't get recalled?"

"Is it chocolate?" he asked.

"It's chocolate."

"Do you want anything?"

"No," I said. "I'm good." Not really, but I was trying hard to calm my heart rate down. "I'm not keeping you from some wild Hollywood party, am I?"

"That's not really my scene," he said after swallowing down a big gulp. "I like going to the theater, but that's a little harder to do these days. I spend a lot of my time reading and watching movies. Cheesy as it may sound, it helps me hone my craft. And if there's one thing I learned in the military, it's the importance of doing things right."

Yeah, and he was going to show me the right way to kiss. My knees buckled slightly, and I leaned against the wall for support. "Do you ever watch your own movies?"

"No. You know how when you see a video of yourself or hear a recording of your voice and it just sounds off or wrong? And it makes you cringe, because that's not how you hear yourself in your own head?"

"Sure."

"It's like that for me, but for some reason it bothers me a thousand times worse than it seems to for other people. Plus, I see all my mistakes and all the different choices I should have made for a scene, and it drives me crazy. I basically just run them over and over again in my head. So I've learned not to watch my own work."

I couldn't help it. My face fell. I had totally wanted to watch the last movie in the Duel of the Fae trilogy with him and demand answers.

"What's that look for?" he asked.

I should have known that he, of all people, would notice. "This means I can't ask you what the writer and director of the third movie were thinking when they freaking killed Malec. He joined the good guys, risked his life to save Aliana, they admit their love, and then . . . he's just dead? How is that a happy ending?" I was so caught up in my indignation that I accidentally added on, "You know, he doesn't die in the books. Instead of having to live up to some masculine fantasy of being a noble martyr, he gets to pay for his misdeeds by actually physically atoning for them and making reparations to the people he's hurt. And he gets to be with Aliana and get married and have little fairy babies. I guess it doesn't matter now that the movie's over, but I'll never not be mad that they killed Malec Shadowfire. That ending was so bad it should be tried at The Hague." It also infuriated me that the movie studio had severely underestimated Malec's popularity and had walked away from hundreds of millions of dollars in continuing his story through animations, novels, or comic books.

Noah just looked amused. "Given this a lot of thought, have you?"

"Yes. And now I'm getting upset all over again. So before that happens, we should just, you know, kiss or whatever. That's what I'm here for, right?"

"That is why you're here." He set his bowl down in the sink and walked over to me. I was already pressed up against the wall, so there was nowhere for me to go. "So, Juliet Nolan, are you ready?"

CHAPTER EIGHTEEN

I was so not ready. My adrenaline grabbed me by the throat, making my heart beat out of control. "I want to say yes, but can we, like, be sitting down or something?"

"I should probably go brush my teeth. Like you already did." He winked at me, and it annoyed me.

What was he implying? "Did you consider that maybe I just have a dedication to good oral hygiene?"

"You were getting ready for our kiss."

"That wasn't it."

"Your minty breath says otherwise." He said it as a parting shot as he left the kitchen. I made my way into the library and found Magnus already there, lying in his oversize dog bed near the fireplace.

I sat down on the couch, rubbing my wet palms against my pant legs. I tried telling myself that I was okay. Noah was a good guy and I had nothing to worry about.

Before I could get too into my own head, he returned. "Hey, would it help if I got you a drink?"

"No." I shook my head harder than I needed to. "I've tried that before, and it didn't work. If anything, alcohol just made things worse, because everything seemed even more out of control. I need to be sober for this."

"Okay." He sat on the couch next to me. "So I stayed up late last night doing research."

"You did?" Why did that make my heart quiver? It seemed so sweet and thoughtful. I hadn't bothered to look up my phobia at all, but he'd stayed up to do just that?

"Of course. You're my friend. I want to help you. And from the things I read, your reaction to kissing is a hardwired, conditioned response, and you can't just logic or reason your way out of it. That's why it's a phobia. It's not supposed to be rational. There's actually not a ton of information about philemaphobia, although it's not supposed to be as severe as other phobias. With other phobias you might have to get cognitive behavioral therapy or exposure therapy. What we're doing is kind of like a home version of exposure therapy. And supposedly just the act of kissing and getting through it can help you overcome it."

I wanted that to be true so badly. I couldn't picture myself going to a professional's office and doing therapy. Not only because I couldn't afford it, but it was so hard telling Noah the truth that I didn't want to have to do it all over again. I realized that there was a possibility this wouldn't work, but I was still hopeful that it would.

If things got worse instead of better, maybe I'd have to consider seeing a therapist. I hoped it didn't come to that.

Noah was still talking, and I made myself pay attention. "One therapist called it sexual stage fright, and I know stage fright. You want to throw up and run away, but then you have to go out there and per-form. And it gets a bit easier each night. You just start off small and then build up from there."

There was a pounding in my head that was so loud it made it dif-ficult to hear him. My lungs were starting to constrict as my body got itself ready to jump immediately into fight or flight. "That makes sense."

"And I want to make some promises to you. I am not going to make fun of your kissing or tease you about how you do it, and I'll never judge you. I won't do anything that you haven't asked me to do. You're the director here—what you say goes. Nothing will happen unless you want it to, okay? So I'm promising that I'm never going to get caught up and forget myself."

"Even if you really want to?"

"Even if I really, really want to," he said, and there was a note in his voice that made my stomach feel like it was going to float away. "I promise that you'll always be a hundred percent safe with me."

"Thank you." It seemed like such an inadequate thing to say, but his promises meant a lot to me. They didn't stop my shins from sweating, though.

"I was also thinking that you should probably kiss me first. That way you're totally in control."

"But I don't know what to do." Didn't he get that's why all of this was happening?

"It will be fine. Don't use your teeth. Ramming your teeth into someone is not sexy."

Ha. Lies. His teeth were extremely sexy.

He was still talking, and I tried to concentrate. "And maybe no weird licking in the beginning."

"What's weird licking?" I asked, alarmed. "What if I do it by accident?"

"I'll let you know if it happens. Just know that when you're kissing someone you want to kiss, it can feel a lot like the sensations you've described from your attacks. Your heart beats fast, you're out of breath, you feel light-headed, only you shouldn't feel like you're going to die. Those feelings should be happening in a pleasurable way instead of a frightening one. Which is why people keep doing it. I hope there comes a point that you fall on that side of the scale."

"Me too."

"Look. I want to show you something. Is it okay if I take your hand for a second?"

"Yes."

He wrapped his long fingers around my wrist and pulled my hand to his chest, placing it over his heart. It was beating fast. "You're not the only one affected."

And we stayed in that moment, his chest feeling strong and sure, his heart pounding beneath my palm.

"Do you want to kiss me?" It wasn't something I had asked him before. He'd volunteered to help me out, but I didn't know if he was just being a nice guy or if he was actually into it.

His words were low, and I could feel them rumbling inside his chest. "Very much so. And you?"

"I want to want it, but it's all sort of abject terror right now."

"You'll do it, and we'll keep doing it. It's why actors rehearse. We practice it over and over again until it feels natural. Okay?"

I nodded. "Okay."

"Rome wasn't built in a day. We got this."

"If you tell me 'Go, team,' I'm going to punch you," I informed him.

"If I said that, I'd deserve it." He shifted a little closer, but I kept my hand on his chest. I liked it there, liked the feeling of his strength and warmth. "So, come on. Let's go, team!"

That made me laugh, and I realized that had been his intent all along. It did help me to relax slightly.

And then there was no more delaying. If I was going to do this, I was going to do this. I had to move quickly. So many of my alarms / warning bells were already sounding in my head. I wanted to make a move before they could stop me.

So I did it.

I leaned forward, pressing my lips to his. There was a moment where I registered his warmth, the softness of his lips.

But before he could respond to me at all, I was moving away from him, crouching on the floor because I felt like I was falling. The room was spinning, and I was convinced I was going to pass out. My heart thumped hard against my chest, and my rib cage was constricted, like someone was sitting on me. I couldn't breathe.

Then Noah was there next to me, not touching me, but he made me feel like I could draw on his strength. "Breathe. Five things you can see."

I struggled to focus, to be in charge of my hysterical brain, trying to drag air in and out of my chest. I saw his robot socks. I saw Magnus, who had come over to investigate why we were on the floor. I saw a pile of Noah's books, the gross avocado carpet. The couch where we had been sitting.

My limbs were shaking so hard.

"You're okay. Keep breathing. Four things you can touch."

I dug my fingers into that carpet. I felt my soft T-shirt against my skin. The hair from my ponytail against my cheek. My shoes straining across my feet.

"Now three things you can hear."

Noah's voice. Magnus's panting. My own strangled breathing. I tried hard to slow it down. To keep breathing in and out. In and out. Inhale, exhale.

"Two you can smell."

Noah's clean scent. Magnus's not-quite-so-clean scent.

My stomach was clenching so hard. I was going to throw up. I gritted my teeth against it. I could beat this thing. I could be stronger than this . . . what had Noah called it? My hardwired response. I would rewire it.

"One you can taste."

"There's nothing to taste," I told him, finally able to catch my breath enough that I could talk. "Maybe my bile in a second after I puke."

"I've definitely never caused that reaction before. My reviews tend to be more on the positive side."

He was trying to make me laugh. I wished I had the lung capacity for it. "Are you Yelping out your kissing? Are there online reviews?"

His smile was enormous, and I both saw and felt his relief that I was able to joke with him. Magnus seemed to sense my lingering distress, and he leaned in to lick my face. Noah got up and left the room but came back quickly to sit down next to me on the floor again.

Noah commented, "You know, as much as that dog of mine loves his own vomit, it's a safe bet he'd enjoy yours, too. So it would probably be better if you didn't throw up, because neither one of us needs to see that."

"But if I puked on this carpet, how would you even be able to tell?"

He laughed. "Here."

I heard a crinkling sound and looked up at the Snickers bar he was handing me. He said, "The next time you're thinking of a taste, think of something you love. Like chocolate."

My stomach had calmed down enough that I wanted to take a bite. My fingers were shaking so badly that he had to help me open the candy bar. I took a bite, and that sugar rush actually soothed me. Why hadn't this ever occurred to me before? "This chocolate thing works. Like in Harry Potter."

"I hope I kiss better than a dementor."

OMG. He spoke nerd. If I didn't know what the end result would be, I might actually consider kissing him again. It took a few minutes to calm down, for my body to realize we weren't about to die and that things were okay. That I had panicked, once again, over nothing.

But Noah didn't seem to view this as a failure. "You did it. It was hard and scary, but you got through it."

"Maybe it'll be easier next time," I said. He had really impressed me through this—how calm and gentle he'd been, how encouraging. The research he'd done, the way he'd memorized the steps to help keep me grounded through the attack. He was definitely the right guy to help me get past this.

He looked surprised. "You want there to be a next time?"

"I do. I want this to get better." Another guy would be running for the hills, arms flailing like a maniac. But Noah sat next to me, helping me eat my chocolate.

My heart warmed, and I didn't recognize what I was feeling. There were too many things racing around in my body for me to figure out what it was.

He asked, "Do you want to stay and hang out? We could watch a movie that doesn't have me in it."

My anxiety attacks were exhausting on so many different levels. I was going to crash soon. "Maybe another night. These things wear me out."

"Understandable. How about tomorrow night?"

"Yes. Let's try this again tomorrow."

I sat on the floor and finished my candy bar, with him sitting right next to me. Supporting me, being close.

After I was done eating, he said, "You're really brave, do you know that?"

"It doesn't feel like bravery. You shot at people and got blown up."

"I only ever shot at targets," he corrected me. "And I think you doing something that terrifies you is very brave."

"I feel more like an idiot than a hero." I shoved the candy bar wrapper into my pocket.

"You're not. That was amazing."

"Okay. Now you're just saying stuff to make me feel better." I put my hand on the wall, intending to get up, and he immediately stood, offering me both of his hands.

When I got to my feet, I swayed toward him, my head still a little woozy. We stayed there, close together, while I regained my bearings.

"I'm okay," I told him, letting go of his hands. I was going to take a step back but realized that I was good where I was, standing so close to him. Now that I'd done it, kissed him, and knew that I was going to do it again, some of that fear had been mitigated. Maybe some of that also had to do with his kindness and respect, but I welcomed not feeling so terrified.

"I should get going," I told him.

I saw his Adam's apple bob, and he nodded. "Yes. Do you want me to take you home?"

"You're not planning on calling a car, are you? I'm just over at Gladys's house."

"No, I meant, do you need help? Do you want me to carry you?"

If another man had said this to me, I probably would have laughed, because I would have imagined that particular feat to be impossible. But with Noah? I totally believed that he could pick me up like I was some dainty feather and carry me all the way back without even breaking a sweat.

I got hit with another new feeling I didn't quite recognize. Something that appreciated his masculinity and strength and how him having those things made me feel more feminine. Which wasn't a feeling I had experienced before.

I liked it.

"I'm okay to walk. I've been fortified by a Snickers bar, remember?" I wanted to say something else, something to let him know what tonight had meant to me, but I couldn't find the words. So I settled on, "I'm sorry about all that. My reaction. But I did warn you."

He held up both hands as if he meant to put them on my shoulders, but he let them drop back to his sides. "You have absolutely nothing to apologize for. I feel like I'm the one who should be apologizing to you, for you having to go through that."

"This is so not your fault." Well, a licensed professional might think it was a little bit his fault, since it was his face on the pillow that had started all of this. "I wanted to do this. I want to keep doing this. If you're okay with it."

"I told you, I'm all in. That hasn't changed."

"Not for me, either."

"Then it's decided," he said with a nod. "Let me walk you out."

"No, I know the way. You stay here." I told Magnus good night and gave Noah a dumb little wave and left. When I got outside, I thought about the enormity of what I'd done. I'd intentionally kissed someone. I'd intentionally kissed Noah Douglas. And that anxiety attack, where I'd really kissed someone and hadn't just come close to doing it, had felt less intense than the others. Whether that was because of the method Noah had me use or just how he'd supported me through it, I didn't know. All I did know was that it had been better.

He'd been right—I had accomplished something important, and I deserved a little celebration. So I jumped up and threw my fists in the air, feeling like I'd just won a battle. Well, maybe I hadn't won it, but I hadn't died in the end, so that was good, too.

Twirling around, it was then that I noticed Noah standing at the front window, apparently keeping an eye on me as I walked back to Gladys's. I stopped my spinning, dropping my arms. His grin let me know he'd seen all of it.

Thankful he couldn't see me blushing because it was dark, I bowed to him instead and laughed out loud when he bowed to me in return with a big, courtly hand flourish.

I nearly skipped the whole way back.

I'd forgotten what hope felt like.

CHAPTER NINETEEN

The next night Noah texted me to come by at nine. This time I decided to make a little effort. My clothes were pretty much the same, but I showered and actually blow-dried my hair so that it was soft and shiny. I left it down. I put on some eye makeup. Not a ton, but enough to give me a mental boost. I scrubbed my teeth again within an inch of their tiny white lives and left off the lip gloss, because I didn't need to make an already difficult situation worse by adding pink stickiness on top of it.

When I got to his house, it was the same routine as the night before. I knocked, he yelled at me to come in, Magnus ran over to check things out. And Noah was in the same spot in the kitchen where he'd been before, again, eating a bowl of cereal.

"Your hair," he said, with a mouthful of milk. He swallowed and then said, "I've never seen it down before. I like it."

The look in his eyes was soft and appreciative, and it made my stomach do somersaults. I found my brain wanting to head into a sarcastic place where, to protect myself and my feelings, I'd say, "I didn't do it for you," but that was untrue. I'd totally done it for him and I'd wanted him to notice and I was glad that he did.

So I just said, "Thanks." Then I cleared my throat and told him, "There are things you could eat besides cereal, you know."

He shook his head. "It's my favorite food."

"Cereal is not anybody's favorite food."

"I know I should probably say it's something sophisticated like sushi, but it is definitely cereal." He drank the rest of the milk in his bowl before placing it in the sink. Then he started opening upper cabinets. And every single one of them was filled, top to bottom, side to side, with boxes of different brands of cereals.

"You're some kind of weird cereal hoarder," I said in awe. I liked that he wasn't this stereotypical macho movie star but had these quirky and nerdy sides that he let me see. Because those were the parts of him I related to.

And liked.

"It's not hoarding if I eat it all. Which I will." He closed the cabinet doors and said, "I thought we should watch a movie tonight."

"What? Why?"

"Come with me." He stopped in front of me, offering his hand. My heart jumped up into my throat in both surprise and anticipation. He'd never done that before. But to be fair, our entire situation consisted of things happening between us that had never happened to me before. I slid my hand into his and loved the way his closed around mine, how strong and warm he felt.

I was holding hands with Noah Douglas. It was like my brain couldn't process that this was actually happening. I wouldn't want to be overly dramatic or anything, but my teenage self literally would have died if she could have seen what I was doing right now.

Tingling shivers were running up and down my arm as he led me into a room I hadn't gone in before. There was a couch and a TV mounted to the wall, and other than yet another dog bed that Magnus was currently occupying, that was it.

He sat and pulled me down next to him. Really close next to him.

"I've been trying to think of ways to make this easier. Which made me think of when people typically get their first kisses. When they're teenagers. So maybe part of the problem is that we're not doing any teenage courtship rituals. There's been no physical buildup to our kiss."

I held up our still-connected hands. "Like holding hands?"

"Yes. I've held back from touching you before because you seemed so skittish. Which I understand now, but if you're okay with it, I think we should try to do those physical things, like cuddling and holding hands, and I don't really know what else we should be doing because all of my knowledge about what normal teens do is based on a TV show, so I'm guessing they're not entirely accurate."

My heart again had that glowy, fluttery feeling. "You are giving this an extraordinary amount of thought."

"Aren't you?"

"Honestly, I'm worried if I think about it too much, I'll go running into the hills and never return. In case you didn't notice, I'm all about avoidance as a coping mechanism."

He nodded, serious. "I noticed. I told you, I tend to overanalyze things when left to my own devices, like our current circumstances."

"I'm trying to be in the present with you. Not thinking about it but just doing it."

"Would you be okay, then, with us touching each other?"

This was something I could definitely get on board with. I had been, like he said, skittish when it came to men touching me, because touching had always led us down a road that ended in kissing. So I stayed away from it to avoid the end result.

But this time I was trying to get to that place.

"I would be okay with it. And you don't have to ask me every time. This is my blanket permission."

His wolfish grin momentarily made me think maybe that had been the wrong decision. Then he reached up with his free hand and ran his fingertips along the edge of the sapphire pendant necklace I was wearing. I felt little tendrils of fire every place that he touched me. My skin was flushing from the sensation. "So you'd be okay if I told you this was pretty. That you look pretty wearing it."

It was like somebody had slammed into me, leaving me momentarily breathless. "What?"

"Where did you get it?"

"It was a college graduation present. Sapphires are my birthstone. My mom worked extra hours to get it for me."

The next thing that occurred to me was that this was just like the scene in the second Duel of the Fae movie where Malec ripped the truth-telling locket from Aliana's neck, and instead of being upset with him for destroying a piece of her magic, she kissed him.

I was understanding her reasoning.

"Or you're fine if I do this," he said.

Now he moved his hand from my collarbone to my hair, running his fingers through the ends, watching the way the strands twined around his fingers. "So soft," he murmured, saying it in a way that made me think he hadn't meant to say it out loud.

"That happens when you have nice conditioner." I was trying to joke, but it was like I could barely get the words out. I wondered if it was okay for me to touch him, too. Would his hair be soft? Would he let me twist and turn it with my fingers? Maybe make little braids in it?

"That kind of reminds me of the other thing I think we should be doing." How could he speak so calmly when my insides were being jumbled like crazy? "We should get to know each other better. Like, I don't even know if you're from California."

"I am. Born and raised."

"Okay . . ." He was still playing with my hair, and I was still loving it and wanted to lean into him and purr like a cat. "What about your favorite color?"

"Teal, like my work polo shirts. What about you?"

"Black, like my soul."

I laughed at that and then said, "My turn. What's your favorite movie?"

"Pass." He shook his head. "Too many for too many different reasons. Same with books. I do have a soft spot for *Fight Club*, though. Favorite vacation? You already know mine. It was the only one I've ever taken."

"My mom used to take me up to Big Bear and we'd spend a couple of nights there. We couldn't really afford to go anywhere else." I was suddenly realizing the gift I'd been given. I could ask Noah Douglas anything I wanted and I knew he'd answer. He was notoriously tight lipped in his interviews and would often just refuse to answer certain questions that he deemed too personal. And I could find out all of his favorite things while he was playing with my hair.

Talk about a win-win.

"Favorite sport?" I asked.

"Football."

"Favorite team?"

"The Portland Jacks."

I didn't care all that much about sports. I'd only asked because for some guys this was the most important question ever, but since Noah wasn't waxing on about his eternal love for his team, I figured I was okay to shift questions. "Favorite ice cream?"

"Vanilla, I guess. I don't really eat a lot of ice cream."

"Don't . . . eat . . . ," I sputtered. "I don't even know what to say to that. I feel like my people have been dishonored or something."

He laughed at that and it looked like he was going to ask me a question, so I rushed in first. "Favorite candy bar?"

"Snickers."

I smacked him on the leg. "You can't choose that. It's my favorite."

"Just one more thing we have in common." His words had a weight to them that I didn't want to examine. Just friends. That was it. We didn't need to overcomplicate things.

To stop where he was headed, I asked, "So who is your favorite director?"

"There's too many with different forms of artistic expression that it would be impossible for me to pick. Do you have a favorite director?"

I nodded. "I never used to before, but I do now, since I binged that trilogy of yours. Rian Johnson. That dude's amazing. So talented." That he'd directed the second and vastly superior movie in the trilogy was the main reason I'd chosen him. I had really liked *Knives Out*, too. "So if you won't pick a favorite director, what about a favorite costar?"

"Easy. Lily Ramsey."

"Good choice," I told him. She'd seemed so nice. "What do you think is the best feeling in the world?"

He looked at his fingers, still running through my hair, and hesitated. His eyes met mine, and then he was the one to quickly look away. "I feel like I should say something trite, like climbing into a newly made bed. But I don't make my bed."

"Me neither," I confessed. It drove Shelby crazy. Which was why I kept my bedroom door shut.

"So I'd say it's probably sitting with Magnus while reading a book."

Aw. "That's nice."

"But I imagine that the best feeling in the world would be getting to be with the person you love most."

"That's mine, too." I hadn't meant to say it out loud. Mostly because I'd never let myself dare to dream that it was possible that I could ever be in a relationship. But I wanted to be. That was why I was doing all this. So that I could get to that point. But it embarrassed me to admit it.

"You like snuggling with Magnus, too?" he teased, letting me off the hook.

"I do. He's such a good boy."

Magnus thumped his tail against the floor, pleased at being included.

Before Noah could maneuver the conversation back to something I wasn't ready to talk about, I asked, "What's up with the socks?" Tonight he was sporting penguins on his feet.

"Too many people in this industry get caught up in their own self-importance and believe their own hype. They're a reminder to not take myself too seriously. And don't think I haven't noticed how you're hogging this conversation. I want to know about you, too."

"Like what? You already know my secrets."

Not all of them, that pesky internal voice reminded me, and I shut it out.

"Um, did you make any New Year's resolutions?"

"No. As far as I can tell, January is just the month where everybody lies to themselves about getting in shape, and I refuse to become victim to the gym- and weight loss–industrial complex. If I ever do make a resolution, it's to eat more chocolate, and I usually meet that just fine."

At that he laughed and then said, "You're delightful, do you know that?"

"Did you just call me delightful? I'm not your four-year-old granddaughter."

"Sorry not sorry," he said while shrugging. "It's how you make me feel. You delight me."

"In that case, you may delight me just a little bit, too."

"Just a little bit?" he teased, moving in closer to me. I wondered if he realized that he was doing it.

"A teeny bit." Not wanting things to get too flirty, I thought of a question to shift the mood. "So what is your biggest regret?"

I fully expected him to talk about the army again, or some part he'd passed on, so it surprised me when he said, "Never having a birthday party."

"You've never had a birthday party?" That was so immensely sad to me. I'd been pretty poor growing up, but even I'd had birthday parties.

"No friends," he said. "I was a working actor from the time I was six years old. And I always had to work on my birthday."

My plan had backfired. That feeling was back, the one that made me want to kiss him. Not just because I was attracted to him—because believe me, I completely was—but because there was a connection there and the only way to express how I felt was to kiss him.

I gulped, knowing what would come next, my heart already racing and my stomach churning, but it was worth it. "Would it be okay if I kissed you?"

The smile spread slowly across his face, and I felt the warmth of it all the way down to my toes. "You never have to ask me. The answer is always going to be yes."

The way his voice sounded, the low, urgent tone to it, had me catching my breath. In a good way. I asked, "Does that mean I'm allowed to touch you, too?"

"Juliet, you can do whatever you'd like to me and there's no way I'll ever object."

With a smile of my own, I leaned forward to press my lips against his.

CHAPTER TWENTY

That kiss lasted slightly longer than the first one, and he talked me through the ensuing anxiety attack. He kept his hands on my shoulders, and I wrapped my hands around his wrists, holding on for dear life. That contact was another thing to ground me, to tether me to the here and now so that I could center and focus on what was real. I wasn't in danger. Noah would never hurt me. He had promised he'd never do any of the things that ran through my head before I'd almost kissed other guys—that I'd be mocked or tormented or found lacking.

When the attack had subsided, he asked, "Are you okay?"

"I wasn't as scared as before. I was still afraid, but not as intensely. I still wanted to vomit at the end and it felt like I was going to hyperventilate for a while there, but it seemed better? Or maybe that's just wishful thinking."

"I was reading that another part of trying to overcome this is to challenge negative thoughts about your phobia. If your brain tells you that it's awful and you hate it, you remind your brain that I'm a great kisser who cares about you and will help you through this."

I smiled. Again I was touched at all that he'd done to help me. How much time and effort he was putting into this. Why was he doing all that? Was it just for the part? To be as realistic as possible? This could hardly be worth it. I felt bad for putting him in this position. I reminded myself that he'd volunteered and maybe instead of trying to figure out what his motives were, I should just appreciate that he was willing to do it and not get hung up on it.

There was one thing he'd said to me about himself that didn't quite match what I was personally experiencing. "You told me you were impatient and easily annoyed. So far you've been incredibly patient and understanding with me. I don't get it."

He shrugged one shoulder. "It's just different with you." Then he cleared his throat and said, "How was that kiss? Any change there?"

"I'm not really getting anything from that part yet. It's almost like kissing the back of my own hand. And I still want to puke and have a faux heart attack right after."

"You are doing so many wonderful things for my self-esteem."

I laughed.

"Time for phase two," he said. He reached for the remote and turned the television on and pulled up his InstaFlicks account while I wondered what phase two meant. "Anything in particular you want to watch?"

A new rom-com had recently premiered, and I'd been wanting to see it. I was actually supposed to watch it with Shelby, but if I explained to her that I'd watched it with Noah, she would be all kinds of understanding and excited about it. I told him the title and he found it, then turned toward me. "I know I'm no Magnus, but would you be interested in cuddling with me through the movie?"

Oh. That was phase two. I waited a second for my body to react, but no part of that scared me. I knew he wouldn't try to kiss me suddenly, and I liked when he touched me. I scooted over to him. He leaned into the corner of the couch, extending his powerful legs out in front of him, crossing them at the ankle. I snuggled against his broad chest, leaning my head against his shoulder and curling my legs up next to him. He put his arm around me, hugging me tightly for a moment before relaxing his arm.

There was that pleasure he'd been talking about, those happy hormones that were giddy about my current situation and filled me with endorphins that almost made me feel like I was floating. Warmth filled all of my veins, making me melt against him. I really did love the way he smelled.

He started the movie, and I listened to the sound of him breathing, mesmerized by the way his chest went up and down. Without thinking, I put my hand on his chest, just like last night. Now his heartbeat was solid and steady. Like I could rely on him for anything. He put his hand over mine, which somehow made it infinitely better.

I felt the fingers on his other hand playing with the ends of my hair again, and I wondered if he even realized that he was doing it. We were almost like this real couple, sitting here enjoying one another's company.

And I had that feeling of belonging again, just like I had when we'd been close together for that picture.

My eyelids felt heavy, and I let them drift shut for just a moment.

The next thing I knew, Noah was gently shaking me awake. "Hey, sleepyhead. You missed the entire movie."

I felt warm and cozy and safe, and it was difficult to drag my eyes open. But then I did and realized where I was and what had happened.

"Why didn't you wake me up earlier?" I asked, realizing that I had drooled all over this poor man and he hadn't said a word to me. Just stayed where he was and let me sleep and soak his hoodie. I was mortified.

"It seemed like you needed to sleep."

He was still holding me; my hand was still on his chest with his on top. His head was resting against mine so that I could feel his words against my scalp. Which made my head feel all tingly and warm.

"It's late," I said. "I have an appointment early tomorrow. I should get home."

I don't know why I said this. It wasn't like I was going to be able to go home and go right back to sleep. I was pretty sure I'd be up for hours dissecting this entire evening. And given the overwhelming desire I had to stay right where I was, that was a signal to me that I needed some space to get my head on straight. This wasn't supposed to be about pretending Noah Douglas was my boyfriend. This was about fixing my fear of kissing and both of us moving on with our lives. I wasn't dumb enough to think that we could do that together.

I started to disentangle myself from him, and I could sense his reluctance to do the same, but he did.

"I'm walking you home." He didn't ask, but he wasn't commanding me, either. More like it was what was going to happen even if I objected. But I wasn't going to object. He took me by the hand again while I briefly wondered how insane my hair looked at the moment.

We went outside and the stars overhead were bright, as were the lights in the valley below us. The air was cold and biting, and I sucked in a breath.

"Cold?" he asked.

When I nodded, he released my hand and stopped to take off his hoodie. He handed it to me, and I happily put it on. It was still warm from his body heat and smelled just like him.

He was never getting this thing back. "Thank you."

"You're welcome." He took my hand again, and we started walking. We didn't say anything else, but it wasn't an awkward silence. More like a comfortable one where we didn't need to speak and could just . . . be together.

Then we were on Gladys's front porch with the half moon out and the crisp, slightly pine-scented air surrounding us. He took both of my hands, holding them gently.

"Good night, Miss Nolan. Thank you for allowing me to escort you home."

He was such a dork, and I loved it. "Good night, Mr. Douglas." Everything felt like a perfect romantic movie moment that I didn't want to go to waste.

"I want to try something," I told him. I couldn't kiss him normally without losing it, but what if . . . ? I leaned up and kissed him on the cheek. His skin felt warm underneath my lips, and I stayed there, breathing him in. I could feel his surprise, his sharp intake of breath as I stood there and waited.

Huh.

My pulse had quickened, but in an understandable and manageable way. I wasn't afraid. I pulled back, reluctant to do so.

"Did that feel like kissing the back of your hand?" he asked.

"Definitely not." I wouldn't have been able to describe how it had felt to someone else—the relief I was feeling that I wasn't a complete freak, how my stomach had flipped, not with nausea, but with anticipation and longing, the urge I had to do it again.

It was too dark to see his eyes clearly, but I heard the hesitation in his voice. "Does that mean I can kiss you on the cheek, too?"

"I don't know. Try it."

He took my face in his hands and then leaned in slowly, softly pressing his warm lips against my skin, his rough stubble pressing against my face.

My legs gave way, and it was a good thing he was holding on to me. Although, being held up by your head wasn't actually very pleasant, so I ordered my legs to start working again and straightened up.

"Good or bad?" he asked, worried.

"Um, definitely good." There was no mistaking the breathiness in my voice, the way I was shaking from the contact.

"Good. I like good."

I definitely liked good, too.

"This could be very interesting," he mused. "Can I do that again? And maybe in some other spots? To test a theory?"

"Anything in the name of science," I said and smiled when I heard him laugh.

He still had his hands on my face, and I closed my eyes as he pressed soft kisses against my cheek, one after another, almost as if to soothe where his stubble grazed me.

This was . . . amazing. Incredible. How had I not known about this loophole before?

He continued his careful exploration, kissing my cheek, up to my forehead, down to each eyelid, which felt exquisitely sensitive. He went over to the other cheek and then down to my neck, and my legs almost stopped functioning again. My breath caught at the sensation of his mouth exploring my throat. I grabbed his waist, needing something to hang on to.

It wasn't fear that was flooding through me. It was fiery want. I wanted his touch, his mouth on me, the little trails of fire that followed his lips everywhere they went. I wanted that hollowed-out feeling deep in my gut that was entirely pleasurable and made me light-headed. A good light-headed.

"So nuzzling your neck is okay?" he asked, his words against my skin.

"I am a fan."

I could feel him smiling. "Me too."

"Then you should let me do it." I didn't know where this confidence was coming from—it was totally unlike me when it came to physical stuff.

"Yeah?" He lifted his head up.

"I want you to feel this way, too."

"For future reference, that's the great thing about kissing," he told me. "Both of us get to feel the same thing at the same time."

"Uh-huh." This was no time for talking. I tugged at his shoulders, getting him to lean down slightly. I ran my lips over his stubble along his jawline, liking the contrast between his five-o'clock shadow and the skin of his cheek. He put his hands on my waist, and I felt his fingers dig into my hips when I moved to his neck. I ghosted my lips along the surface, barely touching him. He smelled so amazing, that unique scent that was just Noah.

I pushed my mouth against the skin where his neck and collarbone met and felt a surge of delight when he groaned at the contact. One of his hands moved up into my hair, lightly holding me in place and stroking my scalp, and I sighed with the pleasure of it.

This was thrilling in a way I hadn't imagined possible. Knowing that I could have that sort of effect on him. I wondered where else I could kiss him that he'd enjoy. While pondering my next move, my brain demanded to know what Noah tasted like, and I thought it was an excellent question. So I flicked the edge of my tongue against his skin, and he let out this throaty sound that was exhilarating, but then he put both of his hands on my shoulders, pushing me back slightly.

"You have an early appointment tomorrow, remember?"

Did I? Oh yeah. Well, forget Mrs. Rabinowitz and Fifi. I was much happier here. There were many, many things to explore. "That's a whole six hours away. Plenty of time."

He let out a sound that was a mixture of laughter and regret. "Please don't tempt me, Juliet. I'm not as strong as you seem to think I am, and I have promises I intend to keep."

Great. He had to go and be honorable. But to be fair, that was probably the only reason I'd been enjoying myself. I knew, as much as I'd ever known anything, that he wasn't going to push me or try to kiss me, and it made me feel safe and unworried.

I tried to come down from the surge of adrenaline that was raging through me. I'd had rushes of adrenaline before, but they'd always been negative. This one was mixed with want and desire and made my blood feel too thick for my veins.

It was a heady sensation, and I liked it.

"So I'm going to go." He said the words, but he wasn't moving. He lifted a hand up, running his fingers over my lower lip. That didn't bother me, either. Then he was moving to hug me, holding me tight against him.

Leaving me to wonder why we hadn't been doing this all along, either. I adored the feeling of his strong arms being wrapped around me, the hard planes of his chest pressed against me, his face touching mine. I almost turned to kiss his cheek again when he withdrew.

"Now I'm really going," he said. To my disappointment, he actually did start walking away. But then he called over his shoulder, "By the way, you snore."

"I do not!" I called back.

He turned around so that he was walking backward. "You a hundred percent do, and it's adorable."

I waved to him, and he returned it before turning around. I watched him go, again admiring the view, and then sighed as I fished in my pocket for my key. I will admit that it took me much longer than it should have to get the key into the stupid lock and get the door open.

When I got inside, a strange mixture of fear and doubt swelled up inside me, whispering insidious lies about how I should be worried and scared and run away from Noah.

Nope. I shook my head. I was going to do what he'd suggested and replace those negative thoughts with positive affirmations.

"Listen up, brain. I'm going to kiss Noah Douglas as much as I want to, and you're not going to overreact or melt down over it. I will kiss him and enjoy it. This is going to happen."

And I was going to keep telling myself that until it became reality.

CHAPTER TWENTY-ONE

I made it to my appointment despite the fact that I was exhausted because I'd barely slept. I just kept running what had happened on the porch through my mind over and over again. It felt like everything had changed, and I was eager to see how that would translate when I saw Noah again.

To my dismay, he sent me a text that said:

> Have to fly to New York for some unexpected voiceovers for my next movie. I won't be back until Friday afternoon. Can I see you then?

> I can't. My mom has her play thing at six.

> Do you want some company?

> If you insist.

> Sounds like a plan. Don't kiss anyone else while I'm gone.

That made me laugh, and I sent him an emoji with its tongue sticking out.

I texted Shelby, thinking maybe we could hang out. I felt like a bad friend—we'd been just sending general "hey, how are you, thinking of you" kinds of messages. I hadn't told her about Noah or how we were hanging out, because those were conversations I wasn't ready to have yet. Maybe that was selfish of me, but I wanted to fix this phobia and it felt like this might work and I wasn't willing to jinx it.

She texted me back a sad face, saying she had been so busy and that we'd catch up soon. She did ask:

> Have you been bored and lonely without me?

> No, I'm finding ways to keep myself occupied.

And she would die if she knew what those ways entailed.

And that's how the next few days went, me finding ways to amuse myself, taking care of Sunshine, going to my appointments, and doing everything in my power not to spend every minute of every day thinking about Noah.

I failed miserably. He was on my mind constantly. I also kept reliving those moments on Gladys's porch, wondering what it would be like when I saw him again.

Because he didn't contact me. I guess part of me had expected him to since he'd become so important to me, and it hurt a little that he didn't seem to feel the same way. I tried to be fair—he was there to work and was probably very busy. I guess I had expected phone calls or a face-to-face chat, a text, something. But it wasn't his fault that he couldn't read my mind. And I could have reached out to him, but I didn't want to give the wrong impression—that we were anything more than friends who cuddled and kissed a bit.

My disappointment in not hearing from him surprised me. And was more than a little troubling.

Friday finally came, and I could hardly wait for him to get back. My heart sank into my stomach when I got a text from him that said:

> Had to switch my flights and I'm going to be a few hours later than I'd thought. Can I meet you at the play?

> Okay.

I texted him the address.

> Will I be able to get a seat?

Had he never been to a student production before?

> You'll be fine.

> Can't wait to see you again.

I wanted to text back *Really?* Because he seemed like he was doing just fine without me while I was missing him terribly.

And although I was annoyed with him, I did leave my hair down for him. I considered wearing his hoodie to the show but figured that was a step too far. We were cool and casual, and I needed to remember it. He obviously had.

Traffic made me slightly later than I'd planned. I had wanted to hang out with my mom backstage before she went on. It had been one of our traditions when I was little. When I got there, the play was just about to start. Tickets weren't required, so I went down to the third row and sat near the aisle, putting my jacket on the seat next to me so that Noah could sit there when he arrived.

There were only about twenty people in the theater, and I figured most of them were drama students who had been offered extra credit to come and see the shows of their fellow performers. The curtains lifted, and we all applauded.

What happened over the next hour was a mishmash of things I didn't want to know about my mother, as it was some kind of one-woman confessional that started with a re-creation of her birth and ended with her current situation of being a student and feeling out of place. I kept checking the door for Noah, but he never came in. He'd probably gotten caught in traffic, too, and I didn't know whether to feel disappointed or relieved that he'd missed this.

The lights came up and I stood, cheering for my mom. I was easily the most enthusiastic applauder. I felt a hand on my shoulder and I turned to see Noah in a ball cap, wearing the hood from his sweatshirt over the hat. He also had a denim jacket on and dark pants.

"Hey," I said, feeling surprisingly awkward, both from the lack of contact and not knowing where things stood between us now.

Apparently he didn't feel the same way, as he said, "I missed you," and then wrapped me in another amazing hug. I buried my face against his neck, breathing in deeply. I felt like I could happily live in the circle of his embrace.

"You didn't call," I said without meaning to.

"I should have. I was so busy every minute of the day. I'm sorry."

And just like that, all was forgiven. His touch was just that over-powering. "Why are you dressed like that?"

He pulled back. "What do you mean? This is to disguise myself so people don't mob me. It works."

"How? You look like the Unabomber. How does that not draw more attention to you?"

"What's drawing attention to me right now is you loudly compar-ing me to a serial killer and bomb maker."

"Whatever you say." He was holding my hand, and I laced my fingers through his. My heart sighed happily. "Did you see the show?"

"I missed the first ten minutes."

"What did you think?"

His face went blank, and I realized that he was trying to hide his real reaction from me. "It was . . . interesting."

"Is that doublespeak for it was terrible and you don't want to hurt anyone's feelings?" Because it had been pretty bad.

"I can tell that your mother really loves acting and the theater," he said diplomatically.

"She does. Why do you think she named me Juliet? Most of my memories with my mom revolve around being at our community the-ater with her."

"Do you love it the same way she does?"

195

"It's never really been my thing. But you said you liked the theater. Do you have a favorite play? Or maybe a favorite playwright?"

He seemed to be thinking, and I loved the way he always took all my questions seriously and how he always answered them. "That would be hard to choose. I've been reading Sam Shepard's plays lately. I enjoy them because he wrote from the perspective of someone who was an actor, too. But if you spent all that time in theaters, you must have a favorite playwright."

"I am a fan of musicals, to my mother's eternal dismay. Do I lose cool points if I say Rodgers and Hammerstein?"

"Yes, you lose all the cool points. But that's okay. I'll still let you kiss me."

I slapped him lightly on the forearm, and he laughed.

Someone walked up behind us, and I turned, half expecting that we were about to be interrupted by one of his fans.

It was my mother. I hugged her and congratulated her and then said, "Mom, this is Noah Douglas."

They said hello and shook hands. Then my mother asked, "And what is it you do, Noah?"

He couldn't suppress his amused smile. "I'm an actor, as well."

"Good for you," my mom said. "It's a hard profession!"

"It is," he agreed, very good natured about the whole thing.

"Did you study it in college?" she asked.

"I didn't get the chance to attend college."

"It's never too late to go back. You could have a show just like this one."

"That would be . . . something," he said, and I felt like I needed to intervene before this got too far off the rails. I wondered if I should tell her that he was a professional, but given how much Noah seemed to be enjoying the anonymity, I decided against it.

"You seem familiar to me," my mom said thoughtfully. "Like we've met before."

"I get that a lot." Which was probably because people weren't expecting to meet a movie star in real life and it took their brain a minute to catch up with where they recognized him from. Because he definitely didn't just have "one of those faces." He was much more unique than that.

His phone buzzed, and he took it out of his pocket to look at it. "My car is here. I'm sorry to do this, but I've got to get going. It was nice to meet you!" He waved to my mother and then leaned in to kiss me quickly on the cheek.

"Wait." I grabbed at his arm, confused. "I thought we were going to hang out tonight."

"I have plans. But I'll call you tomorrow, okay?"

Then he was gone, and I was left feeling bereft. This was not at all how I'd hoped this evening would go.

And what kind of plans did he have? My heart lurched as I considered that he might be seeing someone else. That maybe that's why he didn't call me while he was in New York. Because he was out on dates with women who would actually kiss him. Who would more than kiss him.

For the first time in my life, I understood the phrase *green with envy*. Because I felt sick with jealousy at the idea of him being out with other women. Which was totally irrational, because I was the one who set up our situation. I was the one who had said friends only. If he was seeing other women, he wasn't doing anything wrong.

"Is that your boyfriend?" my mom asked.

"We're just friends. We're not dating."

She raised one eyebrow like she didn't believe me. "How old is he?"

Given that I was currently embroiled in my own jealousy spiral, and while I adored my mother, getting into this weird hang-up of hers was going to make me roll my eyes so hard that my ocular muscle would spasm and make me go blind. Even if I was the last person who should be judging anyone's weird hang-ups. "He's twenty-seven. Not fifty-seven. He's only three years older than me. We're basically the same age."

She must have heard how unwilling I was to have this discussion with her, because she immediately backed off and then proceeded into territory that made me want to roll my eyes even harder. "He's not very conventionally handsome, is he? I can't really see him ever getting a leading man part."

"Okay, I'm making an appointment for you with your eye doctor, and we're getting your vision checked. I know opinions are subjective, but yours is wrong." Maybe it was because she'd never seen him act. The intensity, the sheer talent, the vulnerability he conveyed, the way he made every character into a real person who deserved to find love and their happy ending.

I shouldn't have been surprised at her reaction—my mom had always looked to find the bad in every guy that I'd ever expressed an interest in. During my Felix Morrison obsession, she'd reminded me more often than was necessary that he was a fictional character and that I'd never date him.

Ha. I'd showed her. Well, sort of. Since we weren't technically dating.

But she seemed to always find the flaws in guys that I had crushes on. To discourage me. Did that have something to do with my dad? Did she think she was protecting me from feeling the same kind of heartbreak she had? I wondered if her bringing up what was wrong with guys I liked played into my phobia issues at all. And why hadn't this ever occurred to me before?

My phone beeped, and there was a message from Shelby.

> Can you hang out tonight?

And while there was no way to parse out her tone, I felt in my gut like something was wrong. Maybe because the text was so short, with no greeting, no flowers or emojis. I knew that she needed me.

But before I could tell my mother that I had to go, she hugged me and said she was off to have a small get-together with her professor and a few of her classmates. She kissed my forehead. "Love you, kiddo!"

"I love you, too. And you did a really good job tonight." Then I practically sprinted out to my van.

Fortunately the campus wasn't too far from my apartment, so it didn't take me long to get home. When I burst through the door, I expected to find . . . I didn't know what I expected. It certainly wasn't Shelby sitting on the couch watching a Noah Douglas movie and eating chocolate chip cookie dough.

"Hey." She didn't make eye contact with me.

I closed the door and said hi back. I shrugged my jacket off, leaving it on the back of one of the kitchen chairs. "Is everything okay?"

"I just wanted a girls' night."

That wasn't it. I heard the pain and sadness in her voice. But whatever was wrong with her, she didn't seem quite ready to tell me yet. I'd just wait until she was. I grabbed a spoon from the kitchen and sat down on the couch next to her. In this movie Noah played a medieval knight avenging the murder of his wife and child. We watched the movie for about an hour until it got to the scene where Noah's character was about to kiss the princess he'd fallen in love with during his quest.

Shelby paused the movie just as the kiss started and put her spoon and the tub of dough on the coffee table and announced, "I'm going to break up with Allan."

She immediately burst into sobs while I put my arms around her. "What? Why? Did something happen? Did he do something? I'll kill him if he cheated on you. I'm not even kidding."

"No," she said in a muffled voice. "Tonight Allan's mother told him that if he married me, she would never speak to him again."

Why would that make Shelby want to break up with Allan? "So? That sounds like a good deal to me. You get Allan and you don't have to deal with Harmony."

"But how can I do that? I don't want him to have to choose. I don't want to come between him and his family."

"You're going to be his family," I told her. "That witch should be thrilled she's getting you as a daughter-in-law. I wish I had a brother so that you could marry him and we'd always be related."

Her crying started to subside, and I asked, "What does Allan say?"

"He said he loves me, he chooses me. But I don't want him to have to give up his family." Her voice wobbled and broke, like she was going to start sobbing again.

"So he wants to be with you and you're going to run away? That doesn't seem right. It's not your fault Harmony's a psycho. And I'm sorry you're going through this, but I think pushing the man you love away is probably the worst thing you can do. And take that from someone who is slowly learning that avoiding things isn't the answer. If you love him, which you do, and he loves you, which he does, and you want a life together, then that's what you should do."

"You're right. But this is going to cause him so much pain. And I don't want to be the reason he's in all that pain." She reached for the extra roll of toilet paper we kept on the coffee table because neither one of us ever remembered to buy Kleenex. She blew her nose and then put her face in her hands while I rubbed her back.

I kept trying to make her feel better. "You aren't the reason he's in pain. His mom did that, not you. And think about how much worse it would be if you broke up with him. I'm pretty sure that would destroy him. You're his entire world."

She nodded. "I can't even imagine my life without him. But I would give him up so that he could be happy."

"Which is why you're the one he deserves to be with. The person who puts his happiness above their own." Unlike his stupid mother, but I refrained from adding the last part on.

"Okay!" She straightened back up. "I'll call him after this movie's over and talk it out with him. But thank you, Juliet. You're the best friend a girl could ask for." She hugged me tightly. "Let's finish this and then I'm going to have a difficult conversation."

She pushed play and the movie started up again. After a minute or two, she said, "I wonder if Noah Douglas kisses like that in real life. If he'd be all aggressive and take charge."

Without thinking, I said, "He's actually very sweet and gentle." I immediately realized my mistake, and it was like time came to a complete stop.

Shelby stood up and shrieked, "What?" Only she lengthened the vowel sound in the word for, like, twenty seconds. "You've kissed Noah Douglas? Where? When? How? Anywhere interesting? What else should I know? How is this happening and you haven't said one word to me? You've been sending me these texts saying 'what's up' and what was up was that you were making out with Noah Douglas! Details, now. All of them."

I sighed. Now I was the one who was about to have a difficult conversation.

CHAPTER TWENTY-TWO

When I didn't respond, I saw her suck in a big breath, ready to barrage me with another round of questions. I held up my hands to ward her off. "In order for me to tell you anything, you have to stop talking first and sit back down."

And there was no way to tell her about Noah without giving her the full picture. I wasn't terrified or frozen by the idea of telling her. Maybe it was because I'd already told Noah everything? My secret no longer felt earth-shattering. These stories had somehow just become part of who I'd been, and they didn't define me.

I didn't know who to give credit to for that.

So I filled her in, starting with what had happened to me in high school (which she'd never known about, since we'd gone to different schools) and about my full-blown phobia over kissing. I also told her about my arrangement with Noah—how he was helping me to overcome my phobia, but that we were strictly friends and nothing more. While I talked her eyes kept getting bigger and bigger until she resembled an anime character.

When I had caught her up on everything that had happened between him and me through the events of tonight, I tensed up, some small and scared part of me still believing she might think I was weird or make fun of me. But I should have known better. There was a reason she was my best friend.

"That's why you never date," she said sympathetically, taking both of my hands in hers. "I wish I'd known. I was always pushing you at guys and this was how you felt? I'm so sorry."

"You didn't know."

"I should have."

"How?" I said with a laugh.

"I just should have had best friend ESP or something. You really think that trying to kiss Noah Douglas is going to fix this?"

"That's kind of the plan."

She gave me a sad smile. "Is falling in love with him also the plan?"

What? That wasn't going to happen. "I told you, we're just friends."

"You like him as a person. It sounds like you guys click really well and get each other's sense of humor. You are friends. You add in attraction and intimacy and physicality? Like, that's going to go somewhere."

She wasn't seeing the big picture. "It isn't. We're compartmentalizing. I've compartmentalized for a really long time. I can do it here, too."

"You'd have to be superhero-level strong to avoid falling for this guy." She gestured toward the TV.

"Call me Supergirl. I got this."

"Okay. You can claim friends only, but you do realize that you're dating him, right?"

"How do you figure that? We've been very clear with each other on what this is," I said. Even if my heart sometimes wanted to forget.

"Why don't you want it to be more?"

"So many reasons. Trying to work through my phobia is sort of sucking up all of my emotional energy. The fact that I know things aren't going to work out between us. That I'm pretty sure he'll get bored with me and cheat with some groupie and leave." I let out a shaky breath. Why was this upsetting me? I knew how things had to be.

"I don't believe that. He was in the army. Don't they breed them to be loyal? He'd probably make an excellent boyfriend."

"Being monogamous for Noah Douglas means beating off thousands of women with a stick. For me it means not matching with somebody on Tinder. Unless he defines faithfulness as small bursts of devotion that are followed up by him having the freedom to do what he wants."

She frowned. "How would you even know that?"

"I'm pretty sure he's on a date right now." That sickly jealous feeling returned, making my stomach queasy.

"Do you know that for sure?"

"No. But look at him." Now it was my turn to point at the TV. "Who wouldn't want to date him?"

"That's not what matters. He can make his own choices, and just because someone wants to hook up with him doesn't automatically mean he's going to do it. He's not an infidelity robot set to 'accept all requests.'"

Maybe I wasn't being fair to him. "I don't know why I feel this way. Maybe it's some internalized thing I have because my dad cheated on my mom and she's spent my entire life resenting him for it."

"Which means you should ignore the negative voice in your head and try trusting him."

Did this mean I had another false voice in my head, telling me something was true when it wasn't? "Putting that aside, you're operating under the assumption that he wants to date me."

"Why wouldn't he? You're amazing."

"You have to say that because you're my best friend."

"I'm your best friend because it's true." She let out a little wistful sigh. "And have you considered the possibility that you're making him want you more by refusing to date him?"

"How do you figure that?"

"Don't you remember that one interview he did for *Entertainment Monthly* where he said something about how one of the reasons that he joined the military was because everything in his life was too easy, it was all being handed to him and he wanted something he had to work for? Something that not everyone could do. That's you. You're making him work for you, and it's probably a novel experience for him. Keeping him at arm's length is probably just going to have the opposite effect."

That was just Shelby speculating. She didn't know that for sure, so I said, "I don't think that's true."

"Maybe it is, maybe it isn't. But let me just say—ahoy, mateys. I'm onboard this ship." She playfully saluted me.

Now it was my turn to sigh. "What ship? There's no relationship."

"Just because you're in denial about what's happening doesn't mean it's not happening. You certainly are dating him. You go places with him. You spend your evenings together. You're kissing him. You are in a relationship."

That panicky feeling, the one that had been my almost constant companion lately, returned, making my pulse race. "I can't be."

"Why not?"

"He doesn't know." I whispered the words, barely able to say them. I'd pushed this thing so far out of my head that it was painful to be speaking them out loud.

"Doesn't know what?"

"The first time we met, I told him . . ." My throat felt dry and I swallowed, hard. "I told him I didn't know who he was. That I'd never heard of him."

This got her back to her feet. "Are you serious?"

I nodded.

"You have to tell him."

"I can't. It would ruin everything." I felt tears forming at the edges of my eyes, and I tried blinking them away.

She sat next to me. "I think we both know that the right thing to do here is for you to tell him."

"Do we, though? Despite what you think, we're not in a relationship. We haven't made any kind of commitment to each other. We're hanging out. I'll hopefully get over my kissing thing, and then he'll fly to some-place like France to film a movie and this will die a natural death. There's no reason to upset everything right now. Not to mention, I'm not going to get you fired from this job. You're the one that said it's your last shot."

"I'll find another job."

"Not like this one, you won't. And we both know it."

She let out a little groan. "Now I almost wish you hadn't told me. Like, as your friend I'm so glad you felt like you could confide in me, but as a person in a professional relationship with Noah, I feel like an accomplice or something."

"You're not an accomplice. There's no crime being committed here. I will tell him. After the work is done. I'll deal with the fallout then."

"Do you know how unreliable construction is? I'm hoping to be done in three months and that's only if nothing goes wrong, and things always go wrong. Isn't it better to tell him now than six months from now? And weren't you just telling me how I shouldn't be avoiding things? Neither should you!"

I blurted out, "I can't lose him." It was probably one of the most honest things I'd ever said, and it surprised me how deeply I felt those words. I'd constructed all these walls, some intentional, some not, and he hadn't just broken them down. He'd flattened them with a steamroller and taken up residence in my heart. I really cared about him. He was the first man I'd ever felt this way about, and I just . . . I couldn't lose him. I accepted that there was an ending coming for us. But not yet. I wasn't ready to let go. "He's this incredible person and so unlike what I imagined. I mean, he's definitely all alpha and he would beat the crap out of somebody who tried to hurt me, but then he'd take me home and make me dinner and read me a sonnet he'd composed. He's so strong and masculine, but he plays with my hair and makes me laugh and is so smart and worldly and adores his dog and I just . . . I need him."

Something in my response saddened Shelby, and she said sympa-thetically, "Oh, sweetie."

I brushed away the few tears that had managed to escape. "I'll tell him. I will. After you've finished. When the time is right. Okay?"

"Okay. All I want is for you to be happy. You know how much I love you." She hugged me tightly, and I ignored the burning lump in my throat that urged me to cry.

"I know. Don't worry about me. I'll be fine." And I had to hope that it would be true.

~

I woke up the next morning to the sound of loud banging at the front door. Sunshine was whining outside my bedroom, apparently unhappy at there being a guest. I got up, grumbling the whole way.

When I opened the door, I was surprised to see Noah standing there. He was rocking on his heels, looking far too gleeful for this early in the morning. Okay, technically it was almost noon, but I hadn't slept well.

He grinned. "What are you doing today? We should hang out. My new dog sitter, Joe, is at my house, and he's agreed to keep an eye on Sunshine, too."

"Um, okay." My brain wasn't working yet and he was all dazzling and bright and I was sure that I looked like a coffin had just thrown me up. "What did you have in mind?"

"I was hoping maybe you could teach me how to drive."

I blinked slowly. "You don't know how to drive?"

"My parents didn't want me to drive, so I never got a license as a teenager. It wasn't my job to drive in the army and then I was living in New York and didn't need it there. But I read this script that I'm excited about. I'd be a getaway driver and they would have someone show me how to do stunt driving, but I figured I should probably learn the basics first." He seemed to think I was reluctant. I was going to do it—I was just still sleepy. "Come on, I teach you something, you teach me something."

"Kissing and driving are not the same thing. Plus, so far you haven't really taught me anything."

"Not yet." His voice was low and appealing and cut through my tiredness better than a jolt of caffeine.

"Let me get me and Sunshine ready and I'll come up to your house."

"Okay. See you soon!"

As I closed the door, I realized that I hadn't even considered the fact that he might be a morning person, and it was kind of annoying. Good thing he was superfluously handsome.

It didn't take me long to do everything I needed to, and now it was my turn to knock on his door. When he answered, he leaned down to kiss me hello on the cheek, and my heart sighed a little at the way it felt. He introduced me to Joe, and Sunshine's and Magnus's tails were both wagging as they sniffed one another. Joe promised to take good care of the dogs, and I figured if Noah trusted him, then he was probably good at what he did. I wondered how much he charged and decided I should ask him when we got back. For comparative purposes.

Deciding it would be best to get Noah out of the hills and canyons and onto a flat surface, I headed for a church I knew of nearby, figuring the parking lot would be empty. On the way he told me about how he had spent his morning talking to an army friend he liked to keep tabs on because he had been chaptered out.

"Chaptered out?" I asked.

"Basically kicked out. He tried to hurt himself."

My hand flew to my mouth. "That's awful!"

"He's doing really well now. The director of my charity helped him get a great job, and he met someone recently. And I don't know that his heart was really in what he did back then, because he tried to overdose with cough drops and vitamin supplements. I'm still not sure how he expected to nourish himself to death."

It was very cool that his charity was able to help one of his friends. Sometimes those benefits weren't always tangible, and I thought it was neat that Noah got to see some of the fruits of his labors. "I'm so glad he's doing better." I paused. "It would be inappropriate for me to laugh, right?"

"Yes, and know that I would judge you for it," he said, his tone light and teasing. "It's one of the reasons I have my charity. It makes me feel like I can keep serving even if I'm not still in the army." Then he told me more stories about his friends from his company until we got to the parking lot.

For some reason, I was hearing my mom's voice in my head, reminding me of our age difference. *Which is practically nonexistent,* I said back. But then I realized that it wasn't an age gap but an experience gap, with all the things he had seen and been through. He had done so much and accomplished so many things, and I . . . was scared of kissing and had started a dog-grooming business.

Why would he want to be with someone like you? the voice whispered at me, and this time I didn't have an answer.

I put my van in park and turned off the ignition. I got out of the car to switch places with him, and when we crossed paths in front, he stopped to give me a hug. "Just in case I get us into an accident and we don't make it," he teased.

"Don't wreck my van," I told him.

"I'll do my best."

We got back in and put on our seat belts. I told him to put his foot on the brake and turn the key to start the engine.

"Your check-engine light is on," he said, pointing at the dashboard.

"I checked it. The engine is still there."

"Funny," he said in a tone that indicated he didn't think it was funny at all. "It seems ominous."

"It's fine."

"I'm pretty sure that it's more of an order than a suggestion. I don't think cars give you a heads-up just in case you feel like investigating."

"I can't afford to take it in." There was a silence that hung there and I could feel how much he wanted to offer to pay for it, but it was my responsibility, not his.

We were just friends.

Then I went and blew my own inner declaration by asking, "Where did you go last night?"

"I had to go have drinks with this journalist, Mike something, for an interview about my upcoming release. Have I told you about that yet? It's about the life of Blackbeard. It was fun playing a pirate. Anyway, I ended up being a little bit late for it because of your mom's play."

Given Noah's loose relationship with time, I realized that his little bit late was probably quite a bit late, and I melted at the thought that he had done that for me. I'd been jealous for no reason.

Not that I was even allowed to feel envious of what he was doing or who he was with.

"Wait," he said. "What's with that tone? Are you jealous?"

"No."

"You are," he practically gloated. "You're jealous. You thought I was with another woman."

"You're allowed to date whoever you want. We're friends. It's fine."

"You don't seem fine." He was enjoying this way too much. "But you don't have to worry. You're the only person I'm sort of kissing and then making ill."

"Good." I hadn't meant that word to slip out, and I ignored his goofy grin. "Back to driving. Have you ever played *Mario Kart*?"

"No."

"That's a relief, because real driving is nothing like video games. You have to take the car out of park and put it in drive. You steer with the steering wheel and let your foot off the brake and then press slowly on the gas. Don't run into stuff and press the brake when you want to stop. That's pretty much it."

He did as I'd instructed him, inching the van forward. And he didn't accelerate. At all. While he didn't strike me as a cautious person, he was driving like he was eighty and had cataracts.

"You can go a little faster," I told him. "If you were driving any slower, we'd be going backward."

He had hunched over the steering wheel, and I could see the strain in his shoulders and his forearms. His very excellent forearms.

The van lurched forward as he gave it too much gas.

I put my hand on his thigh. "You have to do it slowly. You can't push it that hard. Ease into it. Just go slowly."

He glanced down at my hand. "That's not helping me relax."

I quickly pulled back. "Sorry."

We did more lurches and slamming stops, and I was glad that I was wearing a seat belt. Part of me wanted to tease him, but his frustration was palpable. This went on for about five minutes before he'd apparently had enough.

He swore and put the car in park. "I don't like being bad at things."

"I can't imagine it happens to you very often."

"Nope."

"Welcome to my world," I told him.

His body softened at that, finally relaxing. He reached out to caress the side of my face. "You're not bad at kissing. You're just scared. There's a difference."

Noah really was an amazing man, and I felt so lucky to be hanging out with him. I was struck with the desire to do something nice for him, to show him how much I liked him.

"We need a break," I announced. "Switch places with me."

Instead of getting out of the van, I climbed over the seats so he could move over, and then I got into the spot he'd just vacated.

I did a quick search on my phone and started following the directions. He reached for the phone, but I swatted his hand away.

"Where are you taking me?" he asked. "If you don't tell me, that's basically kidnapping."

I just smiled. "It's also called a surprise."

CHAPTER TWENTY-THREE

"Where have you brought me?" he asked when we got out of the van.

"You really were sheltered, weren't you? This is called an arcade."

He frowned briefly at me. "I know what an arcade is. I suck at driving so your first thought was, what, let's play video games?"

"Not quite." This time I reached for his hand and brought him inside. Just as I'd hoped, the two party rooms were filled with screaming kids and balloons. "You said your biggest regret was not getting to have or go to a birthday party as a kid. I found you two."

"We can't just crash some kid's party. Or two parties."

"Sure we can. You're Malec Shadowfire. They're going to be thrilled that you're here." I went into one of the rooms and waved. "Hi, everyone! Is it okay if we join you?"

At first there were a lot of confused looks from both the adults and the kids until one little blond toddler came over to him, his mouth hanging open. He stared up at Noah and then uttered a single word. "Malec."

Then all of the kids were swarming Noah, shouting questions at him, hanging on to his legs, tugging at his hands. One of the parents approached, asking if she could get a picture of him with the children. He said sure, and there were excited giggles and some very adorable pictures taken.

After dozens of photos had been shot by all the adults, I said, "You guys, I think Malec Shadowfire needs some birthday cake." One of the moms nearly broke her own neck in a rush to cut Noah a piece of cake.

I, however, did not get one.

He ate his cake with everyone staring at him, and then the apparent birthday boy said, "I want to open more presents!" That got everyone's attention and the boy, who, according to the giant poster hanging on the wall, was named Tucker, climbed into a chair to keep opening gifts. And seeing new toys held more appeal than Noah apparently, as the kids migrated over to watch him tear into wrapping paper.

All except for one little girl. She had to be about four or five, her curly brown hair in two pigtails, and she was wearing a Disney Belle dress. Her eyes were enormous and sad-looking. Noah crouched down to her eye level. "Hi."

"Why did Malec have to die?" she asked, her lower lip trembling. "He was good. He shouldn't have died."

If I'd ever had any doubt about Noah's talent, he quashed it as he shifted into Malec right in front of me. His posture, his voice, even that dangerous glint in his eye. "You're right, I did choose to be good. And I didn't go anywhere. See? I'm here."

The girl rushed forward, throwing her arms around his neck, and I swear, my ovaries exploded. The hug finished and she asked, "Do you want to play Skee-Ball with me?"

"I do." He stood back up, and she wrapped her tiny hand around one of his fingers, and my heart squeezed at the utter adorableness. I heard him ask, "Are you a princess?" as she led him out into the arcade.

There was a lightness to my whole being, a joy I couldn't remember feeling before at how happy he looked and how good it felt that I was the one who put that smile on his face. He started playing with the little girl, at one point picking her up so that she could roll the wooden ball up the ramp easier.

How had he so quickly become my favorite person in the whole world?

Then I flashed back to my conversation with Shelby last night. Was I doing this because of a guilty conscience? Trying to fit in a bunch of good memories before I told him the truth?

I was going to tell him. When the time was right. He turned around to grin at me, and I waved back. Not yet. The time wasn't now.

Then the second birthday party noticed that he was there and emptied out of their party room to come over to him at the Skee-Ball game. He did more pictures and talked to more kids, and I saw when his face shifted from a real smile to a pretend one. He was looking overwhelmed.

I gently pushed my way through the crowd and said, "Sorry, guys! We have to get going. Thanks for letting us come to your parties!"

There was a chorus of sad protests, but I'd brought Noah into this mess, and it was my job to get him back out of it.

One boy seemed particularly upset about Noah leaving—he started screaming and throwing a tantrum. His mother, trying to cajole him into behaving, said, "Maybe if you're a good boy Malec will come to your birthday party, too."

Noah's face darkened, and once we were outside I asked him, "What's wrong?"

"That mom lying to her kid. I'm not going to be at his birthday."

"She was just trying to calm him down."

He shrugged angrily. "I hate lying. My parents always lied to me my entire life to get me to do things."

My stomach went queasy and my heart beat dangerously hard as I tried to figure out what exactly he meant. "Like about Santa?"

"No. Like one more take. One more hour of rehearsal. You're almost done shooting for the day. Talk to one more reporter on the red carpet."

I didn't know what to say. What could I say? Anything that came out of my mouth would be adding to my ridiculously high amount of hypocrisy.

When we got in the van, he had shaken off his anger and seemed like himself again. "Up to the end, that was fun. I wish I'd experienced it when I was six years old. Or that it had been my actual birthday. Which is ten months from now."

I caught my breath. Did he . . . did he think we'd still be hanging out ten months from now?

My guilt was threatening to suffocate me, and I did not know what to do with that new piece of information.

I was going to tell him. I was.

"That cake wasn't enough to fill me up," he said. "I'm starving. We should go grab something to eat."

There was a pain at the back of my throat that I didn't want to identify. I was going to push these feelings out. Like I'd told Shelby, I'd been compartmentalizing things my entire life, and I was going to spend whatever time I had with Noah enjoying him and his company.

I said, "You don't want to eat here and have paper-thin-crust greasy pizza topped with a cheese by-product?"

"I was thinking something more substantial. Do you know of anywhere good to eat?"

Did I . . . "Are you ready for this conversation?"

He laughed. "I was being polite and trying to find out if you are on any kind of dietary plan. Like gluten-free, vegan, keto, paleo—"

"I'm on the eat-eo diet. That's where if I want to eat something, I do."

Another laugh. "I have the perfect place in mind. The food is incredible. Head west on this road."

I started up the van. "When you're giving me directions, you can't use words like *west*."

"Go left."

It took us about twenty minutes, but he had taken me to . . . a tiny hole in the wall called Quixote's. I'd expected a super nice, fancy place, and this was like its evil twin. We headed in, and somehow the inside was worse than the outside.

"Does the health department know about this place?" I whispered, and he nudged me with his elbow.

"It's good food and everybody here leaves me alone."

A hostess approached us. "Two?"

"Yes," Noah said, and we followed her to a table. We sat down and she left us with menus. "Their burgers are amazing."

"Doubtful."

"You're going to eat your words."

"Yeah, that may be the only thing I eat," I told him.

We silently read the menu and he asked, "Do you want to get appetizers? The oysters here are pretty good."

"Oysters are disgusting. They look like somebody already ate them. They're basically sea vomit."

"The ones here are fried."

"I'm not interested in fried ocean puke," I said.

"Well Miss Appetizer Snob, do you know what you want?"

"I'll try one of their burgers that you promised are good. And know that our entire friendship hangs in the balance, because if they're terrible, I'll never get over it."

That twinkle I loved sparkled in his eyes. "I'll take my chances." He raised his arm to gesture for our server to come over. "I'm about to order enough food to freak out the other patrons," he informed me. I was good with that.

We placed our orders, Noah making good on his threat to order an insane amount of food, and I asked for a cheeseburger and fries along with a side of ranch. The server took our menus. Noah reached across the table and took my hand, and I loved the happy blue butterflies that twirled around my heart at the expression in his eyes.

"I missed you when I was in New York," he said.

Those tiny butterfly wings flapped more intensely. "You already said that when you got back."

"I just wanted to make sure that you knew. That I thought about you the whole time while I was away. And I almost called you half a dozen times, but I didn't know if it was okay for me to do that because we're just . . ." He let his words trail off.

"Friends can call each other," I said, ignoring the warm feelings that were bubbling up inside me at his words.

"Right." An expression I didn't recognize crossed his face. "Friends can do that."

There was an awkward silence, and it had been so long since that had happened between us that I didn't know how to respond to it.

Thankfully, he spoke first. "Speaking of New York, I found this article online that said staring into each other's eyes is supposed to increase intimacy and put our brains in sync with one another."

"That sounds made up."

He made an X on his chest. "I swear it's not."

The server returned with glasses of water for both of us, and we thanked him. When he had cleared out, Noah asked, "Do you want to try it?"

"Sure."

We leaned over and began staring into each other's eyes. Even if people did normally leave him alone here, I had the feeling somebody was going to call in a padded wagon if we kept doing this. I felt silly.

Until I didn't. I was focused on his light-brown eyes, the way there was a darker-brown ring around his pupils and another one surrounding his iris. How had I never noticed that before?

He spoke, and it startled me because I was so caught up in staring at him. "I love your eyes. The way the color seems to swirl between green and brown, depending on how the light hits it."

Why did this make me uncomfortable? Him seeing me this way? I pitched forward slightly so that my hair would fall like a curtain around the sides of my face. "They're just eyeballs. Almost everybody has them."

"It's not just your eyes. Do you know how beautiful you are?" he asked, reaching up to lift my chin, and then tucked my hair behind my ears.

I accepted myself, flaws and all, and considered myself pretty average, but for him to call me beautiful? That did something to me. Some kind of exhilarating free fall was happening in my gut. Like he'd somehow infused me with some of his confidence and strength. I believed him, that he thought I was beautiful. His words shifted something inside me, and I found myself saying, "I want you to kiss me."

There was only a slight glimmer of fear, so faint I almost didn't feel it. There was more anticipation than anything else. I knew what would happen after, but I was willing to risk it.

"I was planning on it."

He wasn't understanding what I was saying. I put my hand on top of his. "No. I mean, I want *you* to kiss *me*."

I saw the moment when comprehension set in. "Now?" he asked.

"No, not now."

"In the van?"

"We can't kiss there," I said.

"Why not? A lot of kissing happens in cars. Are you worried people will see us?"

"Maybe."

"And that they'll judge you?" he asked, and it was a bit annoying how perceptive he was and how he seemed to understand things about my psyche that I hadn't even considered. "No one's going to judge you or laugh at you. If anyone does notice, they'll just be jealous that you're kissing me."

He was teasing, and it was a bit on the egotistical side, but also quite possibly true. However, I also didn't want to end up on a magazine cover with him. Because even though he thought himself safe here, I'd seen enough paparazzi photos to know that they sometimes lurked and got personal moments on film.

The server arrived then with our food, and it was enough to completely cover our table.

I picked up my burger and took a bite and couldn't help but let out a little moan of appreciation. This was amazing.

Noah asked, "So was I right or were you wrong?"

"Okay, yes to both, and I am definitely eating my words, because this is worthy of being offered as a sacrifice to the old gods. But good doesn't necessarily equate to healthy." I waved my hand at the stuff he'd ordered.

"If I'm not eating right, at least I'm eating a lot," he quipped back. "I don't see any vegetables on your plate."

I pointed at my ranch sauce.

"Ranch dressing is not a vegetable."

"I eat it with vegetables, so it's basically the same thing. Your onion rings aren't vegetables, either. I think the healthy parts are negated after you dip them in batter."

I was halfway through my cheeseburger when I realized he hadn't eaten anything and was looking around for our server.

"What are you doing? You're the one who said this place was amazing."

The server came over, and Noah said, "Can you box all of this up and bring us the check?"

"What?" I laughed.

"We have plans," he said with a wolfish grin. "I wanted you to have a chance to eat it hot, and you did, so now we can go."

I wanted to ask him if he was being serious, but it was plain that he was. The server brought over a mountain of boxes and two bags while I ate a bunch of my fries and put the rest of my burger into a box. I didn't take the fries, because they were never good once they were cold. Noah was busy shoving boxes into bags until everything was packed up.

He stood up, throwing several (American) hundred-dollar bills on the table, while I marveled at how well this server was about to get tipped. He grabbed the bags with one hand and mine with the other and said, "Let's go."

I was surprised by how excited I was to leave with him.

CHAPTER TWENTY-FOUR

Noah definitely was in a hurry. He even asked me about how committed I was to the idea of driving the speed limit. "I'm against tickets, so I'm practically married to it," I told him.

"I could pay the fine," he said and I wanted to laugh, but he was kneading the back of my neck with his long, clever fingers and his touch was turning me into a pool of jelly. We weren't going to break the law; I was going to get us into an accident.

It seemed to take forever to get back to his house, but when we arrived, everything happened very quickly. In a matter of minutes, Noah had paid Joe and sent him on his way, put the food away, and grabbed dinner for the dogs. While I stood in the kitchen and watched him. Like his touch had numbed my mind and made it so that I wasn't thinking clearly and couldn't pitch in and help.

He took off his bomber jacket and hung it up on a hook.

Then he came over and said, "Let me help you with your coat." He turned me around and slid it off slowly, and it fell to the floor. Then he pushed aside my hair with one hand and pressed his lips to the back of my neck.

It was like being held against a live electrical wire—sparks popped all along my skin. It felt incredible.

"Oh, wow" was all I could manage.

"This is pretty good for me, too." He murmured the words near my hairline and those sparks turned into currents, snaking along my nerve endings. I closed my eyes against the onslaught of sensation from him running his lips across that sensitive skin.

"I can, uh, I can see why people pay you to be the romantic lead in movies. You're very, very good at this."

I felt his smile against my neck. "You're not even getting my best stuff."

"Someday, I will." And whether that was a promise to him or to my misfunctioning brain, I didn't know.

Thinking of him in the movies prompted me to ask him something I'd been wondering about. "You said once that you could be anyone I wanted when you kissed me. What did you mean?"

"I meant that I could be, like, aggressive." One of his hands went to my hip and pulled me straight back against him, and I gasped at the contact. "Taking control. Knowing exactly what to do to push all your buttons and drive you wild."

He released me and then gently ran his fingers up my right arm. "Or I could be shy, unsure of myself, but eager. Using light, feathery touches until I figured out what you liked."

I turned around to face him. We were so close together that I could practically feel him against my skin, even though we weren't touching. I drank in his warmth, his strength. "What would you, Noah, do when you kiss me?"

He framed my face with his hands and just looked at me, and his expression . . . I couldn't have named it, but it felt soft. It caused a lump in my throat and made my limbs shaky. "I would be gentle and kind and patient for however long you needed it."

My heart skipped at his words. "I think I like that one the best."

And my breath caught in anticipation when he reached down and rubbed his nose against mine, breathing me in. The fear was there; I worried the fear would always be there. But it felt different. Manageable. It felt more like an echo than something I had to worry about.

Again, like he could read my mind, he asked, "Are you feeling afraid right now?"

"I'm not going to dignify that with a yes," I told him. "But, a little bit. Although it's not like before. This is different. Like it's changing."

"I'm glad," he said.

So was I.

"Come on," he said, moving to take my hand. "You should be sitting down for this."

I followed him but said, "Oh, should I?"

"Yes. I noticed what happened last time."

When my legs had given out on Gladys's porch? What could I say? He was right.

He led me to the couch in the library and sat us down close together. He was stroking my hair, almost like he was trying to calm me down. To reassure me that everything was fine. I was all pins and needles waiting for him to make his move and kiss me. To see how differently it would feel when he was the one to initiate, how I would react. Especially after all the positive affirmations I'd been doing. Did he know that I'd been looking forward to all of this? Maybe I should tell him.

"Can I confess something?" I asked him. "I thought about this while you were gone."

"This?" he asked, letting his fingers trail along my jawline, over my ear, down my throat. Everywhere he touched he left behind a trail of goose bumps, like they were chasing his caresses. Then, as if he couldn't stand waiting any longer, his lips replaced his hand, and all of my bones turned completely liquid. I was just a gelatinous mess, incapable of doing anything other than reveling in what he was doing.

"Uh-huh. I wanted you to touch me just like this. Kiss me like this."

I both heard and felt his groan against the underside of my jaw. "Do you know how hot that is?"

"Saying what I want?"

"Yes."

His mouth seemed to melt against my flesh, and I reached up and put my arms around his neck, pulling him closer. There was this onslaught of sensation, the feel of his lips on me, his hypnotic scent, his soft hair against my fingertips. I tried to pull him closer. He was so good at everything he did, like he was a master musician and I was his instrument.

When he reached the part of my throat where my scars were, there was no hesitation. It was no different to him than any other area of my skin. He didn't seem grossed out by it like I imagined a man would be. He didn't even seem to care, which made me blink back some unexpected hot tears. It was just another part of me that he wanted to touch and kiss, and my heart utterly melted over his actions.

Then I kept opening my eyes to look at him, to make sure I wasn't making this up. How could it feel this amazing? I tried exploring him with my touch, to follow the shape of his high cheekbones, his strong jawline, the cords in his neck, the way his shoulders flexed beneath my hands. But I kept getting distracted by what he was doing. Currently he was teasing the skin along my collarbone, and my abdomen tightened, swirling with heat and want.

He was enchanting me, using my body's reactions against me. Not against me, against my phobia. And it seemed to be working. I wanted this feeling to go on, to expand. So that when he kissed me, it would be like this, only a thousand times better.

My skin felt pinprickly and warm, overly sensitized from his lips, and he was acting like he had all the time in the world to explore and enjoy me. His kisses were so delicate and gentle and swoonworthy that I had to imagine it would be the same when he finally kissed me.

Along with this fear/anticipation/excitement mixture I had going on, I was starting to feel frustrated. I wanted more. Even if it meant I was going to have what felt like a ten-minute-long heart attack, it would be worth it.

So worth it.

"Were you planning on kissing me sometime tonight?" I asked, and my voice sounded airy and desperate.

He pulled back, and the grin he was sporting reached into my chest and wrapped itself around my heart.

"I'm working up to it."

If he worked any harder, I was going to be rendered unconscious. I didn't know how much more of his teasing I could stand. "I think you've sufficiently worked up to it."

He ran his fingers over my lips, and I trembled, closing my eyes for a second against the warmth that crashed into me.

"Juliet." The sound of his voice, rough with longing, made me open my eyes again. "Can I kiss you?"

"Yes," I responded impatiently. "And if you drag this out any longer, you're not going to get the chance to kiss me first," I warned him as he put his hands around my waist, pulling me close to him. He leaned in closer so that we were breathing the same breath.

My threat seemed to amuse him. "Because you're going to kiss me?"

I tried to say, "Yes," but he swallowed up the word by finally, finally, finally putting his soft, full lips on mine.

He pressed against me, holding himself there for a second, hesitating in the moment, like he was trying it out but ready to pull back quickly if I told him to.

I had no intention of doing that. Those blue butterflies had returned, and they were everywhere, underneath every inch of my skin. They fluttered and sent warm, shimmery shivers in waves throughout my body. This was incredible.

Then he kissed me for real, his mouth sweet and impossibly tender, almost loving, but strong and insistent.

It felt like I was drowning in him, and I wanted to let him pull me under.

I made it an entire ten seconds before my nervous system freaked out. I tried reassuring myself, saying I was fine, but I couldn't just mind over matter this thing. I wanted his kiss and hated that this was my response. Those ten seconds had been transcendent.

Because he'd been right—we both got to feel the same incredible sensations at the same time, and I loved that.

I pulled back and he immediately released me, taking his hands away and stopping all contact.

Which was not what I wanted.

So I put my arms around his neck and held him close. His breathing was labored and harsh in my ear. A second later his arms slipped around me and pulled me against his chest. When he breathed in, I felt the expansion of his chest, the way his heartbeat thundered against me.

All of this soothed me as I clung to him, letting this anxiety attack out and knowing that he'd do whatever I wanted, would support me in any way that I asked him to.

When his own breathing had calmed, he asked, "Are you okay?"

"I will be."

I will be. I repeated the words in my own head. It was going to be true. I loved kissing Noah and how it made me feel during those precious ten seconds, and I was determined to keep doing it.

So an hour later we tried again with all his teasing and showing me what he'd called earlier his "best stuff" and just how capable he was. And we tried again an hour after that. Each kiss lasted a bit longer; each anxiety attack seemed a bit shorter and less intense.

After the third round, when I was feeling exhausted from pushing so hard, he was cradling me on his lap, holding me close.

"You're really good at kissing," I told him.

"I told you so."

He had. I hugged him tighter. "You're also the only person I'd want to do this with."

He kissed my forehead. "Same."

~

I settled into a pretty awesome routine—I spent my days cleaning up dogs and taking care of Sunshine, and my nights were all spent with Noah. We kept practicing our kissing, and things kept improving. My attacks were definitely lessening in intensity and length.

And he was so good at the touching and caressing and non-mouth kissing that he got me all worked up until I couldn't think about anything but kissing him. And he made me want him and his kisses so badly.

I'd never imagined I would feel that way.

It was almost like exercising. The more we did it, the more comfortable I got, the less it seemed to take out of me.

Everything between us became more enjoyable and delicious. Like, I hadn't known there were so many different ways to kiss someone. The light, delicate butterfly kisses. The playful ones that had us both laughing. The intense, hormone-driven kisses that drove me out of my mind. The exploratory, give-and-take ones where we discovered new things that we liked. The intimate ones that seemed to make us even closer. Where it was like he could see into my soul.

The kisses where he made me feel like I was the only woman in the world who mattered to him, and I always would be.

Our homemade exposure therapy was working remarkably well. I thought maybe we should write a book.

And when the two weeks with Gladys were up, I was actually delighted when she texted me from Montana and said that she needed to keep helping her sister and asked me to stay on for another two weeks for another fifteen hundred dollars. I happily accepted. I loved being this close to Noah and Magnus.

Some nights he cooked for me. Others we watched movies. A few nights he read out loud to me, and he was like the world's best audiobook, because in addition to dramatizing the voices, he couldn't help but make faces while he was reading—a wry smile, a raised eyebrow, a frown. I loved how expressive he was.

But most of them were spent talking. We laughed and shared stories and kept getting to know one another. One of his secrets that I uncovered was that he knew about *Days of Our Lives*, a soap I used to watch with my mom and still occasionally caught up with. Noah's on-set tutor had also been a fan of the show, and we bonded over our favorite story lines.

It was also how I found out he had very strong feelings regarding his grandmother.

Noah had finished with rehearsals early one afternoon and called me up to join him for a late lunch. Like most days, my schedule was very open, and I said yes. He decided he was in the mood for some steak, and Magnus was by his feet in the kitchen, desperate for any scraps that might "accidentally" fall his way. I was cutting up some lettuce for a salad that I hoped Noah enjoyed. By himself. This was going to be our last home-cooked meal for a while, because Shelby's crew was going to demolish the kitchen tomorrow.

"But where will your cereal live?" I asked.

"In my bedroom until I have cabinets again."

Then I noticed one of those DNA testing kits on his counter.

"Are you testing out your genes? I told you already, they're good."

He smiled over his shoulder at me and then put the steaks into the oven. "My publicist sent it over. The company wanted to hire me to be their spokesperson. I said no. I'm not interested in doing genetic testing. I don't like the relatives I have now. Why would I go looking for more?"

"You mean your parents?"

He grabbed some baby spinach from the fridge and came over to the counter to join me. "No. My grandmother is the actual worst. She's racist and anti-Semitic and a host of other fun -ist and anti- things that are awful. She likes to spend holidays insulting everyone and telling us how much she has everybody and how we've all fallen short of her extremely high expectations."

I knew it was no excuse, but maybe she'd been a product of her times. "How old is she?"

"Ninety-one."

"Wow. That's pretty old."

"Yeah, well, she's in fantastic shape and sharp as a tack. I figured she made a deal with the devil at some point and he's in no hurry to have to live with her. And technically she's only twelve in evil hag years, so . . ." He finished adding the spinach and threw in some cheese. "She was a stage mother who forced my mom into the business."

"Maybe that could help you understand your own mother a little better." It made me sad that Noah didn't talk to his parents. He was such an amazing man that they were the ones who were definitely missing out. And I heard the note of loss in his voice when he talked about them. The one he tried to hide.

I told myself to stay quiet, but I did not like things that hurt him, and this did. "I know it's none of my business, but I think you should consider calling your parents. I think it would be good for you and that some part of you does miss them and does want things to be better between you. People deserve a second chance."

Instead of responding, he went to take the steaks out and let them rest. He started plating lunch while I put the salad on the table. I decided not to bring it up again unless he did. He was a grown man who could make his own decisions. We sat down to eat, and Noah changed the subject, telling me the story of the last time he took Magnus with him to a pitch meeting. And how Magnus had peed on the director's shoe— something he'd never done before.

"Is that why you get a dog sitter when you go to work?"

"Yes," he said. "I can't exactly bring him with me anymore. But to be fair to Magnus, the director was later prosecuted for sexual harassment and I'm glad we didn't work together. This also means that Magnus is obviously a good judge of character. Like how much he loves you."

"Of course he does. I give him steak," and I slipped him my last bite, which he started munching on. "Which makes me your favorite person, right, Magnus?" But Magnus just ignored me now that he had his prize.

Noah put down his fork and reached for my hand. He had this thing he did where he would lean toward me and I couldn't help but be drawn in. He would drop his chin and look up at me, and it was totally disarming.

"Juliet."

"Noah."

"Magnus isn't the only—" Whatever he'd been about to say got cut off by a knock at his front door. He furrowed his eyebrows at me and asked, "Who could that be?"

Why was he asking me? George Lucas could be at his door, for all I knew.

He went to answer the door, and it surprised me when I heard Shelby's voice.

I got up to join them, and she was standing in the doorway with Allan. She hugged Noah hello and introduced him to Allan. It was weird to remember that she had her own relationship with Noah because of her working on his house. I liked that they knew each other and were friendly. It joined the two big parts of my life together. The men were shaking hands, and she came rushing over to me, her eyes bright and happy.

We'd been in touch mostly via text where I sent her updates as to what was happening with me. Not explicitly detailed updates, but she basically knew what was going on. I wondered what she was doing at Noah's house.

"What are you guys doing here in the middle of the day?" She could have been there to work, but she had Allan with her, and that seemed odd.

"Juliet!" She hugged me and pulled back to say, "I don't mean to interrupt, but I couldn't wait one second longer and had to tell you in person. I did what you said. I got a new dream."

"What's going on? What do you mean?"

Allan came over to join her, putting his arm around her shoulders.

Shelby grinned at me. "Allan and I are going to Las Vegas to get married. Right now. And we want both of you to come with us and be our witnesses."

CHAPTER TWENTY-FIVE

Now it was my turn to shriek in happiness for her. "What? That's insane! I'm so thrilled for you guys!" I hugged both her and Allan while Noah congratulated them. "But Vegas? Why now? Why not wait until the weekend?"

Allan said, "We were talking this morning, and we decided that we wanted our forever to start now."

"We don't have to worry about anyone else being there, so there's no reason to wait," Shelby added, but I heard the way her voice faltered at the words *anyone else*. I knew that it was in part due to her mother not being here, but given that Allan was so flagrantly choosing Shelby, just like he said he would, she must have also been talking about Harmony.

I wondered if Harmony knew. And if she didn't, I would have liked to be there when she found out and her head exploded.

"Do you already have airline tickets?" Noah asked.

"Not yet," Shelby said. "We wanted to make sure you guys could come so we could all fly together."

"We could drive," I offered, but that quickly got shot down.

"I have a photo shoot tomorrow afternoon," Noah said, right as Allan added, "I have a deposition," and Shelby jumped in, "Demolition for this needy movie star I'm working with."

"And I have to feed and walk a dog," I announced, feeling a little less than.

"Let me make a call and get us a flight so that we can go on our own schedule," Noah said. It took me a second to understand what he meant, but Allan got there much faster and protested, "You don't have to do that."

But Noah had his phone out and walked away from us with Allan following at a bit of a distance, presumably to try to talk Noah out of it.

That wasn't going to happen.

"You're getting married!" I said to Shelby and hugged her again. "I can't believe it. I mean, I can, but you're going to be a married lady."

"I know this puts you in a bind, but I'm going to keep paying rent until you make other arrangements."

This hit me hard, like running straight into an accidentally closed door. Of course she would be living with Allan after she got married. But that was supposed to be two years from now, not tomorrow. "You're moving out."

Her lower lip started to tremble. "I don't want to leave you. I think that's one of the reasons I held on to the idea of a double wedding for so long—that neither one of us would be leaving the other. I don't want you to be alone."

"I can get another roommate." At her crestfallen expression, I hurried to add, "Of course she won't be you. No one could ever replace you. And I'll come visit you and you can visit me and we'll do girls' nights."

"Right."

But my promise felt a little hollow. Things were going to change completely. While I was ninety-nine percent thrilled for her that she was marrying the man she loved, that one percent twinged with sadness at the idea that we weren't going to be living together anymore.

Noah and Allan were arguing. Allan said, "You can't do this. You can't hire a private jet to fly us to Las Vegas."

"It's already done."

"I'll pay you back," Allan insisted.

"No, you won't. It's a wedding gift. I also made hotel arrangements for all of us."

Allan looked exasperated and like he didn't know what to do.

"Give it up, Allan," I called out. "You won't win."

Noah grinned at me and winked, and Shelby sighed. "I love how he looks at you. Do you even see it? How soft his gaze is every time you speak? It happens when he and I are talking about you, too."

They talked about me? Like how? I wanted to ask her, but given that we had company, I couldn't really dive into it. So I settled on, "I don't know what you're trying to say here."

"He's about to fly us on a private jet to Las Vegas, which I personally have always dreamed about doing, and he's made hotel and car arrangements. And no matter how good I am at interior design, this is not for me. This is all for you. Because I'm your best friend and he wants to make you happy."

"No," I protested. "He's a really generous person. We—"

"I swear on all that is holy, if you say that you are only friends, I will hurt you. This is my wedding day. You have to humor me. And I say you may not know it yet, but that boy is falling for you."

My throat suddenly felt too tight, and my head went a little woozy. That couldn't be true. I was about to say as much, but Shelby continued, "I am also officially asking you to be my maid of honor. I stopped by our favorite rental shop and picked up a white dress for me and a purple one for you."

"I've been waiting my whole life to be your maid of honor." We hugged again. Allan came back, wanting to talk to Shelby—probably to tell her this was all too much—but Noah seemed determined, and Shelby was even more determined to get her way and seemed enthusiastic about the luxury setup.

I made my way over to Noah and pulled him aside.

"You don't have to do all this," I told him.

"I want to. And technically, I'm not doing it. My new assistant is."

"You hired another assistant?" His last one had moved to Florida, and I knew he'd been looking to replace her. "When?"

"A few days ago. Reina helped pick him out. His name is Kyle. He's very good. I needed one."

"For things like last-minute Vegas weddings?" I asked, shaking my head. I was pretty sure this didn't fall under poor Kyle's job description.

"Exactly. I did try to tell you about hiring him, but then you did that thing to my earlobe that makes me lose track of space and time and so I forgot."

I blushed at his words and hoped that Allan and Shelby hadn't overheard.

Noah cleared his throat and announced to everyone, "The plane will be ready to go in about three hours, which gives us time to pack up and head out to the private airport. Let's meet back here and I'll have a car ready to take us over."

Both Allan and Shelby thanked him profusely, but Noah just waved it away. They left, promising to rejoin us soon, and when the door closed, I hugged Noah. "Thank you. This means a lot."

"You're welcome."

I breathed him in. "Chartering a private plane is expensive."

"It's not that much to go to Vegas. Only a few thousand."

I let out a short laugh. "Oh. Silly me. Just a few thousand."

This made him pull back to look down at me with an amused smile. "I do have a lot of money."

"Like, my brain knows that, but I forget because of how you live. You could be in a mansion with servants, and instead you're in this hovel."

"Soon-to-be completely renovated hovel," he reminded me. "And I don't know. I don't need more house than this."

I so liked that he was practical, because that's exactly how I was, too.

"And," he continued on, "I think you should spend money where it matters."

There was that reminder again at how completely different our worlds were. That he had money to spend on the things he deemed important. "Does it bother you that I'm a dog groomer?"

His face became perplexed. "Why would it bother me?"

"It's not some glamorous job."

He paused for a beat. "When it comes to your job, what do you feel like you were put on this earth to do?"

"Take care of animals," I answered quickly. There was no question of that.

"And for me, it's acting. It's in my blood. It's what I'm meant to do. So I admire you for doing what you love and having the guts to go after it."

"I admire you for the same reason."

"As well you should," he said and kissed me gently on the nose. "Joe is on his way. Go get packed and bring Sunshine back with you."

Some part of me probably should have felt bad that Joe had watched Sunshine on more than one occasion, but there was no way I was going to miss Shelby's wedding.

Everything happened in a big flurry of excitement and activity after that—we rode in a black SUV to the airport and got on our private plane, where we were treated like royalty. Also, the flight attendant was definitely making eyes at Noah, and I found it infuriating. Another SUV was waiting for us on the tarmac at the small airport in Las Vegas, and Allan opened a bottle of champagne for us. We toasted their marriage, and I realized how glad I was that Noah was with me for this moment. Not because he was financing the entire thing, but because I wanted to share it with him.

We checked into the Waldorf Astoria, where Kyle had reserved three rooms for us. We went up to the twenty-second floor, and I realized that they weren't actually rooms but massive suites. Ridiculous-size suites. What was I supposed to do with two bedrooms and a dining room and my own kitchen? I was about to call Shelby when I got a text from her.

> My room has a massive bathtub that overlooks the entire city!!! OMG THIS IS SO AMAZING, YOUR BOYFRIEND IS THE BEST!!! I can say that because my boyfriend's about to be my husband and I will have THE BEST HUSBAND!

I laughed and texted her back, asking if she needed help getting ready. She said she was good and told me to come over when I was done, as Allan was getting ready in Noah's suite so that they technically wouldn't see each other right before the wedding. And we were going to take two cars to ensure it. I thought that was sweet.

Her room was at the opposite end of the hallway, and when I knocked on her door and she opened it, I gasped. She looked stunning in her strapless ivory dress with a huge poufy princess skirt. "You're so beautiful!"

"So are you!" she said and hugged me. "But no crying. I'm not putting my makeup on again."

"No crying," I agreed, even though my eyes were a little shimmery. "Are you nervous?"

"I know I should be," she said as she led me into her massive living room. This suite was even nicer than mine. It was decorated in off-white leather, black marble, and dark wood, with red accent carpets. "And maybe I am a little nervous. But this just feels right. I'm doing what I'm supposed to be doing, and that's a fantastic feeling."

"I'm so glad. You deserve all of this and more." I looked out at the Vegas Strip, where lights of different colors danced and twinkled through her windows. "I can't believe you convinced Allan to say yes to all this."

"I know he loves the way I nag him and talk him into things. He's never actually said as much, but I can read his nonverbal subtext."

That made me laugh, and I asked her, "Is there anything I can do for you right now?"

"Distract me. Tell me about how things are going with Noah. For real. Not the friend thing you keep telling yourself."

She wanted me to be honest. Maybe that was something I should be doing with everyone. "We've never talked about us being in a relationship. We're both really clear that this is just friends."

"Trust me, he does not want to be just your friend."

"No interrupting," I told her. "I'm trying to open up here. Anyway, I don't know what he wants or if he's happy for things to keep being how they have been. But he makes me feel . . ." What was the best way to put it into words? "He makes me feel like a little piece of metal slowly making its way toward the overpowering magnet in the center of the room."

"Like resistance is feudal."

"Feudal?" I said with a laugh. "I think you mean futile. Although a feudal resistance would be pretty cool. Lots of swords and pitchforks."

"I know the right word. Maybe I'm more nervous than I thought," she said, putting her hand over her stomach. Her phone beeped, and she looked at it. "The boys already left and our car is here, down in the lobby."

"Noah really thought of everything, didn't he?"

"So did Allan. Look at this." She pointed at the small table in front of us, and I saw a bouquet of daisies. Her favorite.

"So sweet," I said, handing the flowers to her. "So if that's everything, we should get going."

"Wait!" She stood up. "That's not everything. I need that bridal poem thing. Something old, something new, something borrowed, and something blue."

"Okay. Your dress is borrowed. And I'm your oldest friend, so I can be your something old."

She smiled. "Right. And my earrings are new—Allan gave them to me as a wedding gift."

I reached up to the clasp of my necklace. "And here's your something blue." I put it around her neck. "You're ready. Let's go get you a husband."

CHAPTER TWENTY-SIX

While part of me had expected the ceremony to be cheesy, it was surprisingly perfect. There were no Elvis or Michael Jackson impersonators officiating. Just a nice older gentleman whose wife was playing the organ. Shelby got her walk-down-the-aisle moment, and the way Allan's eyes lit up at seeing her—it made me feel better knowing how well she'd be loved and cared for.

Then I saw Noah, and even though I'd seen him in a tux twice before, him in his suit still hit me like a frying pan to the head. He was so handsome that I had to remind myself to stop stealing peeks at him and pay attention to the wedding.

But during the ceremony, while they were promising to love and honor one another, I couldn't help but glance over at Noah again. Who was looking directly at me with the expression Shelby had described— there was so much softness and tenderness in his eyes that it made my heart stutter, and I had to look away.

Because I could see this. I could see having this. With him.

Which was obviously insane.

Once they were declared husband and wife and they kissed, we cheered for them along with the officiant and his wife. Then everybody had to sign their marriage certificate, and some part of me liked the permanency of both me and Noah being their witnesses. No matter what else happened, we'd at least always be linked in that way.

"We're off!" Shelby said. She hugged me. Then she hugged Noah and thanked him again for everything, as did Allan.

They ran out, and we followed behind. Shelby stopped in the doorway to turn and give me her bouquet. "There's no one else to catch it," she told me with a wink before linking her arm through her husband's as they headed out to the waiting SUV.

And I felt . . . at a loss. I don't know what I thought was going to happen after the wedding, and I should have fully expected Shelby and Allan to ditch us, but it was still strange.

Noah seemed to sense this, and he put his arm around my shoulders to lead me over to the other car. When we got in, he asked, "What would you like to do? It's too late to see a show, but we could walk around the Strip or maybe try gambling."

"I don't gamble. Accounting major, remember? I don't play games when I know I won't win."

"Huh."

"What was that sound for?"

"Nothing. Just an interesting piece of insight." He unbuttoned his suit jacket and leaned back against the seat. "I have something in mind. A surprise, if you're up for it."

"Is this where I accuse you of kidnapping me?"

He grinned and leaned forward to press a kiss against my throat, in that hollow near my ear that I loved so much. It both turned my knees to melted butter and caught me off guard. This wasn't technically in public, but it was the first time he'd kissed me anywhere besides his house.

Then I saw his eyes, the way they danced, and realized he was teasing me. He'd wanted to see what would happen if he did exactly what he just did.

"Two can play that game," I told him.

"As they can most games," he responded, ignoring my challenge. So I did the thing he'd mentioned earlier to the bottom of his ear, and he lost his smugness pretty quickly.

When we got back to our rooms, our faces flushed and our hair more than a little messy, he handed me a key to his room and told me to meet him there after I got changed. He kissed me quickly again, and I went inside to take off this infernal gown that was starting to constrict my lungs. I wondered what his surprise was and found myself rushing to see him again, leaving the dress in a purple pool on the floor and slipping on some yoga pants and a soft T-shirt. I used the bathroom quickly and brushed my teeth. Just in case.

It felt a little strange to let myself in his room, so after I did I called out, "Noah?"

"In here." That was a sign of how massive these suites were: I had to go looking for him. He was by the bar, having a drink. He hadn't yet changed; his jacket was off, his tie was loose, and the top three buttons of his shirt were undone.

How did this make him even sexier?

His expression softened again when I came around the corner, and I saw the way his whole body seemed to relax at catching sight of me. "Hey, you."

That made my heart flutter. "Hi."

"That was fast," he commented.

What could I say? *I missed you for the five minutes we were apart and wanted to see you again, so I hurried?* "You said there was a surprise. I like surprises."

"Do you want a drink?"

"No, thanks." I hoped that wasn't the surprise; I had alcohol in my suite, too. In fact, I was pretty sure I had everything in my suite. This hotel was not kidding around when it came to comfort.

"Do you like your room?" he asked.

"You mean the mini-mansion you put me in? Yeah, I guess it's okay. I mean, I don't know if you were trying to impress me, but if you were, mission a hundred percent accomplished."

He smiled. "Let me go get changed, too. I'll be right back." I watched him walk into the open doorway of his room and had a moment where I saw him take off his shirt, revealing the muscles flexing in his broad back before he walked out of view.

I let out a sigh of disappointment and wandered over to the window. His suite appeared to be the same as mine, but given that I didn't have a bathtub that would let me flash all of Vegas, it seemed as if he'd made sure Allan and Shelby had a nicer room than we had. Given that they only had one night for their honeymoon, it was so thoughtful of him to give them the best.

Everything he did was thoughtful.

Maybe Shelby was wrong. Noah might not have been falling for me, but it felt like I had fallen for him. No matter how hard I fought it or how much I wanted to keep the kissing thing separate from our friendship, it hadn't worked. I cared about him so much. I'd never been in love with a man before, so I didn't know if this was what it felt like, but it had to be close.

Should I tell him? But what would I say? I didn't even know.

I drew in a shaky breath. Before I'd figured anything out, he was back in a black T-shirt and fuzzy-looking plaid pajama pants and his bare feet. He went into the kitchen and came back out carrying a cake. "Ta-da!" he said as he set it down on the dining room table.

The cake was blue and white, and was I mistaken or was that a Star of David on it? I came closer. It said MAZEL TOV.

"Is it my bat mitzvah?"

"No. After a wedding you're supposed to have a reception. Which has a cake."

"A wedding cake."

"Kyle called a local bakery and they only had one that resembled a wedding cake, and we sent that over to Allan and Shelby's suite, along with a bottle of champagne. You and I get this one."

"You are the cutest," I told him, again so touched that he was being nice to my friend.

"I might be," he agreed. He took out his phone and turned on some slow music. "We have cake, and now we're supposed to dance. That's the other thing that happens at receptions." He started walking around the table toward me.

"Um, no. I wasn't kidding about the not dancing thing."

"You weren't kidding about the no kissing thing, either, and yet here we are."

He took me into his arms, settling my arms around his neck while he pulled me close, slipping his hands onto my waist. I loved being pressed up against him, and so I didn't resist.

Which he'd probably expected.

"We just have to move slowly, together." He murmured the words against my ear and sent little heated shivers down my neck. "Do it for thirty seconds. If you hate it, I'll stop."

He was slowly running his hands up and down my back, making sure I wouldn't hate it. As the song progressed, he moved his hands back to my waist and shifted his fingers under the hem of my T-shirt. I loved the feeling of his fingertips against my skin, the way he left mini-fires burning everywhere he touched me. I sighed against him, easing into that mindless pleasure he was good at invoking.

"Was this your plan for the rest of tonight?" I asked when he kissed my cheek, wondering if things were about to turn into the kissing portion of our night.

"It wouldn't be the worst way to spend the evening." He wasn't wrong.

"It is late," I reminded him. "And we've all got work tomorrow. Some more than others."

He stopped swaying but didn't let me go. His fingers pressed against my back, slightly digging into the skin there. "Don't go back to your room. Stay with me."

That made my pulse skip and my legs feel a little weak. Was he asking what it sounded like he was asking? "What?"

"I hate when you go. It's the worst part of my day."

I pushed against his shoulders and backed up so that he wouldn't keep wooing me with his masculine wiles. I crossed my arms. "That doesn't sound very friendish."

"You sleep in the same place as Shelby and she's your friend."

"Not in the same bed."

"We don't have to sleep in the same bed. I'll sleep on the floor," he said as he approached me cautiously, reaching out for my hands and kissing the backs of them gently.

"There's another bedroom. And several couches," I said as I willed myself not to respond to his soft, firm mouth on my heated skin.

"That would miss the point. I want to be with you. I don't want tonight to end."

I still hesitated. We'd been doing some pretty serious making out over the last few weeks, and my anxiety attacks had practically become a thing of the past. In this moment, though, it felt like one might return. I didn't think I was ready for things to move to the next level.

"There are no expectations here. Nothing's going to happen unless you want it to happen," he promised. "But then I'll have to think about whether or not I'm up for it."

That made me laugh and broke some of the tension I was feeling. Thing was, I didn't want to go, either. Leaving him every night was easily the worst part of my day, too.

"Plus," he added, "we can eat cake for breakfast."

"You had me at cake," I said, smiling shyly at him, my mind made up.

He grinned and stepped back, pulling me toward him as he walked backward to his room. When we walked in, he let go of my hands to walk around and turn off the lights, leaving on a single lamp on the nightstand. He grabbed a blanket and a couple of pillows from the bed and made himself a makeshift bed on the floor.

I'd thought he was kidding about the sleeping on the floor thing, but apparently he wasn't. "That can't be comfortable."

"Ever sleep in a cot? This is about the same," he said.

He came over and pulled me in close. "I'm going to kiss you now."

"I know," I said and let him make all the rest of my anxiety disappear.

When things started to get heated, he stopped the kiss, shaking his head ruefully. He stepped back and lay down on the floor.

I climbed into the very soft and very comfortable bed and immediately felt guilty. He was paying so much money for me and my best friend and her new husband to sleep in these amazing rooms, and he was going to sleep on the floor. He was willing to forsake his own comfort just to be close to me.

It says something about how he feels about you, an inner voice whispered, and I didn't know whether to trust it. I'd spent so much time ignoring the voices in my head that discouraged and disheartened me that I wasn't sure what to do with one that told me there might be something more here.

I pulled the leftover blanket up over my shoulders and tugged at the corners. I hated when they were all tucked in. I needed my feet to hang out. I turned onto my side to face him and felt my phone in my pocket. I took it out and placed it on the bed next to me. Then I reached over and turned out the last lamp.

"Try not to snore too loudly," he teased as the darkness descended, and I threw one of the pillows at him, which he easily caught while laughing.

He put the pillow under his head and said, "Good night, Juliet."

"Good night, Noah."

"I'm glad you stayed."

"Me too."

I watched him, the way his chest expanded in and out, how his breathing started to slow, and I wanted to reach out and touch him. To have his warmth envelop me and spend the night in his arms.

I realized that I needed more than to just be in the same room with him. I had to see if that voice of mine was right.

"Noah."

"Hmm?" He sounded like he was on the edge of sleep.

"Come here."

I scooted over, pushing back the blanket. He turned his head toward me. "Are you sure?"

"Just to sleep," I said. "You shouldn't be on the floor."

"Is that the only reason?"

I hesitated and felt the weight of the word I was about to say. "No."

He got up, leaving his bedding behind. He paused next to the bed, staring down at me. He put his hand over his chest, and I didn't recognize the emotion on his face, but he almost looked . . . pained. Maybe even a little overwhelmed. But his expression was gone before I could understand it. Then I felt the mattress sink under his weight as he climbed into bed next to me and the covers being lifted up as he pulled them over his body.

"Turn over," he said in a voice that sounded rough with feeling, and I did, my heart pulsating in my throat. He pulled me against him and put one of his arms under my head, the other around my waist. His legs curved into mine. I put my arm on top of his, holding him the only way I could as he spooned me. His warmth surrounded me, and I sighed happily. We fit so well together.

He reached down and gently kissed my shoulder once before laying his head against the pillows.

His breath was warm against my neck, and I felt the tension leave his body as he drifted off to sleep. But he didn't let go of me. Not even once sleep overtook him.

I smiled. I wasn't the only person in this room who snored.

My eyelids started to feel heavy—cuddling like this with him was making me feel utterly relaxed. It was almost funny: a month ago the idea of this would have terrified me.

But now? This was where I always wanted to be.

CHAPTER TWENTY-SEVEN

The next morning I woke up to the sound of my phone buzzing repeatedly. I was facing Noah, our legs intertwined and our arms wrapped around each other. I carefully extricated myself as much as possible and then turned over to find my phone, which was only a few inches from my head. I turned it on, glancing at the battery indicator. It was almost dead, since I hadn't charged it last night.

Then I looked at my messages. They were all from Shelby.

Hi! You up yet?

Where are you?

I'm knocking on your door.

> Why aren't you answering?

> Wake up. I brought you leftover cake. Your boyfriend got us a wedding cake. Can you believe it?

> Get out of bed.

> Hello????

I texted her back as quickly as I could, although my eyes weren't exactly cooperating. I felt like Noah had drugged me with his expert sleep-holding skills.

> I'm not there. I'm not in my room.

Her response was instant.

> What do you mean you're not in your room? Why not? Where are you?

Then:

OMG ARE YOU WITH NOAH DOUGLAS RIGHT NOW???

Bow, chicka, wow-wow.

There was no bowing, chickaing or wowing. Get your mind out of the gutter.

Too late! My mind is actually past the gutter, down the storm drain and hitching a ride to the sewers.

I smiled and texted:

Ha ha. Go back to your husband.

We have to leave soon. Better wake up your lover.

I grimaced. I don't know why, but I'd always hated that word. *Lover*. It was like the word *moist* in my book.

I turned toward Noah and pushed back his hair from his face. He looked so boyishly handsome while he was sleeping, all the worries of the world wiped away. His lashes were thick and dark against his cheeks.

"We have to get up," I told him as I kissed his forehead. "Shelby's looking for me, and we're supposed to head back to LA."

His arms tightened around me and he mumbled, "I'm very happy where I am."

"So am I, but we do have to go."

He released me and turned onto his back. I propped myself up on one elbow to look at him. He yawned and then stretched, his shirt hiking up. I very much enjoyed that particular view.

"I was going to call room service this morning," he said, "but I didn't wake up when I expected to. You're like a real-life Ambien."

"Are you saying I'm boring?"

He cracked open his eyes to squint at me. "No, that you knocked me out. I haven't slept that well in a long time."

"Me neither," I confessed. I leaned down and kissed his neck. "It's going to be weird to go back to our real lives."

"Things don't have to change from how they are now."

Things didn't have to change? What things? Us sharing a bed from now on? Did that mean what I thought it meant? Should I be concerned here?

I hated that I was so inexperienced with relationships and didn't know how to interpret the things he said.

Or was that a reference to our friendship? That despite what Shelby thought and what I was maybe sort of in some small way hoping for, this was never going beyond the parameters I'd set up in the beginning?

Shouldn't that make me happy, that he only wanted to be friends? It didn't.

Plus, there was still that small matter of telling him that I'd lied to him the first night we'd met. I'd been planning on telling him when Shelby was done with his house, but maybe this trip was proof that my hypothesis was mistaken. He must have cared about Shelby if he was willing to do all this for her. Maybe he wouldn't fire her. Maybe he would even forgive me quickly and we'd move on.

Then I remembered how much he hated lying and realized a snowball in Arizona had a greater chance than I did of coming out of this unscathed.

Before I could ask him to clarify, he kissed me quickly and left to go use the bathroom. Confused by what was going on and feeling a little freaked out, I retreated to my own room to pack up my things and get ready. Which mostly consisted of me throwing things into my suitcase while trying not to panic. I got everything in my bag and put it by the front door. Then I wandered around to make sure that I hadn't left anything behind.

I had to tell him. I had to. I couldn't let things get more serious without him knowing the truth.

That sent a spike of pain through me so intense that it literally felt like I'd been stabbed. I doubled over, grabbing on to the back of the couch to keep from falling.

You're going to lose him.

That was what I feared most. Him being out of my life. Never having another morning like the one I'd experienced today.

There was a knock at the door, and I took in a deep breath, practicing the exercises that Noah and I had worked on, and made my way over to open it. It was both Shelby and Allan, and I could tell that she wanted to question me but didn't because she knew I wouldn't say much with Allan standing there.

"Are you ready?" she asked, her eyes bright with unasked questions. "The concierge called and said the car was ready."

"Yep." I grabbed my suitcase and walked out into the hallway.

Noah stepped out of his room with his bag at the same time, and I didn't know what to say. But he, either missing my awkwardness or deciding to ignore it, came over to take me by the hand, which was a relief.

Outside the hotel there was a bit of a traffic jam, and one of the valets apologized and said our car would be up front in a minute.

But a minute was all it took.

I heard murmuring and noticed people taking out their phones. Their voices became louder. "Isn't that the guy who plays Malec Shadowfire?" "It's Noah Douglas!" "Hey, can I get a picture with you?"

Then there were bright flashes. It wasn't just hotel guests. There were paparazzi, and they started crowding in on us. Just a tsunami of strangers coming straight at us. Somebody must have tipped them off that Noah was here and would be leaving this morning. They were shouting questions at him, some of them about me.

"Get behind me," Noah said, stepping in front of me, shielding me.

He turned to the paparazzi and barked a single word: "Back!" He was so furious sounding and so intimidating that they did exactly as he commanded them. That didn't stop them from taking photos or all the other people from shooting videos.

The valets sprang into action and assisted in keeping the crowd at bay and helped us to get over to our waiting SUV.

Once we were safely inside, Shelby let out a loud breath. "That was insane! I thought they were going to crush us."

But Noah only had eyes for me. "Reina's right. It's time for me to get a bodyguard. The idea that someone might have hurt you . . ." His voice trailed off, and he kissed me as if to reassure himself that I was okay.

Meanwhile, he was the one I was worried about. We'd been happy in our little bubble for so long, behaving like normal people, that I'd forgotten myself. I'd forgotten who he was and how those pictures were probably going to end up on the ENZ website and in my favorite magazines with everybody wondering who I was.

But the thing that concerned me most was how he could have gotten hurt. I'd already seen a fan physically attack him in the name of adoration—what if the next one had a knife? Or a gun? "I definitely think you should look into getting more security," I said.

Shelby added, "We can get somebody out to your house to install a state-of-the-art home system, too."

As we drove to the airport, Noah's arm around me and holding me tightly against him, I wondered if I could always live like this. Zoe Covington was doing it, but even she'd admitted it was hard.

I squeezed his hand. I could do it for him. I could find a way to cope with all of this craziness, if that's what it took.

Problem was, I didn't think I was going to get that chance. Not once I told him everything.

~

So I did what I'd been doing—I didn't say anything. It was so much easier to pretend I didn't have this secret looming over our heads and to just continue life like normal. Gladys came back and paid me the rest of my fee, and I realized that I was going to really miss Sunshine. I asked if I could come by and visit sometime, and she replied by shutting the door in my face.

I was also going to miss being so close to Noah. But me moving back to my now-empty apartment didn't change much. Either I went to his place or he came to see me every night. Then about a week after Las Vegas, he asked me if I had plans.

"Depends. There's this movie star I hang out with, and he might want to do something."

"Forget that guy," he said. "There's this film festival I have to go to. I'm getting an award for Best Actor for *The Last Goodbye*. You should come hang out with me instead."

"I could do that."

"There's going to be press. And fans," he warned me.

"I've already been through all that with you before. I can handle it. You don't have to worry about me. I'd enjoy seeing you win an award."

He told me it was casual; he was going to wear just jeans and a T-shirt. I got a little more dressed up by putting on one of my nicer button-up shirts and my fanciest pair of jeans. The ones I only broke out for special occasions. Just in case I was photographed again.

The night of the festival, he came to pick me up, and when we arrived at the event, the car had to go through several checkpoints, as the streets had been closed down, just like they'd been at the Oscars.

He explained, "This film festival is tied into a street carnival that the city throws. Traffic will be insane afterward, so I rented a hotel room across the street so we can wait it out."

I could see for myself why such a thing would be necessary. There were people everywhere; the car was moving along at a snail's pace.

We finally made it to the theater where the awards were being given out. I saw a glimpse of his costar, Rubie Jorgenson, talking to a reporter. Reina and Morgan met us at the car. Reina was going to take Noah around to the fans and journalists, and Morgan was there to babysit me again and do whatever Reina needed.

Noah kissed me, promising to see me soon, and I could tell the exact moment when everybody realized that he was the one getting out of the SUV because of the explosion of lights and people screaming his name.

Once Rubie and Noah had both gone inside, Morgan had me get out of the car, probably under the assumption that nobody would care about me once the stars had left. She gave me a badge to wear and told me to guard it with my life, because it provided me with all access to the venue.

She took me backstage, and I really enjoyed listening to Noah talk about his role in the movie. He was witty and self-deprecating and intelligent and all-around delightful in his responses. Someone from the crowd yelled out, "Malec Shadowfire lives!" and he responded by laughing and saying he loved Malec and missed playing him.

After he finished, they brought out Rubie, and she was equally charming and also had the audience eating out of the palm of her hand. They were both skilled performers, on-screen and off.

I watched as the president of the film festival presented them with their awards and they said a few words from the podium, thanking their professional teams, the cast and crew of the movie, the festival board members, and the fans for their support.

Morgan turned toward me. "Noah might take a little while to catch up with you. He's still got some press to do and festival board members to thank personally. I can take you across the street to his room to wait for him."

"Okay."

There were so many people gathered on the streets, and I could smell funnel cake and hear the screams of people on rides. The carnival sounded fun, and I wanted to take Noah and check it out.

But then I realized I wouldn't be able to do that. He had this room because he couldn't mingle with everyone else and had to wait for the roads to clear up. That made me sad for him.

It made me sad for us.

At the hotel, Morgan gave me a key and told me the room number. That was another thing that I had forgotten about when it came to Noah—how often his life was handled and overseen by other people. It made the fact that he'd taken off for Vegas even more amazing.

The room was much plainer than the suites we'd stayed in. More like a regular hotel room, but with a big sitting area. I noticed a small blue-and-white cake on the table that again had the words *Mazel tov* written on it. I giggled, took a picture of it, and sent it to him with a question mark.

> I got another one because we never got the chance to eat it in Vegas.

I'd been right in my assessment. He was absolutely the cutest. Even though either he or Kyle had forgotten about things like plates and forks. So I stole a very tiny (okay, not so tiny) chunk off the back, licking the frosting off my fingers.

Deciding that I probably shouldn't eat any more until he joined me, I sat on the sofa and pulled out my phone. I played a couple of games to distract myself but then ended up doing something I'd told myself I wouldn't—I googled Noah.

The most recent images were of him and me together. The one from Vegas was in such high definition that you could see all the flaws he didn't have. There were also some from the kids' birthday parties. The blogs were speculating about who I was and if I was dating Noah. I didn't even bother looking at the comments, because I knew there wouldn't be anything I wanted to see there.

It felt strange, almost surreal. He was this public person that the whole world knew and loved, but he was just Noah to me. Yes, he was an actor and had these roles, and while my brain understood that he was famous and had been before we'd ever even met, none of that mattered to me.

I looked at his picture from Las Vegas, the defiant look in his eyes, his firm lips, his strong hands, his broad shoulders, and couldn't believe that I got to touch him, got to kiss him.

That I wanted to keep doing those things indefinitely.

About half an hour later, the door swung open, startling me. I'd been lost in thought, pondering my relationship with Noah and what I should do. I hadn't arrived at any definitive solutions, but it struck me all over again how incredibly sexy he was when he grinned at me. "Sorry for taking so long."

"It's okay." And it was. I was willing to wait for him.

Just like he'd been willing to wait for me.

He put his award down on the table and came over to me. His phone buzzed, and he checked it. "It's from Ray. Traffic has lightened up enough that we could go. But one of the tires is completely flat and apparently there's no spare. He has to wait for a tow truck, so we might be stuck here for a while. Any ideas on what we should do?"

"Some," I said, standing up to meet him. My mouth had gone dry and my heart was beating hard in my chest as I thought about what I wanted to do. "I've been thinking about you teaching me and was wondering if maybe we could expand our lessons a little bit."

Another grin from him. "I like where this is headed. Proceed."

"I know how to kiss a guy now and how to not freak out after."

"I've definitely taught you well," he agreed.

"I love how humble you are about it and I hate to encourage you, but yes. So now, oh great and wise one, what would I do if I wanted things to go a little bit further? Not all the way, but maybe next level?"

Before he could respond, an earthquake rumbled through, briefly shaking the room around us. I put my hands against his chest, feeling like I might have another anxiety attack. "I hate earthquakes," I muttered. I'd grown up in Southern California. I should have been used to them, but I'd never gotten to that point.

"It was just a little one," he said. "It's okay."

"I'm someone who relies on the ground beneath my feet. I need that. Something that's rock solid."

"I'm solid." He put his hands over mine on his chest. "Rock solid."

He was. Not just physically, but emotionally, too. He'd always been someone I could rely on and trust.

Do the same thing for him. Tell him the truth. Show him he can trust you, that annoying voice said.

Okay. I was going to tell him. I tried ignoring the drumline that had set up residence in my heart and forced my mouth open to speak.

Then he took a step back and sat on the bed. He reached behind his head and yanked off his shirt in one clean motion.

All my reason and rational thought fled.

CHAPTER TWENTY-EIGHT

"Oh my" was all my brain could come up with to say. He was magnificent. Perfectly sculpted, only the medium was flesh instead of stone. My eyes traveled from his well-formed shoulders to his ripped stomach. My fingers itched to touch him, all those symmetrical ridges and planes.

I wondered whether I should send my handwritten thank-you notes for all his gloriousness to his parents, his personal trainer, the United States Army, or the Academy of Motion Picture Arts and Sciences.

"Is this okay?" he asked.

Okay? I was going to throw him a ticker-tape parade. "Is it all right for me to touch you?"

"Please." The way he said the word, with so much longing in his voice, the way he broke on that word with an emotion I couldn't quite identify. "That's entirely the reason I took it off. Since removing clothing indicates things moving to the next level."

"That makes perfect sense," I said, marveling at my ability to keep forming words.

"You know how much I enjoy being logical."

"I feel like you're using your Noah Douglas–ness against me. All your charm and strength and hotness."

"Is it working?" he queried.

"Little bit. It feels like you're not playing fair."

"I'm not trying to play fair," he said in a voice that made me utterly breathless, my pulse careening out of control.

So I did the only thing I could think to do. I sank down slowly next to him on the bed and reached out to feel his chest muscles. When my hand made contact with his skin, he made a strangled sound and then immediately looked embarrassed. "Sorry. For some reason that surprised me, even though I was anticipating it. It's been a long time."

"Longer than twenty-four years? Because that's how long it's been for me."

"No, not that long. But it feels like I've been waiting an entire lifetime for you to touch me like this."

That sent my blood pulsating in my ears, but I kept touching him, dragging my fingers across his skin. I watched the way his muscles responded to me with tiny twitches. He was both strong and soft at the same time, and I found the juxtaposition infinitely fascinating.

"I think I've created a monster," he said, his wry voice low and delicious.

"Is that a bad thing?"

"It's an excellent thing."

I moved up to his shoulders, which were sprinkled with moles and freckles. I found myself playing a very adult game of connect-the-dots with them. Then I leaned forward to kiss his corded muscles that contracted under my lips. I outlined the shape of his rock-hard biceps with my hands, trailing down to his forearms.

"You're being very thorough," he said.

"I have a lot to explore." I crawled behind him, ready to investigate his back next, to see what I'd only glimpsed in Las Vegas. But he didn't seem to have the same amount of patience that he normally did.

"Kissing you. Now," he demanded as he turned to face me, and I was only too happy to let him. There was that faint echo of fear before his mouth was on mine, colliding into me like a massive wave crashing onto a beach, but there was no hesitation from either one of us. No gentleness or tenderness, either. He was like a roaring fire that I could only barely contain, barely resist. He was going to consume me.

And instead of that scaring me, I wholeheartedly embraced it, the way his mouth was ravaging mine, how he pulled me against him so tightly. We'd really hit the ground running, full throttle. This was more than a kiss. It was like he was going to devour me, and it was utterly intoxicating.

He broke off midkiss, his breathing heavy. "Sorry, sorry if it's too much," he said, like he'd only barely remembered himself and was trying to get back under control.

Problem was, I wanted him this way. I knew he typically held back, kept himself in check, to make sure I was all right. But here and now . . . he didn't have to worry. I was on board for this ride. There was an undeniable thrill that I could render him this mindless and needy. "No. I like it."

Twin brown flames burned in his eyes. "Tell me when you want me to stop."

Never was what I was going to say, but his mouth was back on mine again, insistent and strong, parting my sensitized lips, sending lines of fire down my nerves. My abdomen tightened, filling with heat and want. The attraction I felt for him was so . . . chemical. Intense, overwhelming.

"You taste like sugar," he murmured against my lips, and I wanted to tell him that he tasted like heaven, but he was kissing me again. He was also laying me back against the bed, moving to hover over me.

He hesitated again, and I was the one who made the decision. I reached up to his shoulders and pulled him against me, and sighed with sheer pleasure at his massive frame being pressed against mine, the way we complemented each other and fit together. I wrapped my legs around his, intertwining us like two pieces of yarn being woven together, and was rewarded by his breath catching.

Liking that sound and wanting more of it, I pressed my lips to his throat, moving my hands into his hair so that I could scrape his scalp with my fingertips in the way that I knew drove him crazy.

Sure enough, he shuddered against me and made another strangled groaning, growling sound and his mouth was on me again, kissing me once, twice, three times, and then outlining my jaw before moving to work on my neck. The heat moved up from my stomach into my chest until it almost hurt to breathe. He didn't seem to be having the same problem, as his breaths were hot on my skin, and I felt a pull deep and low that had me moving to capture his lips with mine again.

"Now I think I'm the one who's going to have an anxiety attack," he muttered.

"Oh. I wouldn't want that," I teased. "We could stop."

"Um, no," he growled, and I laughed. But then his lips were touching mine and all of my laughter instantly stopped.

As his mouth skated over mine again and again, he sent blood rushing to every part of my body. It was a little like being caught up in my own personal earthquake. Everything was off-kilter and out of control, except for him. He was rock solid and constant, just as he'd promised, and I clung to him as my head grew dizzy with sensation, my eyes blurring and unable to focus.

He reached down with one hand to grab at my hip, pulling me against him, but we couldn't get any closer. I got the inclination—it was what I wanted, too. To melt into him so that we couldn't tell where one of us ended and the other one began.

His heartbeat raced against my chest, and I hoped he could feel mine, too. He pulled away to look down at me, and for a moment I wondered if I'd done something wrong.

"I love it when you make those sounds," he murmured, and I tried to figure out if what he was saying was true, because I hadn't realized I'd been making any noises.

"What sounds?"

He had on a rakish grin that sent warm shimmers down my back. "These breathy whimpers that mean you can't get enough of what I'm doing. It drives me insane."

"Oh. Sorry?"

"Please don't apologize. It is a hundred percent my pleasure."

He ran his lips over my ear before sucking gently at the bottom of my earlobe, and I couldn't even make fun of him for saying dumb things because my eyes were rolling back in my head and my veins were all throbbing.

"Just like that," he said in a satisfied tone.

"I'll get you back for that," I said, definitely making some kind of whimpering, breathy sound.

"I hope so."

I ran a finger lightly over his chest. "So what would happen next? In this teaching experiment of ours?"

There was a look of brief confusion in his eyes, but he put it away. "You're asking me what should happen next?"

"Uh-huh," I said, and my entire body tensed in anticipation of his response.

"Well"—he leaned down to kiss the tip of my nose—"I would kiss you a lot more, and then I'd reach up"—he brought up his right hand—"and I would do this." He unbuttoned the top button on my shirt.

I didn't say anything.

He undid the second button, but still I stayed silent.

Then his fingers hesitated, and I saw the teasing light fall from his eyes. "Juliet, I don't know how much self-control you think I have, but we are pushing right up against that line."

"Just kiss me," I told him, almost not caring what happened next. I just wanted to be with him.

He did as I requested, devastating my mouth and invading all of my senses.

I became aware of a ringing sound. It was my phone. I wanted to ignore it. Given how clever he was with his lips, I really, really wanted to ignore it. But what if it was important? The only people who called me in the evenings were my mom and Shelby.

"Noah, hang on."

He rolled to his side, and I got up on barely functioning legs to make my way over to where I'd left my phone. I was pulsating with a jittery energy that demanded release. I saw that it was Allan calling. I put my fingers over my well-kissed and slightly throbbing lips and answered it.

"Hello? Allan?"

"Juliet?" He sounded completely distraught, like he'd been crying. I instantly sobered up and turned toward Noah, my eyes wide. He picked up on my distress and sat straight up in the bed.

"What's wrong?" he mouthed.

"Allan? What's happening?"

"We were out at dinner, and Shelby said she was feeling dizzy. That she's been feeling dizzy for the last few days, and we were going to go home, and on our way back to the car she fainted."

Every last bit of color drained from my face; my heart thunked to my feet. That was exactly what happened when Shelby was diagnosed with leukemia. The dizziness, the fainting. This could not be happening again. It could not.

"What did the doctor say?" I asked.

"We're still waiting on the test results. They're going to call her oncologist when they get them back."

I heard the pain and desperation in his voice; I was feeling the exact same thing. "Where are you?"

"We're at Patterson Memorial Hospital. We're in room 1119."

"I'm on my way."

Noah was already throwing his shirt back on. "What's going on?"

"Shelby fainted and has been feeling light-headed. Those were her first symptoms last time, and it's why she went to the doctor and got diagnosed with cancer. She needs me. I have to get to her."

"Ray's still got that blown tire," Noah said, getting on his phone. "If we can wait half an hour—"

"I can't wait that long." The need I felt to be by her side, to support her through this, nearly wrecked me. I got on my phone, too, checking both the Uber and Lyft apps. There were no cars available because of this festival. There was a lump in my throat, but I refused to cry. I had to be strong, to see what the doctor said. "There's no ride-share cars, either. What are we going to do?"

Determined, he took my hand. "Come with me. I'm going to get you there."

"How?"

He took me by the shoulders, looking deep into my eyes. I could see how much he meant what he said next. "Trust me. You're my battle buddy. I've got your back, and I promise that I'm going to get you safely to Shelby's side."

Some detached part of my brain wanted to ask him what a battle buddy was, but he pulled me after him and I followed. We ran down the stairs instead of waiting for the elevator and hurried through the lobby. When we got to the half-circle driveway out front, there were no taxis that I could see, but there was a young woman about to get into her car.

Noah rushed over to her. "Hi. Weird question—are you a Duel of the Fae fan?"

It took a second for her to register who he was, but her mouth dropped open and I understood all too well when she temporarily lost her ability to speak. "You're . . . you're . . ."

But he was too impatient to wait for her to get there. "Yes, I play Malec Shadowfire. I'm Noah. What's your name?"

"I'm Nicole. Wow, it's so great to meet you!" Her eyes flickered to mine, but she seemed to mentally dismiss me.

He shook her hand. "Is there any chance I could get you to drive me and my friend to the hospital? I could pay you."

"Are you okay?" she asked, her eyes big. I noticed she didn't ask if I was okay. To be fair, she probably didn't care.

"I'm fine. There's someone there we have to see right away."

"Of course. I'd love to drive you. And don't worry about the money. Just having the chance to talk to you would be payment enough!"

She got into her car, and he turned to me. "I'll sit up front and chat with her."

It occurred to me as I climbed into the back seat that this woman could be a complete psycho and kidnap us and tie Noah up in her basement while making him read lines from Duel of the Fae. But there was no time to worry.

Nicole didn't seem all that partial to the speed limit, which was good in our current situation. She and Noah talked in the front seat, mostly about inane movie stuff, while I rocked in the back, promising God that I'd do anything if Shelby would be okay.

I'd even be willing to give up Noah, if that's what it took. Because for some reason this felt like some personal punishment for me being a liar for so long.

I just kept whispering the word *please*. She couldn't die.

We rolled up to the emergency room entrance at the hospital, and both Noah and I opened our doors. I heard him thanking her.

She got out of the car, too. "Wait! Can I get a picture with you?"

I saw the pained look in his eyes. "Go," he told me. "I'll catch up."

Maybe I should have waited, but I couldn't. Right as I got to the elevator bank, one of the elevators opened, like it had been waiting just for me. I took it up to the eleventh floor and looked for the door numbers until I found Shelby's.

She was alone in her bed, looking so small. Allan wasn't in the room.

I rushed to her side. "I'm here." Noah had gotten me to the hospital, just like he'd promised. "We'll get through this."

"Everything's okay," she said, putting a hand over her stomach. "I'm just having a baby. Allan's out calling his parents right now."

"What?" For some reason that did not compute.

"They got the blood work back and the doctors didn't see any evidence that my cancer had returned and it's supposed to be virtually impossible for me to get pregnant naturally, but I am definitely pregnant. That can apparently cause fainting and light-headedness, too. So this is a literal miracle. I'm going to be a mommy."

At that my tears finally started to fall; I was so thrilled for her. I knew how much this meant to her. She and Allan had already talked about adopting children because they thought they wouldn't be able to get pregnant on their own. I leaned over to hug her, making sure not to squish her stomach. "Congratulations. You're going to be the best mom ever."

She was crying happy tears. "I wish my mom was here to see this."

"I know. I'm sorry she's not. But for what it's worth, your baby is going to have the world's best aunt, and I'm going to love them with everything I have."

And it was in that moment that I realized no matter how much things might change between me and Shelby, no matter what challenges and obstacles we were going to face, we would still get through them all together. Adding new people to love along the way.

In this case, a very tiny person.

And one oversize one. The person who made sure I was here for this, who did whatever he had to do to get me to my best friend because he knew how important it was to me.

I couldn't deny it any longer. A rush of warmth washed over me, and I could feel my cheeks flush. I was in love with Noah Douglas. I knew it as clearly and as plainly as I'd ever known anything. I wanted him in my life now and forever.

I maybe even wanted to make tiny people with him.

And none of that terrified me.

Allan came back in the room, carrying his cell phone. "My mom's on the phone. She's excited. She wants to talk to you and apologize."

Shelby's eyes sparkled with happiness and I left them alone, glad that Satan's Evilest Minion had finally come around at the prospect of being a grandmother. I found Noah in a small waiting room, a few doors down from where Shelby was. He was on his phone.

"I want you to find out who is the best oncologist in the state. No, it's not for me. But this is important. Find out who that person is and get them on the phone."

I put my hand on his arm. "Hang up."

"Kyle, I'm going to call you back." He studied my face. "What's going on?"

"She's not sick. She's pregnant."

His whole face lit up—you would have almost thought she was having his baby. "That's fantastic!" He picked me up like it was nothing, swinging me around once.

I laughed, and when I felt my feet back on the floor, I told him, before I lost my nerve, "I need to talk to you. There's something I have to say."

CHAPTER TWENTY-NINE

He sensed the people watching us before I did. I was too busy trying to work up my courage. I needed to tell him the truth. About everything. "Come with me," he said, leading me into an empty hospital room and closing the door.

Maybe if I told him the love thing first, the lie wouldn't seem quite so bad. Now that the moment of truth was here, my nerves felt jangly and I shook my hands, trying to get some feeling back into them. My heartbeat was violent in my chest.

"Hey, what's going on?" he asked, his concern evident in every line of his beautiful face.

"What's a battle buddy?" I blurted out, my brain stepping in to create a diversion.

"In the army you're assigned a partner to keep an eye on both in and out of combat. It just means I've got your back and nothing's going to happen to you on my watch if I can help it."

My heart melted at his words. "You did that tonight. You took care of me and got me exactly what I needed. You're always doing that. Taking care of me."

"You take care of me, too. In ways you don't even realize," he said, holding my hands in his.

Why was this so hard? It was so much more difficult than I'd thought it would be. Maybe I should find a way to ease into it. "Tonight . . . I can't even tell you what this meant to me. You finding a stranger to drive me here to see my best friend. And I—I—"

I was such a coward. *Such* a coward.

But still I kept talking, trying to find the words I could actually say. "I don't know how you feel about things and if you only want to be friends I understand, because those were the rules, right? Just friends? But at some point everything changed for me and I don't know when that moment was, but I . . . I want more. I want to be in a relationship with you. I kind of feel like I have been in one and just didn't register it."

He didn't say anything, so I just kept talking. "I thought I was happy with my life. I had my mom and my best friend and my business and I didn't need or want anything else. I can't believe how wrong I was, how I was missing you before I ever even met you. We click. You get me. Hanging out with you is my favorite thing. You're so strong, smart, funny, kind, generous, talented, and a million other things that make you one of the best people I've ever met. You're my person and I want you in my life. If you don't, I understand, and this is a lot to spring on you and I'm sorry about that and if you want to stay friends I'll do that, because you're so important to me and—"

Noah squeezed my hands and said, "My turn. I want that, too. Have wanted it for a while."

My heart soared at his words, sending happy, flappy flutters through my whole body. "You do? Why didn't you say anything earlier?"

"Because you said no and I wanted to respect your feelings and your boundaries. I secretly hoped they would change, but if they hadn't and you'd just ended things and walked away, I still always would have been glad that I'd met you. Even if I was nursing a broken heart."

"A broken heart?" I repeated, those happiness bubbles still fizzing away inside me.

He nodded his head, like I was silly. "I'm in love with you, Juliet. How could I not be? You're everything I never knew I always wanted. Sweet, brave, loyal, willing to fight for what you want, brilliant, hilarious, and, like you said, a million other things that make you the most amazing woman I've ever known. I've been into you since the first night we met and I fell in love with you a long time ago."

"You love me?" Why was I repeating everything he was saying?

"Even more than I love Magnus."

Wow. That was more than I'd expected.

But how could he love me? How could I ever be enough for him? My mom hadn't been enough for my dad, and while I'd never thought I'd actually be in a relationship, now that I was, how could I expect someone like him to be faithful? Because while I didn't have much experience, I was pretty sure cheating would be something I couldn't get over.

"What is that look for?" he asked.

"What if you get bored of me?"

He laughed. "How could I ever get bored of you?"

"Oh, I don't know, maybe because you're constantly around the most beautiful, fascinating, and talented people in the world?"

Noah put his hands on the sides of my face. "There's something Paul Newman said once when asked if he was tempted to cheat on his wife. To paraphrase, he said, 'Why would I go out for hamburger when I have steak at home?'"

My heart lifted at his words. "But hamburgers are really good, too."

"Not as good as steak," he said definitively, as if there were no further discussion to be had. "I'd never cheat on you."

Then he kissed me, and I didn't even have that fear echo. His kiss was so intimate and perfect; it was just love and excited giddiness and promises of so much more to come.

"Wait," I said, pulling back. "I want you to meet my mom."

He smiled wryly. "I already met your mom."

"No, as my boyfriend. If it's okay to call you that."

"Yes." He grinned. "And I'd love to meet her again."

"How about tomorrow?"

"It's a date."

We were interrupted by a nurse, who came in and said, "You can't be in here." Her expression shifted and she said, "Oh. You're Noah Douglas."

"I'm sorry for being in here. We just needed a minute," he said in that confident way that smoothed over everything.

"No, it's okay. Take as long as you need."

"My girlfriend and I were on our way out."

Girlfriend. Why was that the best word in the whole world?

Noah loved me. Noah Douglas loved me. I'd already figured out that I was in love with him, but it seriously hadn't entered into my head that he would love me back. As we walked out of the hospital room hand in hand, I knew that I should tell him. But I couldn't speak. I couldn't say the thing that would make him walk away from me and never talk to me again.

But for some reason, I couldn't tell him I loved him, either. I didn't know why or what was holding me back.

And I didn't know how to resolve it.

~

The next morning I got my phone out to call my mom and saw that I had a text from Gladys.

> Sunshine's bear is missing.
> Do you know where it is?

> I don't. I'm sorry. I can come by tomorrow and help you look for it.

But she didn't respond. I decided I'd go by tomorrow regardless. She wasn't the kind of person to ask for help, but she was going to get it. I knew how much Sunshine loved his teddy bear.

Then I called my mother to inform her that Noah, my boyfriend, and I would be coming by for dinner.

She let out a tormented sigh and said, "I thought you were just friends. Do you think an actor is the best person to be in a relationship with?"

Annoyance exploded behind my eyes. I couldn't keep quiet. "You're trying to be an actor. You cannot keep doing stuff like this. Mom, I love you, but do you know how many weird hang-ups I have because you hated Dad?"

"What do you mean?"

"You always think no guy is good enough for me."

"No guy is good enough for you," she agreed.

"Mom!"

"You're my baby. I want to protect you. I never want you to get hurt the way that I did. And that Noah seems like he could be a real heartbreaker."

I decided to ignore her last sentence. "I know you want to protect me. But you can't protect me from life. You need to let me fly and make my own mistakes."

"I know." She sighed again. "I just love you so much that I want to put you in bubble wrap and keep you in your old bedroom."

"That's not at all creepy."

"Speaking of your room, I've started packing your stuff up. It's been your shrine for long enough. I'm thinking about turning it into an exercise or sewing room. You'll have to take the boxes back to your apartment."

"I will," I promised. "But I want you to meet Noah and really talk to him and I want you to be nice to him and I want you to love him, because I already do." Whoa, I felt that deep in my gut. I'd never said the words out loud before, and it seemed monumental.

"Do you see a future with this boy?"

"Maybe. We'll see." I figured saying, *Yes, absolutely,* would probably freak her out more than was necessary in this moment.

"Okay, then. You bring him over, and I'll do my best to love him, too."

"That's all I can ask for! But don't tell him about the love part. I technically haven't told him yet," I said. The last thing I needed was for him to find out that I loved him because my mom didn't know how to keep a secret.

I told her I'd see her at seven and followed up with a text to Noah, making sure he could show up at that time.

> Try and stop me. Love you.

I actually pressed my phone to my chest, squealed, and spun around. I never thought this would happen to me, and not even in my wildest daydreams did I ever imagine that it would be with Noah Douglas.

The rest of the day passed by in a blur. I didn't have any dog-grooming appointments, but I always made sure to spend at least an hour of my day trying new ways of marketing. Today it was to contact current and previous clients to let them know that I was now doing dog sitting in addition to grooming and that I would offer them fifty percent off their next dog grooming if they referred me to a friend.

Then I got ready and drove over to my mom's. I let myself in the front door and found her in the kitchen, where she was stirring up her famous bolognese sauce.

"It smells good!" I told her, kissing her cheek hello.

"Here, taste. You need to eat more," she said, offering me some of the sauce on a wooden spoon. I blew on it and then tasted it.

"Amazing as always," I said. "What can I do to help?"

She asked me to go set up the dining room table. I got out a table-cloth and the nice china that we almost never used except for holidays. It was strangely thrilling to be setting it for three people instead of two.

Once that was done, my mother had me making the salad while she told me about her favorite class and how she thought her professor might be flirting with her. Even though he was too young for her.

I hoped he was flirting. My mom was still a hottie and deserved the ego boost. Good for her. I took the salad and the bread out to the table.

At exactly two minutes before seven o'clock, the doorbell rang. I wondered who it could be because I'd fully expected Noah to be late and had already prepared my mother for this fact.

But to my surprise, it was him. All cleaned up and wearing a blue button-down shirt and khaki pants. He'd even put product in his hair and pushed it back from his face. He had a mixed floral bouquet with him.

"You look like you just walked out of an Old Navy commercial," I told him as he kissed me hello.

"Hush. I'm dressed like this solely to impress your mother. And before you get any big ideas, these flowers are not for you."

He was nervous. I could see it, and this tickled me. Because he was doing this for me. He wanted to make me happy and knew that this would. He was trying so hard, and it was completely adorable. "I'm glad you're taking this seriously. Because so far she disapproves."

"Does that ruin my chances with you?" he asked, slipping an arm around my waist.

"Actually, it makes it much more likely that I'll keep hanging around you. It would only make you more appealing."

"Good. Because usually mothers hate me. They think I'm the worst."

"Noah!" I laughed. "That's probably the opposite of true. I bet you charm them all."

He grinned. "Okay, yes, mothers love me."

My mom came in the room carrying her sauce and the noodles, setting them down on the table. "Mom, you remember Noah?"

"I do! How are you?"

"I'm good, Ms. Barber. How are you?"

Oh, bonus points for him for remembering that she went by her maiden name. I could see that she felt the same way, given how her smile warmed. "I'm doing very well, and please, call me Caroline."

"These are for you," he said, offering her the bouquet. "Thank you for inviting me to your home."

"Thank you! They're beautiful. I'm going to go put them in water."

"Maybe I misjudged you," I whispered to him. "You're kind of killing it."

"Never underestimate the movie star," he whispered back as my mom returned with her flowers in a vase. She placed them in the middle of the dining room table.

"Please, sit down," she said.

We all took our seats, and my mom offered the pasta to him first. He took it and had just started serving himself when she said, "Oh! Before I forget again, I found something today. Now I know where I recognized you from." She got up, leaving the room.

Weird. I wondered if she'd looked him up online or something.

He got a text and checked his phone. "Whoops. I forgot to call Kyle back last night, and now I have a thoroughly vetted list of California's best oncologists."

"Yeah, we were a little busy," I said.

"We were," he said with a sexy smile, and I debated whether or not I could kiss him senseless before my mom came back.

But she returned right then to majorly mom-block me. When I saw her, my smile slipped off my face. My ears started ringing, and my heart stopped beating. Like, literally stopped and then slowly started up again, so slow that I thought I might pass out.

She was carrying my scrapbook. My Felix Morrison scrapbook that I'd kept throughout middle school and half of high school.

This. Was. Not. Happening.

"I've been packing up Juliet's room, and I found this. She spent so much time on this scrapbook. I threatened to take it away from her more than once if she didn't do better in school and spend less time looking up things to print out." She was so joyful. She thought she was helping. Doing a good thing.

Not ruining my entire world.

"What's this?" Noah asked when she placed it in front of me, reaching out to touch it. I wanted to scream, to tell him not to look, to grab it and run away so that he'd never see it. But it was like being trapped in a real-life nightmare. I was paralyzed in place, unable to move, unable to blink, unable to do anything besides just sit there and watch.

Even if I had been able to act, it was already too late. He opened it and I saw the microseconds when his expression changed—from curiosity to confusion to understanding.

His whole visage darkened. His betrayal and pain were etched into his face. "What is this, Juliet?" he demanded.

CHAPTER THIRTY

My mother might not have known exactly what was happening, but she had the good sense to excuse herself, leaving us alone.

"Noah, let me explain—"

"What is this?" he repeated, his teeth clenched together. I'd seen him angry before, but never at me. I didn't know how to take it.

Even if it was well deserved. "It's a scrapbook I kept when I was younger."

"Of me. Of Felix Morrison." He said the name with disgust. "You told me you didn't know who I was. The first night we met, you said you'd never heard of me."

I reached for his hand and tried not to flinch when he jerked it away, out of reach. I had to explain this. To make him see. "I know I did, but I thought you were being arrogant that night. Now I know it was just to protect yourself from what you thought was a crazy stalker fan, but I was so annoyed that I just wanted to knock you down a few pegs. Which I shouldn't have done and maybe I should have confessed earlier, but what would have happened? You would have walked away from me and never looked back. And I didn't want to lose you."

"You used me. You lied to me and then had me help you learn how to kiss." I wished he would yell instead of utilizing this deadly calm voice he was using and his blank face. "Did you fake your phobia, too? Were you trying to trick me into being with you? Was this some scheme? Was the whole thing a lie?"

"Nothing was a lie. Besides me saying I didn't know you. Everything else was the truth. A hundred percent. I promise."

"Your promises don't mean a whole lot right now." He stood up, clearly meaning to leave.

I couldn't let that happen. I grabbed for his wrist, and he stopped only to pull himself from my grasp.

"Please don't go. We can work this out," I begged.

"How?" he asked. "I thought I'd found this unicorn—this unexpected woman who was perfect for me and wasn't blinded by my celebrity. Who didn't care about the roles I played. Who cared about me. As a man."

"I can't say that I don't care. But I only loved those characters because you were so good at performing them." I saw immediately that that was the wrong thing to say and tried to fix it. "You are not some character to me. This was never about Felix or Malec for me. I couldn't care less about what you do for a living. You're just Noah to me."

Finally, there was anger. "That isn't true! There's a four-inch notebook on your table saying that isn't true!"

"I'm not the same person I was when I was fifteen. I know there's a difference between fantasy and reality."

"I don't think you do," he said, his voice back to being cold. "And right now, apparently neither do I."

He was nearly to the front door when I called out, "You can't go. I wanted to tell you everything, but I was too scared to. I didn't want to lose you. I'm begging you. Please don't do this." My voice was edged with unshed tears. I was struggling so hard to keep myself in check, to not break down.

His shoulders curved in, and relief shot through me. I thought that was it. That I'd gotten through to him and we would talk about this and I would find a way to make it up to him.

Instead he seemed to shake off my words and without turning around, he said in a low voice, "Don't call me. Don't come to my house. I'm done."

Then he walked out the front door, closing it behind him.

I collapsed onto the floor in a sobbing heap, crying so hard I thought my chest might split open. My throat felt raw, shredded, and my whole body shook with my tears. My heart ached so badly I didn't know that it would ever beat the same way again. Him shutting me out of his life was what I was most afraid of and it was what had happened.

I'd ruined everything.

~

Life had to go on, but it was like all the color had been drained from the world. It didn't help matters that I was living alone. It let me really steep myself in my depression.

Shelby came over the night after he walked out of my mother's house and just held me while I cried and told her all the ways I had messed up and how I didn't know how to live without him.

"I'll tell you how. You get up in the morning and take a shower and keep living your life. You build your business. You find a new room-mate. You move on, and hopefully every day it will hurt a little less."

She never said *I told you so,* but maybe she should have. Because she'd been right about everything. Again. And I'd lost the person I loved most in the whole world.

My mother kept calling to apologize and see if I was okay. But she wasn't to blame and it was exhausting pretending I felt better than I actually did. I found myself dodging some of her calls.

One night Shelby stopped by to check on me. It might have been two weeks later. Maybe three. Time had sort of lost all meaning. She let herself in because she still had her key.

"How are you doing?" she asked.

And I knew why she looked so concerned. Despite her counsel to take care of myself, I had fallen into a deep funk that included not leaving my house and forgetting about personal hygiene. I was also wearing the hoodie that Noah had lent to me and I'd never returned. It had never been washed. "Today I wanted to find out how many Snickers bars I had to eat to stop feeling sad. So far it's not ten."

"Sweetie, what can I do?"

Tell me about Noah, I wanted to say but didn't. Whenever we talked or she visited, I was starved for information about him. But she wouldn't talk about him. Even when I specifically asked, she would change the subject. I was torn between understanding why she was doing it, wanting to keep out of it because she had her own relationship with Noah, and feeling hurt that she wouldn't give me every morsel and detail she knew because I was her best friend.

Not that I couldn't get morsels and details of my own. It was really hard to break up with someone when there were millions of images of him online. When with a click of a button I could hear his voice whenever I wanted. See his beautiful face. Watch him gazing adoringly at Aliana the same way he used to look at me.

I'd been so stupid.

But I was tired of remembering how dumb I was. So instead I answered her question by saying, "I don't know. I don't know what I'm doing anymore. Other than the Snickers bars today, I haven't really been eating or sleeping. And those are my two best events. I was also considering giving myself bangs."

"That kind of talk stops here," she told me. "I am not going to let you cut your own hair while you're sad. Just like I wouldn't let you go to the grocery store if you were hungry. Mistakes will be made and regrets will be had. Speaking of food, do you want me to make you something to eat?"

I hugged my pillow tighter. "I don't want you to cook for me." Noah cooked for me and it just felt like too much. "Why did you let me date him? I feel like part of this is on you."

"It is all my fault," she agreed, trying to take the burden from me, only it didn't help. It just made me feel guiltier, because of course, she'd played no part in my downfall. She'd actively encouraged me to try to prevent it. But wouldn't it have hurt just as much then as it did now?

"No, you were right. I should have told him. But either way, he would have left. Just like my dad."

"I feel like that's a whole other thing that I'm not qualified to get into with you, but maybe that's another reason you kept your secret. Because you were convinced that no matter what you did, in the end, Noah would leave. And this way you got to justify your belief by causing it."

Whoa, that was way too deep for somebody who had just eaten ten candy bars. Maybe what she said had merit. I'd have to think about it. When my brain wasn't so sad.

She went into the kitchen. "You have to eat. Actual food." She checked my empty fridge. "Okay, I'm ordering delivery. You're having Chinese."

"Snickers is actual food. It has peanuts. That's protein."

"I'm serious, Juliet. I'm going to tough love you here. You're going to eat, and tomorrow you're going to wake up and go clean some dogs and find new clients. Maybe even take up a hobby or something."

"I was considering alcoholism, but I can't afford it."

"Which is why you have to start working again and stop delaying your appointments." I never should have told her about that. "I understand what you're going through. It would have killed me if I ever lost Allan."

I didn't remind her that she almost had, what with her being willing to break up with him to protect him. I was like her polar opposite, selfishly hanging on to Noah without giving him all the facts. Hiding it from him.

And from myself.

Everything I'd ever asked him to do, he'd done without question. And all he'd ever wanted from me was my honesty, and I couldn't even give him that.

I was tired of thinking about me and my pathetic lack of a life. "Things are better with Harmony?"

She smiled, her first real one since she'd arrived. "She has bought so many baby clothes, and we don't even know the sex of the baby yet. She's very excited to be a grandma. Although she wants us to have the baby call her Gigi, and I'm still deciding how I feel about that."

It was nice that good things were happening in the world. I tried to say that, but instead I started crying again. It happened a lot recently.

"Sweetie," she said, hugging me. "I know. I thought for sure you guys were going to make it. You had this relationship like me and Allan—you would have kept him grounded and stopped him from getting a big head, and he would have reminded you to have fun and done romantic things like fly you to Las Vegas just because."

And the fact that she was willing to say something about him actually stopped my tears. It surprised me; I would have expected her words to make me feel worse, but instead they made me think that I hadn't made it all up. He had loved me and we were good together.

We'd shared something special, even if we didn't have it anymore.

"I never told him I loved him," I confessed.

"I'm not surprised. That wouldn't have been easy for you to say to anyone. Again, dad issues and kissing phobia, but how could you have said that when you knew deep in your heart you weren't being totally truthful with him?"

That hit me hard, piercing me like a knife. That's why I hadn't been able to tell him. How did she always see me so clearly when I ran around not knowing why I did half the stuff I did?

She sighed and said, "I'm going to tell you this and then we have to stop talking about him, because it's going to make you sadder, okay?"

I nodded, probably too eagerly.

"He is so miserable without you. He pretends like he's okay, but I can hear it in his voice and see it in his eyes. He misses you like crazy."

"Does he ask about me?"

"No." Her eyes were full of sympathy, and I told myself I wasn't going to cry again because I was tired of being dehydrated. "But I do tell him some things about you."

There was a knock at the door, and she went to answer it. Our food had arrived from the restaurant around the corner.

And I knew she'd told me the things she had to make me feel better. Maybe feel not so alone because he was just as sad.

But instead it made me feel worse. I didn't want him to be suffering, because I knew that I was the cause of that.

She stayed and ate with me, refusing to leave until I'd eaten half a container of beef with broccoli. Turned out I was hungry for real food. Well, takeout food, which was kind of the same thing. I decided I should probably go to the store and get some vegetables and citrus so that I didn't die of scurvy.

About an hour after she left, my phone rang. A restricted number. My heart lurched so hard in my chest that I was surprised it hadn't accidentally burst through the side. Hope furiously bloomed inside my chest.

"Hello?"

"Hello? Is this Juliet?"

That hope imploded, leaving me hollow again. I was so desperate for it to be his voice on the other end that it almost felt like losing him all over again when it wasn't.

"Yes, this is her."

"This is Lily, Lily Ramsey. We met at Noah's house?"

I straightened up. "Yes, I remember. How are you?"

"Good, thanks. Yourself?"

Oh, well, famous actress Lily Ramsey, my life is in utter shambles right now and I've eaten so much sugar I might actually go into a coma. Thanks so much for asking! "I'm good," I lied.

"I'm embarrassed to admit this, but I forgot to follow up with you about coming over to groom my dog. Noah reminded me earlier, and that's why I'm calling."

My heart went into my throat, beating rapidly. "He . . . reached out to you? Today?"

"Yes. Why?"

Tears blurred my vision, and I was glad we weren't face-to-face. He didn't want anything to do with me, but he was calling his celebrity friends to use my services. Just like he'd promised he would when we'd first met. That had to mean something, didn't it? "No reason. I was just curious. But I'd love to schedule a time to come over and take care of Blueberry."

"I can't believe you remembered his name after all this time! I'm impressed!"

She shouldn't have been. I felt doomed to remember every single thing associated with Noah for the rest of my life. "What day and time would work for you?" I asked, and we set up an appointment.

After we hung up, I realized Shelby was right, as usual, and this time I wasn't going to ignore her advice. It was time to go back out into the world and do what I could to move on.

~

There were other phone calls: one from Zoe Covington, who invited me to stay for lunch after I groomed Nemo, and two from celebrities that

I'd heard of but never met. Noah again, doing what he had promised, even though he was furious with me. This made me feel even more guilty that he was so honorable and kept his word and I just generally sucked.

But I wasn't going to let that get me down. The next morning I was cleaning out my van and reached under the passenger seat and felt something furry. I pulled out Sunshine's teddy bear. I felt bad that I hadn't looked for it sooner and decided to return it to Gladys immediately.

I probably should have texted or called first, but I wanted to see Noah's house, even from a distance. It might have been pathetic, but I wasn't claiming the high moral ground here. When I got to the gate, my heart pounded in anticipation that Noah might have told them not to let me in. But they just waved me through, which was also a testament to how much time I'd spent here.

When I got to Gladys's house, I gripped the steering wheel tightly, steeling myself. And I was not ready to see his house, even though I'd been trying to psych myself up for it. It sent pangs of emotion through me when I caught a glimpse. There were people outside, and I guessed they were part of the construction crew. I wondered if he was home. Probably not—it was the middle of the day. For all I knew he might have been traveling for a movie.

I went up to the front door, and when Gladys answered it, I fell apart. I handed her the teddy bear while sobbing, and she looked at me and said, "Better get in here. What's gotten into you?"

She took me into the living room, and I spent ten minutes trying to fill her in on what had happened in between sobs, but it mostly came out like, "And I love him and"—*hiccup*—"he never wants to see me again"—*sob*—"and I didn't even apologize to him"—*wailing*—"I ruined everything" until she finally interrupted me.

"Do you know how rare true love is? And I'm assuming that's what you think you feel for that movie star?"

"Uh-huh." I nodded.

Gladys scowled at me. "Then go up there and make him see that you love him. Right now. Life is too short, girlie. Despite you being a blubbering mess, I know that you're not weak. Apologize. Fight for what you want. Quit your boo-hooing and be a woman about it!"

Yes. She was utterly brilliant. I should do that. I should fight for him. I should tell him that I was sorry and that I loved him. How could he make a decision about whether or not he wanted to be with me when he didn't have all the information? "I'm going right now to talk to him."

"That's the spirit," she said with a proud look.

"Thank you!" I called, running out of her house and up to Noah's. When I got closer, I recognized his publicist. She was barking at someone on her phone and looked absolutely furious.

"Reina? What's going on?"

She paused her call long enough to speak to me. "Magnus is missing. Nobody can find him."

CHAPTER THIRTY-ONE

Not Magnus. This was like the worst possible news. With everything else that was going on, I couldn't face a reality where Magnus had been chewed up by a mountain lion or coyote. I had to help look for him.

I headed out into the hills, following the well-trodden path that led down into the canyon nearest Noah's house. I'd taken both Sunshine and Magnus down these trails many times. I didn't know what made me think that I might be able to find him. There was definitely some magical thinking happening in my head where I saw myself leading Magnus back to Noah's house and him instantly forgiving me. The reality was, there wasn't a huge chance I would find him. But at least if I helped look and somebody else located him, maybe I'd get some credit?

I didn't let myself think of the worst-case scenario, because it would take my already shattered heart and break the remaining pieces into smithereens. I loved Magnus too much. I loved Noah too much for anything to happen.

"Magnus!" I yelled, and I heard other voices at a distance also calling his name. I decided to head in the opposite direction of the other searchers, thinking I could help cover more ground that way.

Stopping for a moment, I called Shelby. When she answered I asked, "Magnus is missing and I'm out helping to look for him. Did you see him at all today?"

"What are you doing at Noah's? No, that doesn't matter if Magnus is missing. You can explain later. I haven't seen him because I haven't been to the house today. Isn't he microchipped? Can't you track him down that way?"

"It's not a GPS tracker." Although given Magnus's history, Noah should probably get one for him. "It just means if someone finds him they can scan it and get Noah's information to contact him."

"Do you need me to come help you look?"

"No, there are a lot of people here."

She asked me to keep her posted, and I told her I would.

I found myself heading down toward a stream that Sunshine particularly loved to splash around in. It was definitely off the beaten path. I kept calling Magnus's name. It took me about twenty minutes to get there, and when I came over the ridge I saw—the stream. No Magnus like I'd hoped. I decided to press on, still yelling for him. I couldn't hear anyone else's voices, so it seemed like a good idea.

An hour later I was almost hoarse from saying his name, and I could feel the way my skin was burning under the sun. The sky was overcast and it was cooler, so I'd forgotten the very real need I had for sunscreen when I was outside this long.

I came to a stop. I was getting thirsty and burned. I'd have to head back. I tried one last time. "Magnus!"

Then I heard something. It sounded like a whimper. I called his name again, and this time there was a definite bark. I followed it and found Magnus, his collar caught in a bush. My heart leaped at the sight of him, so glad he was safe. And at the very least I could give Noah this.

"You naughty boy, why do you keep doing this?" I asked and hugged him tightly. He licked my face in response, his tail wagging, and he seemed very happy to see me.

It took me a second to get him free, as he'd really managed to tangle himself up in the thorny vegetation. When I got him loose, I held on to his collar, but he sat and didn't seem in a hurry to go anywhere. "Let me check you out."

I wasn't a vet or anything, but he didn't seem to be bleeding, which I figured was a good sign. "Are you okay?" I asked, and he just looked up at me with doggy love in his eyes, and I hugged him again.

It took me a while to get him back to Noah's, because I could only walk so fast hunched over and hanging on to Magnus's collar. I couldn't risk him running off again, and who knew if he had been properly chastened by his adventure or if he was ready for another one?

Someone spotted me as I got closer to the main trail and called out, "There he is! Magnus!"

I saw Noah running over a crest, skidding down until he came to a stop in front of us. I couldn't catch my breath looking at him. It had been so long and I had missed him so much that it made me ache with need.

And it was like he was torn on what to say. I could see his relief at Magnus being found but his uncertainty about what to do with me.

"Juliet? What are you doing here? How did you find him?"

"I was bringing something to Gladys and Reina told me that Magnus was missing and I . . . I couldn't bear the idea of you losing him."

Again, I saw the pain and confusion in his eyes. "Your skin is all red."

I held out one of my hands in front of me. "Little bit. But it was worth it."

"You did that for . . ." His voice trailed off. He looked like he wanted to say something, but instead he stooped down to pick up his dog and carry him back inside.

That was it. Conversation over. I was never going to see him again. Pinpricks of pain lanced my gut, and I put my hand on my stomach, as if I was trying to hold everything in. I didn't want to cry and yell his name.

Then he turned slightly. "Do you want to come inside and get something to drink?" he asked.

"Yes." More than I'd ever wanted anything.

There was a crowd of people at his house, and once they saw that Magnus had returned, they started calling the other searchers and telling them he was safe. Then they began leaving after telling Noah how glad they were that Magnus was back home. Magnus seemed to be loving the attention of everybody who petted him and told him not to run off again.

I went to wait in the library. New hardwood floors had been laid down, but there was rough drywall on the interior walls. The weight of being in this house again pressed down on me. I tried to gather my thoughts, to figure out exactly what I was going to say, but they were scattering in a thousand different directions and I couldn't slow them down.

Noah entered the room, handing me a cold water bottle.

"Thank you," I said, opening it and drinking a large gulp.

Magnus came over to me, resting his head on my lap, as if to tell me he missed me. I scratched under his chin while my heart felt like a bomb about to detonate. Would Noah talk first or should I?

He retreated to stand in the doorway, his arms folded, his body language telling me he didn't want me there.

"I'm sorry," I said, the words spilling out of me. "I never got to apologize to you and I want to do that now. I'm sorry that I hurt you. That was the last thing I would ever want to do."

"But you did it anyway. I told you how important the truth is to me."

"I know," I said, grasping on to Magnus's fur to help me feel grounded. "I should have said something earlier. But this wasn't a scheme. I wasn't trying to trick you. Just deflate your ego a little bit. Then we started hanging out and you hired Shelby and she really needed this job. I told myself that I was protecting her."

His eyes still seemed flat. "I know you'd do anything for her."

"Yes. But once I got to really know you, that didn't work as an excuse any longer. I know the kind of man you are, and you'd never fire her because you were angry with me." Which he'd already proven by keeping her on even though we were broken up. "And the night we met, if I'd had any clue about how gentle and good and loving you were, I never would have lied to you. I thought you were some arrogant jerk. I wish I'd known better. It was never a scheme or a ploy to get you to like me. I'm not insane."

"I know that," he said. "Now that I've calmed down, I know."

Then why aren't you kissing me? I wanted to ask, but I didn't.

He continued, "But that doesn't make what you did any less of a lie. You pretended the entire time we were together that you'd never heard of me before that night."

"That's true. I did. And I shouldn't have. I'll spend the rest of my life apologizing to you if that's what it takes. You were so good about respecting my boundaries, and I failed to respect yours."

He nodded, and hope surged inside me again, wondering if I was getting through to him. But all he said was, "I appreciate that." He paused a beat and said, "Your eyes are all red."

"Yeah, I might have been, you know, crying a little bit earlier." Nonstop since he'd walked out of my mom's house, thank you very much. "I really miss you."

He didn't say anything. Maybe Shelby had been wrong about this. About him missing me and being miserable without me.

But no matter how he was or was not feeling about me, he'd kept his word. "You called your friends to patronize my business. Just like you said you would."

At that, he looked down at his feet. "Shelby said you were struggling, so I made some phone calls."

He'd made the phone calls. Not Kyle or his publicist or anyone else. Noah had done it himself. That had to mean something.

That blue butterfly-wing hope returned. "Speaking of Shelby, there's some things she helped me realize. That my dad maybe gave me more issues than I'd realized. I thought my kissing phobia was my biggest fear, but it turns out it was losing you. And I did want to tell you. You know how I get when I'm afraid. So I didn't say anything. Because avoidance has been my coping mechanism for so long that I—"

He cut me off. "No, you do not get to use my weakness for you against me."

"Weakness for me?" I repeated, surprised.

"You're my kryptonite. So is how much I care about what you've gone through, how important it was to me to help you, how much I love you. You can't play on that now."

I was surprised by the vehemence in his voice. Was his anger a good thing? What about the fact that he'd used *love* in the present tense, not a past one? "I wasn't trying to do that, I promise. I'm just trying to explain why I did what I did. I think I at least owe you that."

He nodded but again was silent.

I sucked in a big breath. "I never pretended when I was with you. I was always me."

"You pretended from the beginning. You lied to me and then you kept lying to manipulate me."

Now I was feeling a little frustrated. "I was not trying to manipulate you. I lied so much to myself that it was too easy to lie to you, too. I didn't know how things were going to turn out between us. I didn't know I was going to fall in love with you!"

His expression shifted and I couldn't read it fast enough, but he was back to anger. "Now you can say it? Now that I know the truth about everything?"

"Yes! That's why I couldn't tell you before."

"Because of a guilty conscience?" he correctly guessed. "You knew what you were doing was wrong, but you did it anyway."

"I did. And it was selfish of me and it was due to my issues and had nothing to do with your job. I never saw you as Malec. Except for that one time you dressed like him. But even then, you were still Noah to me. I see you and I know you and I love you."

He let out a sigh of what sounded like a mixture of disgust and regret, and I wished I knew the right thing to say to him so that he would let me back in.

But I didn't have those words, so I told him what was in my heart. "At Shelby's wedding I thought . . . I could see myself doing that with you. I saw a future. And I'd never, ever pictured that for my life. I wouldn't have imagined it to be possible. But I wanted that—to someday be standing next to you and promising to spend the rest of my life loving you. Because I will. Even if you can't forgive me, I will spend every day from now on being in love with you."

"You think I didn't want that, too?" My breath caught, both at his words and his tone. He sounded so wounded that the only thing I wanted was to hug him and make things better.

But all I could do was try to convince him to understand. "I was so scared to be myself with you, to show you all of me. I opened myself up to you, and I don't do that. Ever."

"Yeah, well, same. You made a fool of me. I don't let people take advantage of me. Not anymore. And you did. You took advantage of the trust I placed in you," he said, his voice fiery.

"I didn't mean to." I couldn't stay on the couch. I stood up and walked over to him and he shifted from left to right, obviously worried that I was going to touch him, so I didn't. "Can you forgive me?"

He let out a shaky breath. "You think I don't want to forgive you? You think I don't want to take you in my arms and pretend it didn't happen? Because I do."

My mouth parted in anticipation, that stupid hope of mine encouraging me, and I stepped forward.

He stepped back. "But that's the problem, Juliet. I can't. This isn't about forgiving you. It's not knowing if I can trust you again."

I put my hands out, wanting to touch him, but instantly dropped them when I realized what I was doing. So strange how I used to be afraid of touching him, but it had become so vital to me. "You can. I promise I'll never lie to you again. You . . . spoil Magnus. Your chicken cacciatore is not as good as you think it is. You should not wear the color yellow, because it washes out your complexion. When I was fourteen, that celebrity pillow I kissed and caught my braces on? It was you. Noah, please."

I saw him swallow, hard. "Maybe I can forgive, but I'm not sure I can forget. Maybe this seems like one small lie to you. But I told you, for most of my life I've been lied to. Not just by my parents. By everyone in this industry who thinks they can get something from me or coerce me into doing what they want. I can't have it in my personal life, too. It's too much."

This time I did touch him, even though I knew I shouldn't. I couldn't stop myself. I rested my hand on his forearm. And he didn't move away. "I want to fight for us. We're worth fighting for. Please, tell me what I can do to make you trust me again. I'll do anything to fix this. Anything."

"That's the problem, Juliet. Short of going back in time and starting all over, you can't fix it." He moved farther back, all the way to the front door. "I can't do this right now. I need for you to go." He opened it.

There had to be something I could do or say. I racked my brain but realized there was nothing. I had done everything I could. I had laid all my cards on the table, but he wasn't interested in playing this game.

So I left. My heart broke a little more with each step I took.

When I got to my van, I turned back.

But this time he wasn't watching me go.

CHAPTER THIRTY-TWO

A couple of weeks later, Shelby and I were going out to look at baby cribs. She didn't want to buy anything until Allan agreed, but her plan was to have it all picked out.

"If I don't, then Harmony will just buy the one she likes." She was trying to sound exasperated, but I could hear the delight in her voice. Harmony had come around in a big way, and Shelby was loving every second of it.

Remembering my resolve to be here, in the moment, I smiled at my friend. I was going to feel sad, probably for a long time, but I was doing my best to move on.

We got to a red light, and she dug something out of her purse. It was her lip gloss, which she handed to me. "Here. Put this on."

"Are you afraid the clerks at the baby store are going to be horrified by me?" I joked. I counted it as a win that I was routinely showering again. But I put it on to humor her, because as she was fond of reminding me, newly pregnant women should always be humored, given the amount of vomiting they were subjected to.

Shelby suddenly pulled over to the curb and brought the car to a stop. "I'm doing this because I love you. Get out."

"What?" I asked. We were in the middle of downtown LA.

"Go into that building, and you're welcome." She leaned over and opened my door. "Go on. Out." She undid my seat belt and started pushing me.

"What is going on?" I asked.

"Go inside and find out."

She'd told me that she wanted me to be the baby's godmother, and if this was some weird kind of surprise party to celebrate that, I was not in the mood. I was about to tell her that when she waved, shut my car door, and drove off.

I stood on the sidewalk for a second, not sure what to do. A uniformed guard called to me from in front of a building. "Juliet Nolan?"

"Yeah?"

She smiled and waved me up the steps. "You're supposed to come with me."

My feet seemed to be moving of their own volition as my desperate curiosity was getting the better of me. She opened the glass door behind her and said, "You're going to row two, seat B."

It was then that I realized where I was. It was the theater where I'd met Noah. And that was the exact seat I'd been sitting in when it happened. Tears welled up in my eyes, and I brushed them away. I wished Shelby had made me dress up. At least she'd given me lip gloss.

Hope beat so hard in my chest, like a captured bird struggling to break free. I was both scared and excited at the same time, and it had been a while since I'd felt that way.

The theater was empty, and I made my way over to the seat, waiting.

I didn't have to wait long.

Noah sat down in the seat next to me.

"Noah, I—"

He stopped me. "You're not supposed to talk to the audience members unless they talk to you first, remember?"

I was about to tell him that he'd just spoken, but he was doing something and I didn't want to ruin it.

He held out his hand. "I'm Noah Douglas. Nice to meet you."

"Juliet Nolan." I shook his hand, and it was such a relief to touch him again, even briefly.

"I'm not going to jump to any conclusions about why you're here, and instead I'll let you tell me. You're in this seat because . . ."

For a second I couldn't speak, because I realized what he was doing. What he'd said couldn't be done. He was taking us back in time and letting us redo this night. "I'm a seat filler. There can't be any empty seats. I'll get up when your date gets back."

He looked thoroughly confused. "I don't have a date. I guess you'll have to stay put."

There was no place on earth I'd rather be.

"I'm an actor. You may know me from some of my more famous roles," he went on. "I played Felix Morrison. And Malec Shadowfire."

"Yes, I know. I know exactly who you are. I had a huge crush on you in middle school, and the Duel of the Fae trilogy is my favorite, even if they did screw up the ending. I think you are so talented and gifted, and I'm excited to meet you."

He grinned at me, and in that moment I knew—absolutely knew—that everything was going to be okay. "And what is it you do for a living?"

"I have my own dog-grooming service."

"That is very ambitious and entrepreneurial of you. I happen to have a dog I think you might like. You should come over and clean him up. He got really dirty recently."

My heart was in my throat. "I would love to."

"But only if you promise to wear those shoes." Of course I had on my pink Converse, because I wore them all the time. "I love your shoes."

He had on a pair of ratty Nikes, but I said, "I love yours, too. You have excellent taste."

"I brought you something. Look under your seat." He sounded like my Noah again, and I couldn't believe how much I'd missed him.

Under my chair was a huge box of Snickers. Like the kinds grocery stores got and put out on their shelves. I picked it up and put it in my lap, fingering the edges. "Thank you."

"It's in case you get hungry," he told me.

"You're really thoughtful."

"I try." He shifted in his seat, putting his arm across the back of my chair. "So, is there any chance you might want to go out with me?"

"Pretty big chance," I said. "But I have this thing about kissing, and you might need to help me through it."

"It would be my pleasure."

"But," I added, "only if you understand that I'm going to fall in love with you. I can't just be your friend."

There was so much softness in his eyes that I melted into my chair. Seriously, someone was going to have to scrape me off this thing. Then he made the melting worse by saying, "I can't just be your friend, either. And I will definitely fall in love with you."

It was all I could do not to throw myself against his chest and sob.

He took his phone out. "Can I show you some pictures?"

"Sure."

He opened his gallery and showed me a middle-aged couple. "These are my parents. You may not know this, but I'd cut off contact with them. I had dinner with them three days ago. It went better than I'd expected. Someone I adore told me that I should give people second chances, so I decided to start there. I think I'm going to try and find a way for them to be in my life."

I couldn't believe that had happened. I'd never thought Noah would try to repair things with his parents, but I was so glad that he had, because I knew he'd missed them.

The next one was of a fence being put up around his house. "My neighbor Gladys told me that she was going to let me have a fence for my yard. My dog tends to run away, and now I won't have to worry. She told me that I would be, and I quote, 'a doddering fool' if I didn't fix things with the woman I love. That my girlfriend was the only reason she was doing any of this and that I needed to man up and make things right.'"

Gladys was the absolute best, and she was getting free dog grooming for the rest of her life. I was also going to buy Sunshine a dozen teddy bears.

The picture he showed me next was him with a mother and daughter. "Reina set up a quick charity auction, and I agreed to take a picture with the highest bidder. It's not how I want my charity to grow, but a very smart woman told me to stop being so precious about this fame thing and use it to help other people."

My heart swelled at the idea that he had taken my words to heart that way and was going to help a lot more people moving forward.

The next screen showed a guy in his midtwenties with a buzz cut and in combat fatigues. "This is Ferguson. He's my other battle buddy, and he and I talked recently because I was having some issues in my love life. He told me I was stupid to throw away the only real happiness I've ever known. That I tended toward the dramatic and could be oversensitive. And that as my friend, while I had a right to my feelings, he thought I was overreacting and was a total idiot. That I had been given multiple do-overs in my life and I should do the same for the woman I love. That the army had trained me to fight for the things I believed in and cared about."

I was going to name my firstborn child after Ferguson. After I found out his first name.

The next picture was of a house surrounded by greenery. "I bought this ranch just outside town. It won't be much more of a commute than I'm doing now. It means I don't really need the fence at my old house, but this one sits on twenty acres. It has a barn and a lot of pens. It's the perfect place for an animal rescue, don't you think? If I can find someone who would want to marry me and live there with me. And have babies, both the fur and human kind."

Joy engulfed my heart. "Oh, Noah." I was choked up, and my chin was trembling. That was my dream. He had bought my dream.

He put his phone down. "Juliet, I told you I'd always have your back, and I didn't. I'm sorry."

I wanted to throw my arms around his neck, but it was difficult to reach him with this armrest between us. "You have nothing to apologize for. I know why you were upset. You were protecting yourself."

He leaned in to kiss me on the tip of my nose, in that way that I now recognized as a signal to me of how much he cared. "I should have been protecting you. I promise you that I'll try not to fall into that overly-sensitive-artist stereotype and will talk to you about everything. I will always give you the benefit of the doubt, because I know how much you love me. You're my whole world and it's like . . . everything is just gray without you."

"I know exactly what you mean. I swear I won't ever keep anything from you again. I will be better about communicating my feelings, even though that's not really my primary skill set." I sighed; my fears and sadness had all been washed away. "You really forgive me, though?"

"I do." Then he made an X across his heart, and I laugh-cried. He added, "My job is different and my life is demanding and hard and we'll have to give up some of our privacy. I know it's a lot to ask, but if Covington manages it, anybody can."

Now I truly understood exactly what Zoe had meant. "I've thought about that. And I would make those sacrifices if it meant I got to be with you. You're worth whatever hardship we might have to put up with. But I need you to remember that I'm not perfect and I will make mistakes again."

"So will I. And I will do my best to always be patient and understanding if you promise to do the same. But if we both swear to love each other and always fight for us, how can we go wrong?"

He leaned his forehead against mine, our breaths mingling, and I had never imagined that this kind of happiness was possible.

"So, the candy is in case you get hungry," he said, "but there's something inside in case you get lonely."

I furrowed my brows, not understanding what he meant. I noticed the box's perforations had already been broken, and I lifted up the top.

Inside there was a ring with a diamond so big I could see my reflection in it, surrounded by a band of blue sapphires. I gasped and then looked up to see that he was down on one knee, on the same gross floor I'd once had to sit on.

"Juliet Nolan, I love you and I want to make a life with you. So does Magnus. Will you marry me?"

There was so much elation and hope and giddiness that for a second I couldn't answer. I just stared at him, wanting to freeze this moment in my memory.

A bewildered expression settled on his face. "If you're not ready, we can wait."

"Oh, I'm ready. I'm ready now."

His concern turned into sheer delight. "I'll call the plane and we can be in Las Vegas in a few hours."

That made me laugh. "No, when we get married, I want everyone we love to be there."

"I can make that happen right now."

He could. He would absolutely round everyone up and get them all out to Vegas if that was what I wanted. I set the box of candy down on the floor and then put my hands on both sides of his face. How could I love him this much? "I know you can. You make dreams come true. Like this one."

"So . . . is that a yes?"

I kissed him briefly, teasingly, and leaned back in my chair before he could respond. "I have some conditions."

"Oh?"

I nodded, trying to look stern. "My answer will depend on the kind of socks you have on right now."

He lifted up his pant leg. They were zebra striped.

"Good. Also, I'm going to need a blue-and-white wedding cake with the words *Mazel tov* written on it."

"You've got it."

"And maybe you could wear your Malec costume again."

He smiled. "Your wish is my command," which was Malec's most famous line, and he said it in Malec's voice, and it made me giggle. "Anything else?" he asked.

"Just love me forever, and my answer will always be yes."

"Done."

Then I joined him on the floor and finally and truly kissed him. The man who was going to be my husband. Who would make all of my dreams come true.

Who already had.

AUTHOR'S NOTE

Thank you for reading my story! I hope you liked getting to know Noah and Juliet and enjoyed them falling in love as much as I did. If you'd like to find out when I've written something new, make sure you sign up for my newsletter at www.sariahwilson.com, where I most definitely will not spam you. (I'm happy when I send out a newsletter once a month!)

And if you feel so inclined, I'd love for you to leave a review on Amazon, on Goodreads, with your hairdresser's cousin's roommate's blog, via a skywriter, in graffiti on the side of a bookstore, on the back of your electric bill, or any other place you want. I would be so grateful. Thanks!

ACKNOWLEDGMENTS

For everyone who is reading this—thank you. I can't tell you how much your support means to me—it is often quite literally the thing that keeps me going when the writing is hard. Hoping that you will enjoy and laugh and swoon and that for a short, brief amount of time, I maybe made your burdens a little easier to bear.

This book was inspired by meeting Adam Driver at the SAG-AFTRA Awards in January 2020. So first and foremost, thank you to Adam Driver for, you know, being Adam Driver and letting me have that amazing experience.

Thank you also to everyone who contributed to Adam Driver becoming the man and actor that he is—including his parents, the Juilliard School, and the United States Marine Corps. A special thank-you to members of his team (especially to Bryna Rifkin and Jordan Schlesinger of Narrative PR) who helped arrange the experience. Thank you to Amy Komorowski for making him even prettier and posting pictures of your excellent work. Another thank-you to Arts in the Armed Forces and the amazing charity work that they do, with special thanks to Lindsay Miserandino. A portion of the proceeds of this book has been sent to AITAF so that they can continue to bring art to those who protect us.

The biggest of thanks-yous ever to Alison Dasho—I can't tell you how much I appreciated your immediate support and enthusiasm for this book and for all of your amazing insight and for having adorable daughters. Your words to me after reading the first draft of this story—I'll always remember them. I'm thankful every day that I get to work with you and the entire amazing Montlake team (Anh Schluep, Lauren Grange, Megan Meier, Kris Beecroft, Jillian Cline, Andrew George, Erin Calligan Mooney, and Jessica Preeg). Thank you for being on my side and fighting for me. And an Adam Driver–size thanks to Charlotte Herscher, who always finds a way to make my stories even better and helps me to dive into what I actually meant to say. Your brilliance and advice are always so appreciated. I'm also thankful this book was a "light edit." It's much more fun that way. We should do that every time.

Thank you to the copyeditors and proofreaders who find all my mistakes and make me follow grammatical standards even when I don't want to. A special shout-out to Philip Pascuzzo for this absolutely delightful cover. I can't even tell you how much I adore it.

Sarah Younger: thank you for letting me call you after I met Adam Driver and gush to you about it and for being completely on board when I said I wanted to write a book inspired by those events. It was super late in New York, but you let me be thrilled about the experience and recognized how it made me excited about writing again. You are the best cheerleader ever, and I'm so thrilled that you're in my corner.

A big thanks to the team at Dana Kaye Publicity for all of their support and getting me to do all the publicity type things I don't like doing. I'm so excited to be working with you!

I have to give a shout-out to all the people who supported me online both in my fandom and through that meeting with Adam Driver—to @AdamDriverFiles, especially Ang for walking me through what would happen and what I should say/do (which I promptly forgot), and to the Adam Driver Fans subreddit for your expertise and enthusiasm. Thanks to everyone on Twitter and Instagram who liked my video and pictures of meeting him and read some of my stories as a result. Love to all the Adam Driver (rats), Ben Solo, and Reylo fans out there—thanks for making me feel like my fangirling is not all that strange. #BenSoloDeservedBetter #BenSoloLives Also sending love to the people in my Facebook reader group—it was so much fun putting up pictures of things that were happening in my story in real time and having all of your giddy excitement for this book. I'm so glad you finally got to read it, and thank you so much for all your suggestions, some of which found their way into the story! You guys are the best!

For my children—I hope you know how much I love you, and I'm sorry for how often you've had to listen to me talk about Ben Solo and Star Wars and how terribly his story ended.

And Kevin, I love you a million times more than I do Adam Driver.